Panther's Prey

Also by Lachlan Smith

Bear Is Broken
Lion Plays Rough
Fox Is Framed

Panther's Prey

A Leo Maxwell Mystery

LACHLAN SMITH

The Mysterious Press
New York

Published simultaneously in Canada
Printed in the United States of America

FIRST EDITION

ISBN 978-0-8021-2503-3
eISBN 978-0-8021-8992-9

The Mysterious Press
an imprint of Grove Atlantic
154 West 14th Street
New York, NY 10011

Distributed by Publishers Group West

groveatlantic.com

16 17 18 19   10 9 8 7 6 5 4 3 2 1

Panther's Prey

Chapter 1

"Not everyone who confesses is guilty. This is the case of a man who confessed to a crime he didn't commit."

I turned and indicated my client, Randall Rodriguez, behind me at the defense table in a borrowed suit. Next to him sat my cocounsel, Jordan Walker.

I went on, addressing the jury. "After a childhood filled with unspeakable abuse, Mr. Rodriguez has spent his adult life on the street, in mental hospitals, or in jail. Three times in the past five years he's appeared at one of the police stations here in San Francisco and asked to be arrested, just as he did in this case. Each confession involved a well-publicized crime: two murders and a rape. Each time, the police proved he couldn't have committed it.

"But that was before he crossed paths with police detective Harold Cole."

I drew the fourteen jurors' attention to Cole, a balding, middle-aged man sitting at the DA's table beside the assistant district attorney.

Medicated now, Randall was passive before his fate. The judge had determined his confession was voluntary, and she'd also found him competent to stand trial and assist in his defense. Jordan had worked wonders with him, but our client's "assistance" was more theoretical possibility than practical fact. One of his diagnoses was autism, another schizophrenia. His raw intelligence was remarkable, however. For instance, he'd begged me to clip the chess problems from the *Chronicle* and bring them to our meetings. Before we could discuss the case, he'd sit down with a chess set he'd constructed from scraps of paper. He began from the opening position and played a realistic game, complete with formal openings and sophisticated tactics, his fat, scarred fingers moving at lightning speed, delicately sliding certain slips of paper and plucking others up, until after five or six minutes the pieces arrived in the formation of the problem. Then, rather than solve the puzzle, he'd move to the next clipping and start again. Wanting the jury to see a homeless man incapable of planning or foresight, I'd instructed Randall to avoid chessboards in jail.

Jordan and I'd been prepping the case for weeks, day and night. It was August. Janelle Fitzpatrick had been raped in January, one of the first cases I was assigned when I came to work at the PD's office. When Jordan had arrived for her six-month stint as a volunteer attorney, I'd enlisted her help, asking her to interview the cops who'd investigated Rodriguez's confessions in the past. Two years younger than I was, she was a slight five four, with red-blond hair, a distance runner. She could get in someone's face when needed, but was accustomed to relying on her more than considerable charm. Most importantly, she was a worker, willing to put in the hours. I hadn't expected her to succeed, but she'd persuaded those ordinarily closemouthed detectives to cross the so-called blue line. Based on this accomplishment, I'd asked her to help me try the case.

After I'd laid out our defense in my opening statement, the grizzled DA, Mark Saenz, called his first witness. This was the alleged victim, Janelle Fitzpatrick. She was young, blond, single, and dressed more expensively than any of the three lawyers in the courtroom. She came from a wealthy family and worked at a downtown investment bank.

At the prelim Saenz had presented only the testimony of the investigating detective, who'd nearly fumbled the case when I confronted him with the shocking fact that the victim had failed to pick out Rodriguez from a lineup on her first try.

She wouldn't make the same mistake today. After they'd spent over an hour walking through every detail of the attack, most of which admittedly had occurred in near darkness, Janelle dramatically pointed out Rodriguez in the courtroom as her attacker.

Next, Saenz asked her what had happened when she returned to the police department's Southern Station three days after the attack.

"They called me to let me know they had a suspect who'd confessed, saying all I had to do was identify him. I thought I was strong enough, that I'd be able to handle that. But I was wrong.

"Being in the same room with him again, even separated by glass, sent me into a panic attack." She stiffened slightly as she spoke these words, and avoided looking at Rodriguez, showing the jury that the fear was still there, though under containment now. "I couldn't breathe. I had tunnel vision. When the light came on, I was so focused on not breaking down I couldn't look at the men. I didn't want to see him. I blurted out a number, but it was just the number that was in my head, and the minute I said it I knew I was wrong.

"All I could think was now they'd have to let him go. And he'd be waiting for me someday again. I told Detective Cole I wanted to go back in. And so we did and I picked out Mr. Rodriguez." Now she looked directly at him across the courtroom, ignoring Jordan and me. I could almost feel her counting to herself—one, two, three—as if daring him to glance up and meet her eyes. Rodriguez went on staring at his hands, hunching lower in a posture the jurors no doubt would construe as shame but that was simply the reaction of a severely autistic, schizophrenic man—or so I wanted the jurors to believe. "It was him. I've never been more sure of anything in my life."

When Janelle looked away, Rodriguez glanced at me and winked.

This crafty look was gone in an instant. I couldn't even be completely sure I'd seen it. The jurors were watching Janelle as Saenz wrapped up his questioning. Jordan hadn't noticed anything, either.

Now Jordan took Saenz's place at the podium. It made sense for a female to handle this cross-examination, and Jordan was more than up to the job. Also, the physical resemblance between her and Janelle couldn't have been lost on the jurors. Janelle's smile at her indicated recognition of a peer, someone who couldn't possibly harm her. The jury saw that, too.

"When you picked out the wrong man from the lineup, how much time had passed since the rape?" Jordan asked.

"Three and a half days."

"Did you watch TV news or look at newspapers, websites during those days?"

"Some. I was staying at a friend's. I needed to know if my name was out there. Because it would dictate how much I'd have to tell people when I went back to work."

"Was there much publicity?"

"More than I expected."

"A media frenzy?"

"I wouldn't go that far, but my father is active in state politics. If something happens to his daughter, that's news."

Jordan led Janelle through a summary of what she'd read in the news, quickly establishing that the rape had been a lead story on the *Chronicle* website and had also featured on TV. A number of details had been leaked, including that she'd been raped, forced by her attacker to shower, then duct-taped and locked in the bathroom. "The press didn't learn any of these facts from you?"

"Of course not. I was screening my calls."

Jordan skipped to the contact from the detective informing Janelle a suspect had confessed. "Was that also reported?"

Janelle didn't recall. But, in fact, Rodriguez's picture, an old mug shot, had been published online by the *Chronicle* a few hours before she showed up at the station to make the ID.

"Do you recognize the story?" Jordan asked, showing her the website printout.

The witness claimed not to remember if she'd looked at that particular article.

"Isn't it true that you viewed online a picture of Mr. Rodriguez immediately before you drove to the police station to identify the suspect in custody?"

It was possible, Janelle conceded.

"You ran a Google search with the keywords 'rape' and 'San Francisco' and 'confession,' correct?"

Janelle again pleaded a faulty memory but didn't deny it.

Jordan moved away from the podium, coming back around to a position beside Rodriguez behind the defense table. She put her hand on his shoulder, the jurors swiveling their heads between her and Janelle, most of them looking back to Jordan. Rodriguez was stone-faced. Again I tried to tell myself I must have been mistaken about the wink. "The reason you couldn't identify Mr. Rodriguez in that first lineup—even right after looking online at a mug shot of him as the guy who'd confessed—was because you were having a panic attack?"

Janelle must have recognized what Jordan was doing with Rodriguez, playing off her physical similarity to the victim, showing the jurors *she* wasn't afraid. "I might be having one now." Her tone was cool but her voice had begun to shake a little.

Jordan remained at Rodriguez's side, her hand on his shoulder. "Thank you, Ms. Fitzpatrick."

Chapter 2

The next afternoon, it was finally my turn again. While Jordan cross-examined Janelle, and during the DA's direct examination of Detective Cole, I'd found myself obsessing over Randall's slightest movements in the chair beside me, with equal parts dread and fascination, both dreading and anticipating another revelatory moment like that wink.

Relieved to be on my feet, I cross-examined Detective Cole, working from the script I'd established based on his testimony at the preliminary hearing. As I moved around the courtroom, approaching the witness and retreating, I was conscious of the jurors, the only audience that mattered. Yet, at every moment, I was also aware of Jordan watching me.

The conundrum for the police was the complete lack of physical evidence implicating Rodriguez or anyone else. This was because in addition to forcing Janelle to shower after the attack, the rapist had taken away the bedding, an act obviously requiring more cunning than I wanted the jury to believe he possessed. (Good thing they hadn't seen him moving his homemade chess pieces . . .) Having confessed to the crime, Rodriguez nonetheless had been unable or unwilling to tell the police what had become of the bag and its contents. Cole kept trying to minimize the importance of this, while I did everything in my power to highlight his evasions. My goal: to show the jury that this cop was incompetent or indifferent or both.

The state rested on Wednesday, after calling the obligatory police, medical, and forensic witnesses. Then Jordan and I took over and put on a demonstration showcasing the beauties of a publically funded defense. Our case lasted the rest of that week and half the next, with closing arguments on Tuesday morning and the jury retiring to deliberate that afternoon.

We'd begun by attacking Janelle's identification of Rodriguez as the rapist. Wednesday afternoon, the jury heard from the computer expert who'd analyzed her hard drive. Then an employee of the newspaper's website host confirmed that on the afternoon in question, a URL listed in her search history had linked to the article with the picture of Rodriguez. This allowed us to argue that her picking him out of a lineup an hour later was a foregone conclusion, tainted by her viewing the photograph online. This was in addition to the fact she'd *not* been able to identify him as the perpetrator the first time she'd tried.

Our main problem, of course, was the confession. The conventional wisdom held that the jury would need to hear Rodriguez deny the guilt he'd previously admitted. Jordan had worked with our client for hours in the weeks leading up to the trial, and I'd considered letting her put him on the stand, but we decided there was no question of Randall testifying. This was owing to his numerous low-level convictions for theft and drug offenses as well as his habit of responding to even the most basic questions with non sequiturs. Not to mention my fear that if he took the stand, he'd revert to his free-confessing ways.

Without the ability to use him as a witness to disown his confession, we had our backs to the wall. Our way out was the testimony of a pair of expert witnesses.

The first we called to the stand was a Michigan law professor who'd published prolifically on the subject of false confessions. Jordan had met Eric Lewis at the airport Wednesday evening and driven him straight to our office, where the three of us sat up late into the night.

Based on his review of Detective Cole's testimony, Lewis testified that in his opinion Rodriguez's confession had been obtained as the result of improperly coercive and suggestive questioning, without the safeguards necessary to ensure key details came from Rodriguez and not from the police. At the same time, Lewis had no choice but to acknowledge that Cole's interrogation of Rodriguez was itself the result of the accused's own prior uncoerced and voluntary admissions.

The research on voluntary false confessions was less developed, Lewis explained to the jury. Yet it was well established there were personality types prone to confessing falsely without prompting from the police. "The reasons for voluntary false confessions are as varied as the confessors themselves. These include a conscious or unconscious desire to be punished because of some real or imagined guilt, or a compulsion arising out of childhood trauma that leaves the individual with a deep-seated conviction of his worthlessness. There can also be simple confusion between fantasy and reality, to the point where a person fantasizes about a crime, then comes to believe he actually committed it. These conditions are often reinforced by a desire to impress or gain approval.

"It is a real phenomenon, recognized by psychological and sociological authorities, to the extent that police interrogation has evolved techniques to minimize voluntary false confessions. One method is to check the suspect's knowledge regarding key details of the crime scene that have been withheld from the public. The most important safeguard is to record the entire interview. Obviously, those precautions weren't followed in this case."

The DA's cross-examination of our first expert focused on making his testimony seem abstract, emphasizing that he'd flown here from Michigan the night before, had a ticket home to Detroit that evening, and had never set eyes on Rodriguez prior to seeing him in the courtroom today and thus had no idea whether he was mentally ill or not, guilty or not. Lewis's own statistics revealed the rarity of voluntary false confessions. Outwardly bored with a witness that his body language communicated was an irrelevant waste of the jury's time, Saenz excused Lewis after twenty minutes. "To catch your plane," he said.

However, his testimony provided merely the foundation of our false-confession defense. More significant was the testimony of Angela O'Dowd, a psychiatrist from Berkeley who'd examined Rodriguez on two separate occasions and worked up a profile that the judge, over the DA's strenuous (and well-argued) objections, had deemed admissible. This was a major victory, owing in large part to Jordan's well-researched brief. Dr. O'Dowd's testimony allowed us to present much of Rodriguez's life story in the guise of the factual basis for her psychiatric conclusions. She'd ultimately determined that Rodriguez was competent to stand trial under California law. However, this did not mean that in the conventional sense he was sane.

On the contrary, she identified him as someone highly susceptible to confessing to crimes he hadn't committed. In her interviews with Rodriguez and in her review of the records generated by the state's involvement in his life, dating back to his early childhood, she'd uncovered a history of physical abuse at the hands of his mother. This mistreatment had ended only when Rodriguez, at the age of nine, was taken by the state and placed in a series of foster homes, where the abuse continued in other forms. By sixteen, he'd been sent to juvenile camp, where suicide attempts and an attempted sexual assault by Randall against a teacher had resulted in his transfer to a series of mental institutions. (We'd been unsuccessful in persuading the judge to exclude evidence of this long-ago crime, even though it bore little similarity to the facts of Janelle Fitzpatrick's case, and so we were forced to integrate it into our narrative as best we could.) In all, he'd spent the next ten years in the custody of the state before funding cuts forced the closure of the inpatient hospital where Randall at the time was being treated with heavy doses of lithium and shock therapy.

With no family to turn to, and no ability to support himself by even the most menial employment, Randall Rodriguez, like so many others, had spent the last fifteen years on the street.

O'Dowd was in her forties, a slight woman with a prematurely lined face who wore no makeup, thus offering an absolutely unpretentious presence on the stand. As I eased her through her testimony, I snuck glances at the jurors. Their faces were skeptical, troubled, as though confronting a problem of knotty complexity. In this case, conviction was the easy answer. Their confusion meant we were winning, I hoped.

Based on her psychiatric training and her examinations of Rodriguez, Dr. O'Dowd hypothesized he suffered from a guilt complex associated with childhood abuse. "Deep down," she testified, "he's convinced he must have done something to deserve it. It's not an uncommon response in survivors. They blame themselves.

"On the flip side, this man shares a universal human need for attention and esteem. Unlike most of ours, his life presents no realistic possibility for fulfilling those needs. The people with whom he comes into contact almost universally seek to end that contact as quickly as possible. Except, of course, for those who regard him as prey for *their* needs.

"For a man like this, confessing to a terrible crime gets him off the street, into a warm room where the attention's on *him*. Suddenly people are listening to him in a way he never experiences at other times. In that interview room, he's able to give those detectives exactly what they want, and in return he receives an intense reward of affirmation and praise.

"Also, let us remember this is a man who's spent his life either homeless or in mental institutions. At least in comparison with the streets, prison is a relatively safe place, and the type of abuse he experiences there is predictable and familiar. So in some ways, the punishment he seeks isn't punishment at all. Rather, the opposite. It's the only safety in his power to achieve."

Saenz listened with a stony face, not writing a word on his pad. This wasn't Dr. O'Dowd's first time on the witness stand. Along with the hearing regarding the admissibility of Rodriguez's confession, there'd been one to determine whether the Berkeley psychiatrist would be allowed to offer her conclusions. After that second hearing, the judge had issued an order defining what Dr. Dowd would and would not be allowed to say in her testimony. Because of this, both she and I were careful not to step a foot beyond the boundaries. She was not to opine that Rodriguez had falsely confessed, nor was she to testify that he'd told her he'd invented his confession. Rather, she was to stick to demonstrable facts based on generally accepted, reliable principles of psychiatry.

When Saenz finally rose to cross-examine her, he simply turned her opinions inside out, showing how each aspect of Rodriguez's pathology could be consistent with that of a criminal who, by actually committing a crime such as the one here, gained the same notoriety and fulfillment—the same "safety"—while exhibiting the same disregard for future consequences of present actions in favor of their immediate reward.

Nonetheless, he couldn't so easily brush aside our next three witnesses, as we moved from the abstract and theoretical to the increasingly—and undeniably—concrete and real. Now Jordan took center stage, questioning the first of the three police detectives who'd rejected Rodriguez's previous false confessions. Each had brought that previous investigation to a successful close, leading to the conviction of another suspect notwithstanding Rodriguez's claim of guilt. One case had ended with the confession of the real perpetrator; the second had been sealed with a DNA match; the third had been closed by video footage of the true suspect leaving the crime scene. Each detective had previously testified either in a preliminary hearing or trial to prove the guilt of the person who was convicted. Each therefore was now obligated to defend that result here in this trial.

Though at moments a bit clumsy, her handling of Janelle Fitzpatrick had been intuitive and successful. This, by comparison, would be like shooting fish in a barrel—and the reason the fish were in the barrel was because Jordan had placed them there. She'd insisted on obtaining the complete records from every case in which Rodriguez had contact with the police, either as a suspect or as a witness. She'd then pored over every page of the nearly ten thousand the DA had produced in a "document dump" containing mostly irrelevant material. Next, after identifying the detectives who'd questioned Rodriguez in prior cases, she'd convinced them to talk. I still didn't know how she'd done this, and I'd suggested it hadn't hurt that she was extremely attractive, but Jordan had discounted this. "They talked because they know this prosecution is a mistake. No good cop wants to see an innocent man convicted, because that means the real rapist is still out there. The guy who did this is going to strike again. You've got to offer them a chance to do what's right."

Testifying in response to Jordan's questions, each of the detectives was reticent but professional. Clearly, none of them was eager to do the defense any favors, and each was conflicted by the unfamiliar role of being called as a witness on behalf of a man accused of a terrible crime. Their obvious reluctance made their testimony all the more damaging to the state.

Jordan used them to draw out the common themes. Each of the three cases, to start with, had been the subject of intense local news coverage across multiple media outlets, including the newspapers that Rodriguez was known to hoard. (His possessions included notebooks in which he'd pasted clippings having to do with notorious crimes.) In each of the cases, following the initial wave of publicity, Rodriguez, a familiar face to the local beat cops, had presented himself at the Southern Station reception desk and asked to speak with the investigating detective. When he was interviewed, Rodriguez's stories had seemed to fit the known facts. In none of the cases, however, had he been able to provide details that weren't contained in the plastic-wrapped scrapbooks in his shopping cart.

"You want to ask open-ended questions in a situation like that," the lone woman, Sergeant Ochoa, testified. "It's human nature to feed the witness details in the hope of jogging his memory, but some of them are like mediums, or fortune-tellers. They've got this ability to figure out what you want to hear and parrot it back, wrapped up in the information you provided. That's why you always look for corroborating evidence. If the case is legitimate, the confession confirms what the physical evidence already shows."

When it was time for me to make our closing argument, I thought I saw disappointment in the jurors' eyes as I stood up, notes in hand. If so, I knew its cause. The jurors wanted to hear from Jordan, the understudy who'd stolen the show. She'd won them over, helped them make up their minds.

Nothing was scheduled in the courtroom that afternoon, so after closing arguments Jordan and I waited for the verdict there, working on our laptops, pretending to each other we were brushing off this trial and moving on to the next. Rodriguez was downstairs in lockup, the deputies ready to bring him up on ten minutes' notice. Sitting beside Jordan, I kept forgetting he was even part of it. Some cases are like that, with the client immobilized at the center of the evidence like a fly trapped in amber.

The jury was out a little over three hours. Then we heard the customary raps on the jury-room door. A few minutes later the deputies brought Rodriguez up. He glanced at Jordan as he took his place at the counsel table, an urgent question in his eyes. She took his hand. He made a sudden, almost violent movement to pull away. Jordan forced a smile and tightened her grip, no doubt feeling he deserved human contact at this fateful moment. I heard his breath catch in his throat.

The judge directed Rodriguez to rise. I glanced over, then quickly looked away, my cheeks burning at what I'd seen. Jordan was trying to disengage her hand now that Randall was standing alone, with the lawyers remaining seated per protocol, but he squeezed her fingers tightly. Jordan, sitting somewhat behind our client, didn't have the same angle I had and might not have seen what I saw. I hoped to God his poorly fitting jacket concealed the bulge in his pants from the jurors.

Their verdict was already rendered, however. All that remained was for Randall's fate to be read aloud.

As their "not guilty" was announced, Randall seemed to sway like someone buffeted by a strong wind. At last he let go of Jordan's hand. He had a look of panic. It was the way most defendants look the moment they realize they're about to be taken to prison.

I glanced over again and saw that Rodriguez was no longer visibly aroused. I couldn't tell if anyone else in the courtroom had seen what I'd seen. The jurors' faces were somber, probably because they knew the real rapist was unlikely to be prosecuted even if he were caught. Rodriguez's confession had been discredited, but it would still serve to provide reasonable doubt for anyone subsequently charged with the same crime.

After the jury had been discharged and the judge returned to his chambers, Jordan and I stood at the back of the courtroom, accepting congratulations from our fellow public defenders. Then we went out into the hallway. At some point during this process, Rodriguez slipped away, without so much as a word of thanks for Jordan or me. I looked for him, then turned back to the half dozen assembled reporters with a shrug, assuming that the chapter in my life that concerned him was closed.

Chapter 3

We went for after-work drinks at Mars, the closest watering hole to the PD's office. Around a dozen other attorneys from our office came along to help celebrate our win.

Normally I'd have gotten drunk and spent the evening going over the details of every cross-examination, rehashing every crisis and triumph. Tonight, for some reason, I wasn't feeling it. I wanted to bask in the glow of our triumph, but I didn't want to think about what it meant. Maybe my hesitancy came from Rodriguez's wink and his visible arousal, making me question whether he might have been capable of this crime after all. Or maybe I was more bothered than I wanted to admit that the real rapist would never be caught. In any event, I found myself drinking steadily but not saying much.

Jordan had spent most of the evening talking with Rebecca, one of her friends from law school. I'd been playing pool but was sitting at the bar watching the Giants on TV when she slid onto the stool beside me. "You don't look like a man who just won the big case."

No point mentioning to her what was bothering me. "I'm just tired. Trials take it out of me. When the work is done all I really want to do is go home."

"I know what you mean. After my last trial I wanted to sleep for a week."

"I heard one of the reporters ask you about Kairos."

"Yeah, that was the trial I did at Baker before I came here," she said. "He was asking me if that verdict had been as satisfying as this one. Obviously, I told him no."

"What was it about?"

"Money." She sipped her beer. "And politics. The whole human spectrum of betrayal and deceit. But, mostly, it was about money. I can't talk about it, and I wouldn't want to if I could."

"Money's not so bad. There's something to be said for a payday at the finish line."

She laughed. "No one never mistook *you* for a crusader."

"I'm a realist. I'm on the side I'm on because I don't think convicting people and sending them to prison solves any of our society's problems. At the same time, I can't fool myself about a guy like Rodriguez. Is it a good thing he walks free? Who knows? I'm just trying to do a job, and hopefully pick up a little human interest along the way."

Hearing myself, I knew I must have been drunker than I realized. Quickly tallying pints in my head, I realized I was starting my fifth. It was time to guzzle water and start thinking about going home before I ended up sounding like even more of an ass.

Jordan had a declaration. "Today's verdict was the single biggest satisfaction of my professional life."

I glanced over to be sure she was serious. The verdict had been something like four million dollars in that case. An entire company had changed hands. "You probably didn't get to do anything in the Kairos trial. Associate work."

"That's not it. It's what's at stake. The values. In public defense, regardless of whether the client's innocent or guilty, we have these principles it's our job to uphold. The right to counsel. The presumption of innocence. The requirement the state prove guilt beyond a reasonable doubt. These are things worth believing in. Civil work, on the other hand, it's just about the score."

Now she was the one who sounded cynical. Six months ago, when I was recovering in the hospital in Fort Bragg from a gunshot wound, Jordan had been a senior associate at Baker Benton. The folks at Baker were still holding her place and expecting her return. This stint as a so-called volunteer attorney was no risk for her. While she gained trial experience, she continued to draw her annual two-hundred-thousand-dollar paycheck.

"So stay here at the PD's office and try cases." I tried to bring our conversation back to the celebration of our victory and Jordan's part in it. "Tonight, because of you, an innocent man is free instead of spending the first night of the rest of his life in Corcoran."

"I'd like nothing more. Unfortunately, I can't just walk away from Baker."

"Why not?" If there was one thing I believed, it was that any of us ought to be free at any moment to turn our backs on a work situation, and walk out the door the minute it was no longer in our interest to remain. In fact, I intended to do just that as soon as I could afford to be my own boss again, or so I'd promised myself when I took the PD job.

"I have commitments. I can't just throw them off."

"Commitments to whom? The partners at Baker?"

"I *really* don't want to talk about it. Let's just enjoy this moment. Right here. Right now. That's a pretty good mantra. Don't you think?"

"Okay," I said, feeling self-conscious for having pried, and slightly angry at her for letting me feel that way. I figured she'd walk away and find Rebecca now, but she didn't.

"I came over here to ask you if you wanted to get out of here."

I looked up. "Are you serious?"

She nodded, draining her beer.

That was good enough for me.

~ ~ ~

We slept together that night, and twice more that week, all at my place.

She'd wanted to know what I was doing living in such a dump, and I'd told her about being shot a year and a half ago, having my law office burned, being forced to sell my condo and losing all the equity.

"My brother once represented the manager here," I said, explaining how I'd ended up at the Seward.

I suppose it was possible trysting in the Tenderloin turned her on. But more likely she was merely safeguarding her freedom, intending to be the one who walked out, who decided when that would be. I couldn't blame her for wanting control, but at the same time I tried not to recognize these precautions for what they were. *Right here, right now*, she'd said. Perhaps she could feel my own hope like an electric charge, a burnt smell in the air.

We'd just made love, and she was studying the scars on my chest and stomach with minute attention. "Have you ever thought about carrying a gun?"

"I have one." I hesitated. "But it's unregistered."

She was both amused and disturbed. "Why?"

"A former client gave it to me. I made the decision a long time ago that if I ever had to shoot to kill in self-defense, I wasn't going to wait around for the cops to show up."

She laughed, then seemed to realize I was serious. "Because of your family?"

"Something like that. If anyone ever wants to kill me, it'll be because of some issues between my father and a man named Bo Wilder. Unfortunately, the backstory would be viewed by the police as incriminating. Bo thinks my family owes him because of a favor he thinks he did for us. We disagree and don't feel it was much of a favor. But if I have to explain any of this to the police, I'd be talking us into prison."

"So your plan is?"

"If it ever comes to that—and I don't think it will—my plan is to shoot the people who are trying to shoot me, run, and ditch the gun."

I hadn't intended to get into these complicated explanations, and I could see my answers disturbed her. "You have it here?"

I took the gun, a Bersa 9mm, from the drawer where I stored it wrapped in an old shirt.

"Just carrying this you're committing a felony," she said. "If you're going to own a pistol, you need a permit."

"I've actually been meaning to get rid of it. You're right. It's a stupid liability." I wrapped the gun back up. I didn't want to look at it, didn't want to deal with it, which was exactly why it was still in my drawer months after I'd resolved to throw it away.

"We could get rid of it together," she said. Then gathering her legs underneath her and kneeling in bed, she said: "It could be a turn-on. We can pretend you just shot somebody, and you came to me for help."

Her eyes were glinting. It was a side of her I hadn't seen before. I couldn't tell whether she was serious or not, and wasn't sure I wanted to know. I assumed that Jordan had lived the sort of sheltered life that meant she couldn't possibly know anything about fear.

I was hoping to let it go. But that Friday she came into my office, told me she was busy tonight but tomorrow I should come to her place and bring the gun.

I almost didn't. Bring the gun, that is—I wasn't about to turn down an invitation to Jordan's apartment. I figured she couldn't be serious about the game she'd proposed, but another part of me had started to come around. It was true. I needed to get rid of the thing. I'd never been into role play, but maybe it would be fun. I was pretty certain I could summon enthusiasm for any game that ended in sex with Jordan.

She'd told me she lived in the Marina District but her building was clearly in North Beach, a high-rise at the foot of Columbus just a few blocks from Washington Square, with views of Coit Tower and downtown. The kitchen and the living room were a single open space, with granite counters and stainless appliances and furniture from some high-end store. One bedroom was set up as an office, outfitted with a full desk and credenza.

The other, of course, was the focus of my intentions.

We sat on the couch, sipping wine. I told her she seemed distracted. She didn't respond. Something seemed to be working its way to the surface of her mind. I was ready for her just to come out with it, whatever it was. I went on: "Sometimes I look at you and I get the sense you're rehearsing conversations in your head. Like you're thinking how to break the news to the other man, whoever he might be."

She lifted an eyebrow, back in the here and now. "What news?"

She ought to have said: "What man?"

"You and me. Whatever this is. We haven't talked about where this is going."

"Do you want to talk about it?" she asked with sufficient detachment to make clear I'd regret that conversation. "Or would you rather just go to bed?"

After we'd made love and were lying between her sheets, she asked me if I'd brought the gun. I said it was in my coat in the other room. "You still want to play make-believe?" I asked.

She told me no. It was as if she'd forgotten all about our role-play fantasy. But she hadn't forgotten the gun. "Leave it with me," she said. "I'll take care of it. I don't trust you to do it yourself. You'd probably just take it home again and put it back in the drawer."

I had to admit she was right. "What are you going to do with it?"

"Get rid of it," she told me. "Think of it as my major contribution to your welfare."

I was puzzled but won over. The idea of someone taking even a small share of the weight from my shoulders was seductive.

Jordan awakened with a gasp, sitting upright and yanking the sheet up over her chest, like there were watchers. But we were alone.

"Was someone here?" she asked. "I could've sworn I heard my name called."

At my place she'd slept like a baby. "There's no one."

"Oh." She fell back onto the pillow and curled against me. "It wasn't you playing tricks?"

Her voice was different now from the voice I'd come to know over the past week. Now it resembled the voice of a scared child waking in the middle of the night.

"Cross my heart."

Her breathing deepened until I thought she was asleep. Then her phone chimed and she started awake again.

She found the phone, looked at it, read something, and set it aside. Turning on the light, she finished dressing and gave me a pointed look. She meant me to dress, too.

When I'd complied, I followed her out of the bedroom. She was on the phone requesting a cab. "Something's come up," she explained. "Even if I had time to explain and wanted to, I'm afraid I'm not free to tell you anything about it. Duty of confidentiality and all. It has nothing to do with any of our cases."

That didn't explain why she was throwing me out. But of course I couldn't say that without claiming a right to her bed I didn't have.

"I'm sorry to kick you out. If I'd known this was going to happen tonight, I wouldn't have brought you here."

Still she didn't explain what this was. In any case, I wasn't sure I believed her. Her phone rang. It was the cab driver. She opened the apartment door and held it for me, but waited, holding out her hand. Looking her in the face, I slowly took the gun from my raincoat pocket and handed it to her. She set it on her kitchen counter, then locked the door top and bottom. We took the elevator down, neither of us saying a word.

"First stop is the Seward," she told the driver.

Chapter 4

As I returned from felony arraignments on Tuesday morning, Rebecca Lorenz appeared at my office door. "Have you seen Jordan?" she asked, with a concerned expression. She was an attractive African American woman, a felony attorney who'd graduated with Jordan in the same law school class. It was Rebecca who'd persuaded her to apply for the volunteer attorney program after Jordan had mentioned, over drinks one night, feeling burned out. She was Jordan's closest friend in the office. If anyone knew about our relationship, she'd be the one.

"Not since Saturday night," I told her. "I left a message yesterday and another this morning."

"You two didn't have some kind of fight, did you?"

"No. I don't know what happened." I hesitated. Then, realizing she obviously knew about Jordan and me, I explained about Jordan getting a message from someone and sending me away.

She looked skeptical.

I thought a moment. "You haven't talked to her?"

"Nope. She hasn't called in, and she missed a hearing today. Something's definitely wrong. I'm freaking out. I was about to drive over to her place and check on her. I have her spare key. Do you want to come?"

As soon as she'd made the offer she looked like she wanted to take it back, but I didn't give her that chance. Rebecca was right. Jordan would never miss a hearing even if she was at death's door.

We retrieved Rebecca's aged Saab from its parking place down by the elevated freeway. As she drove, I learned a few more details about her friendship with Jordan. They'd shared many interests, including criminal law, and had taken a series of trial advocacy classes together, usually ending up on the same team. "I tried to get her to apply to the PD's office with me, but her father convinced her to take the law firm path. He's a city attorney down in Los Altos. Better late than never, I say."

"Really?" I asked. "Do you think she's going to make the switch for good?"

"After that win you two pulled off last week? Who knows?"

I thought of what Jordan had implied about commitments she couldn't get free of, citing her "duty of confidentiality." But I said nothing to Rebecca about any of these things. At Jordan's building she had to circle for nearly twenty minutes before finding a parking spot. Then, at the apartment, she looked over at me before rapping loudly. Receiving no answer, she shook her head and sighed. First looking at me again, she inserted the key in the lock.

The deadbolt wasn't engaged, I saw.

"She put that on when we left Saturday night," I said. I explained about her dropping me off.

Taking a deep breath, then calling out Jordan's name, Rebecca pushed into the apartment. "Jordan? Are you okay?"

She stopped. "Oh, Jesus."

A substance like brown paint had dripped on the tiles inside the apartment entrance. In the kitchen a chair was overturned.

Shattered glass was scattered over the countertop and floor. I had time to notice a handgun—it looked like my Bersa—on the floor. Rebecca had frozen, but I pushed past her and went jogging into the bedroom. The mattress was bare, the bed stripped. An icy shock went down my spine.

The door to the master bathroom was barricaded with a book-shelf and other furniture that had been toppled over, filling the space between the bathroom door and the foot of the bed. At the door I caught the corpse smell and knew it must be coming from inside. "No," I cried. "No, no, no," as my shaking hands moved the furniture out of the way, throwing designer bookshelves and a desk aside until I made a space for the door to swing free. Out flowed a sweet-rot stench I'd hoped never to smell again.

She was on the toilet, head hanging forward and slightly turned, her milky eyes staring at the door as if expecting rescue. Her arms slanted downward to meet beneath and behind the porcelain toilet bowl, where they were bound with duct tape. Her ankles had similarly been forced back behind the base of the toilet, with loops of duct tape wrapped around them, so that she was effectively hog-tied around the commode. Her bindings had forced her breasts against her knees, the flesh a livid purple where skin met skin. Other than the duct tape that bound her and another strip that sealed her mouth, she was naked.

I became conscious of Rebecca standing beside me, mouth open with horror. Then her fingernails dug into my wrist and the scream came. Because of the direction of the corpse's eyes I'd had a moment's illusion that Jordan was still alive, that we'd come just in time to save her, but that illusion was now thoroughly dispelled. Her skin was swollen, mottled purple, her eyes lifeless.

No one could save her.

Chapter 5

The situation, to me, was eerily familiar, with echoes running all through my life. At the age of ten I'd come home from school one day and discovered my mother's naked body in the front hallway of our Potrero Hill apartment, beaten to death with my aluminum baseball bat. My father, Lawrence, was arrested for her murder. He pleaded not guilty and was tried before a jury. The jury convicted him, and the judge sentenced him to life.

After 1983, with our mother dead and our father in San Quentin, Teddy was all the family I had left. He was twenty-two, just starting law school. He tolerated me at the periphery of his life, providing the material necessities but little emotional sustenance as he built his legal career. As a teenager I stifled my loneliness with punk rock music and bong hits. Later, I learned Teddy and our father had stayed in close contact, with my brother visiting him every few weeks.

By the time I finished college, Teddy had become one of the most notorious young criminal defense attorneys in San Francisco, equally sought after and despised. His biggest client was Ricky Santorez, who, I later learned, had used Teddy as a front for his illicit businesses after he went to prison, counting on Teddy to plead his foot soldiers to low-level offenses while minimizing risk to those higher up. Knowing nothing about this side of Teddy's practice, idealizing him and seeking approval he wasn't inclined to give, I followed him to law school, persevering with my studies despite receiving no encouragement from him.

In 1999, the week after I learned I'd passed the bar, Teddy was shot in the head in a Civic Center restaurant during the lunch recess in one of his trials, the gunman reaching over my shoulder to pull the trigger. There were plenty of people in law enforcement who thought he had it coming and told me so. In fact, as I learned through my own inquiries, my brother was shot because he'd been about to reopen the case that had haunted my childhood. He'd tracked down our mother's real killer—the mentally ill son of her lover—and had planned to expose him. For this Teddy had nearly paid with his life. The shooter escaped but I tracked him down. He was now serving a lengthy prison sentence for attempted murder.

The neurosurgeons at San Francisco General Hospital had told me Teddy would never wake up. When he defied this expectation, their revised prognosis was that he'd remain a vegetable, unable to walk, speak, or care for himself. They were wrong. My brother spent months in the neurotrauma ward, nearly half a year after that in an inpatient brain-injury rehabilitation center, and then another year living with me in my Oakland condominium.

He'd changed, becoming a very different person from the ruthless charmer who'd once dominated the criminal courtrooms at San Francisco's Hall of Justice. The new Teddy would never again eviscerate a witness or coax jurors into a verdict that went against the facts. However, just as he'd relearned to feed and care for himself, he'd also taught himself to draft a decent brief through sheer repetitive determination, enabling him to earn a modest living as an appellate lawyer after he regained his law license. Most significantly, he was now a family man, a transformation that astonished his ex-wife, Jeanie, me, and everyone else who'd been innocent bystanders to his former habits. Prior to his injuries, it hadn't been unusual for him to put in sixteen-hour days, sleeping in a room he kept at a residence hotel near his Tenderloin office rather than return home to Contra Costa County for a few hours' rest in the shell of the house he and Jeanie had never gotten around to finishing, plastic sheeting still covering the windows, unpainted drywall inside.

Teddy and his wife, Tamara, had met during their stay at the same brain-injury rehab center, where she was recovering from a virus that had ravaged her brain and left her without short-term memory. They now lived in a bungalow in Berkeley funded by a lawsuit I'd settled on Tamara's behalf. Their child, Carly, was three years old. Though Tamara's impairments remained severe, she, too, had improved, the demands of marriage and parenthood seeming to create new neural pathways, complementing the habits and practices they'd both learned to replace the capabilities they'd lost.

Through all of this, I'd tried to carry on my brother's work on our father's behalf. I'd shopped his case to the Innocence Project and other such organizations, but hadn't yet found a lawyer to take the case. With a full plate of my own cases, and not trusting my ability to represent my father impartially, I was reluctant to shoulder the burden myself. This unjust stasis was broken a few weeks after Teddy had regained his law license. One day he'd dropped a brief on my desk, a habeas petition arguing that my father's twenty-one-year-old conviction should be overturned based on stunning prosecutorial misconduct.

Imprisoned all these years after being convicted of my mother's murder in a tainted trial, Lawrence two years ago had finally been awarded his freedom thanks to Teddy's brief. His newfound freedom didn't last long, however, before he was accused of the murder of Russell Bell, the star witness who'd been slated to testify against him in his retrial, a former cell mate who'd planned to tell the jury my father had spilled his guts.

Lawrence had an alibi for the time of Bell's shooting, thanks to his fiancée, Dot, whom he'd met while he was still behind bars. Due also to the excellent lawyering of his appointed counsel, he was acquitted of murdering my mother, and thus exonerated twenty-one years after the fact. However, the state could still charge him with the murder of Bell. The DA surely would press charges if the truth were known.

As we'd learned soon after my father's acquittal, the truth was that without Lawrence's knowledge—but intending to benefit him—the leader of a white supremacist prison gang named Bo Wilder had ordered the snitch gunned down. Wilder, who'd protected my father in prison, wanted Lawrence working for him on the outside as recompense for Wilder's having eased his life behind bars—with my law practice serving as the front for a criminal enterprise spanning guns, drugs, and prostitution.

When I refused to play along, Bo had sent men to burn my office. After the fire my father had fled the country with Dot. Last I heard, they were in Croatia living off the settlement money I'd negotiated for his wrongful conviction, Croatia being one of the few countries with a decent standard of living and no extradition treaty with the United States.

Having been the one to find her body when I came home from school that fateful day at the age of twelve, most of my life I'd believed Lawrence guilty of her death. I'd suffered greatly during my childhood, but with my father's release and acquittal I'd had to face the fact that his suffering had been far worse. In my teenage years he was a convenient scapegoat for the howling loneliness of growing up fatherless and motherless, eating lonely mac-and-cheese dinners to punk rock music while Teddy worked late nights—but through all the time I'd spent blaming him, my father had sat in San Quentin, wrongfully accused and falsely convicted, proclaiming his innocence to the world but never to me. I'd spent twenty years believing I was the one with the grievance, but now, I'd realized I owed *him* an apology.

As my father and I were finding out, it's far easier to forgive then to forget.

Chapter 6

Eventually we were driven to the SFPD's Southern Station for interviews. Or I was, rather. They told me Rebecca was coming, but after I climbed into the back of the police car I didn't see her again. No doubt she'd reported what I'd told her about being with Jordan Saturday night. In any case, as Jordan's only known boyfriend, I was clearly a person of interest.

A guilty lawyer knows to keep his mouth shut, but an innocent one will talk his way into trouble like anyone else. I wanted to help the police investigation in any way possible, but this wasn't where my need to talk came from. It was part egoism, part loneliness. I had the feeling that what happened to Jordan was something that had happened in large part to me, isolating me from everyone who hadn't experienced it. That isolation fueled a need to talk about the experience with anyone who'd listen.

I was afraid they'd send in Cole, but evidently the SFPD had enough sense not to put me face-to-face with the detective whose credibility and competence I'd recently attempted to destroy in the very public forum of a San Francisco criminal court. Instead, I was questioned by a younger detective, Mark Chen, who stood a slim six four or six five, like a Ralph Lauren model in a thousand-dollar suit.

"I'm sorry to have kept you waiting," he said.

"It's all right."

"I've just been looking at some preliminary forensics. Fingerprint analysis, mainly."

"You'll find mine. I was with her a few hours before she was killed." I concisely narrated the events of that evening, beginning with meeting for dinner, including our lovemaking at her apartment but not the substance of our conversation there. I reported that someone had contacted her, probably via text, after which her mood had changed.

"She mentioned something about her duty of confidentiality, like it had to do with a client. She wouldn't tell me anything more, but made clear it was time for me to go. She dropped me in a cab at my hotel around one AM."

Chen nodded, waiting for me to go on.

I hesitated, gauging the value of speaking the rest versus the risk of remaining silent. I quickly reached the conclusion that he already knew what I was considering telling him, or would soon know it. I'd been arrested before, so the police had my fingerprints on file. "I noticed a gun on the kitchen floor. The Bersa. You may find my prints on that as well."

"I see."

Before the police had arrived at Jordan's apartment I'd examined the Bersa to check whether it had been fired. There were no scorch marks. Though I hadn't touched it, it would have been easy enough to lie and tell Chen I'd held it in my hand, and claim I'd never seen it before handling it at Jordan's place. Apart from my scrupulous nature, the reason I hadn't tampered with the Bersa, or lied and said I'd done so, was because it seemed to me the police needed to know how it got there. I told Chen as much.

"You're telling me that gun in her apartment is yours?"

"It's not registered to me. Probably it's been reported stolen. All I'm saying is my fingerprints are likely on it. You knew that before you walked in here, I'm guessing."

Chen was silent, seeming to process the implications of my admission that I'd handled the gun before, rather than after, Jordan's murder. If it'd been the murder weapon, he probably would have considered reading me my rights.

"Why would Jordan want to ditch a gun for you?"

"She thought it was a risk for me to have it. She was right. It was stupid of me, but it came into my hands at a time when I thought I needed protection." Without delving into particulars, I explained about the arson fire and my belief someone wanted me dead.

Chen wanted to know where I'd gotten the gun.

"The point isn't why I needed the gun, or where I got it," I said. "The point is that Jordan wanted me to leave it with her. The question is why she thought *she* needed it."

"You think she was afraid of somebody."

"I didn't pick up on this at the time, but it seems likely. She wanted me to bring the gun to her apartment—supposedly so we could get rid of it together. Then she received a text on her phone and showed me the door, reminding me to leave the Bersa."

"Janelle Fitzpatrick thinks Randall Rodriguez is pretty scary. You think Jordan might have been worried about him?"

"Randall'd never have done something like this, showed up at her apartment. He isn't capable of it, any more than he was capable of the Fitzpatrick rape." Even as I said these words I felt a tremor of doubt. He'd probably spent the day sifting trash bins for clean copies of newspapers from which to create new versions of his precious scrapbooks, and for the chess puzzles. These scrapbooks would have included articles about his own case—maybe even yesterday's scathing column blaming the police and the DA for botching the investigation. The whole city knew a confessed rapist had walked free.

According to our expert witness, freedom was the last thing Rodriguez had wanted.

"You must have noticed the shared elements with Fitzpatrick," Chen said. "First, the apparent sexual assault, with the bedding stripped and taken away, and the victim locked in the bathroom to keep her from reporting the crime immediately. Of course, our intruder did a better job with the tape this time. *Too* good, as it turns out."

I closed my eyes, suddenly confronted again with the imagined scene I'd tried to shut out all afternoon: Jordan trapped in that bathroom, bound, her legs cramping and finally going numb, her breath forced for hours through the tiny passages of her nostrils, knowing at every moment that if she panicked, she would suffocate and die, hoping only that someone would discover her in time. No one had, and thus appeared to be, for the rapist, a stroke of luck.

"I'm sorry if these questions disturb you. But, as you pointed out in the trial, if he didn't do this, the real rapist is still out there. If that's true, Ms. Fitzpatrick's case can no longer be considered closed. Now, shortly after your client's release from custody, there occurs a second crime that follows the same pattern as the first. Put yourself in my shoes."

Inadvertently complying, I thought of what I'd seen in the courtroom the day of the verdict—Rodriguez standing behind the counsel table after Jordan had taken his hand. And, a few days earlier, his wink, like we'd shared a secret he knew I'd never tell.

"We found this on her desk." The detective took out a file folder and from it removed two clear evidence bags. One contained a ripped-open blue envelope, the other the card that must have come with it. On the envelope, stamped by the post office the day after the verdict, Jordan's home address was printed in block letters. The card was a generic thank-you card like an old lady might send, with a pastel rainbow on the front. Blue fingerprint dust stained both items. "It's blank inside," Chen said. "Unsigned. You ever see it?"

"No."

"You didn't receive one?"

"I didn't. Have you identified the fingerprints?"

"Rodriguez's are on both the card and the envelope. Jordan's address was unlisted, but evidently he was able to find out where she lived and send her this card. The way you spun things at the trial, you'd think he didn't have the mental wherewithal to find her even if she was in the phone book. Now I'm wondering if the picture you painted was accurate."

I didn't tell him about Randall's chess skills, the wink he'd given me, or his reaction before the verdict to Jordan's touch. "He's no imbecile," I confessed.

That seemed to be all Chen needed. "Just for the file, where were you Sunday?"

"Most of the day I was alone. I left a message for Jordan in the morning. I took BART to Oakland around nine and went for a bike ride in the hills, stopped at my brother's in Berkeley for lunch, and rode BART home in the afternoon." I fished out my wallet and pulled out my Bay Area Rapid Transit ticket, which I'd saved because it still had a dollar-and-a-half credit. "Here."

He slipped it into the chest pocket of his shirt and rose. "Thank you. We'd like to talk to Mr. Rodriguez. You wouldn't happen to know how to reach him?"

"Try the shelters. Under freeway overpasses. I doubt he'll be hard to find."

I felt my grief and anger boil over and knew I was getting out of this little room just in time, but I couldn't resist delivering unwanted advice. "Do me a favor. Videotape the interrogation this time," I said as Chen walked me to the front desk. "Document Rodriguez telling you something you didn't already know. Because if you guys had done the job right the first time . . ."

Chen made no response, just opened the door for me and held it. As it clicked shut between us, I had a sudden fleeting feeling I was standing on the wrong side.

Chapter 7

As soon as I walked out of Southern Station I called Gabriela Alame, the elected public defender and my boss, to tell her I'd be in tomorrow. She tried to convince me to take at least the rest of the week off, but I knew too well that work was the only antidote. The prospect of the empty hours I'd have to fill would otherwise be intolerable.

I let my brother know what had happened and that I was okay. He offered me his couch, a consideration that would never have occurred to the old Teddy, his concern yet another sign of the changes the bullet had wrought. I thanked him but declined. No matter how awful my little room and the recent memories it contained, I needed to spend this evening alone.

I slept only fitfully and was ready for the dawn when it came. By 7:30 AM I was at my desk. Several colleagues stopped by and spoke a few words, but my affair with Jordan hadn't been common knowledge, and it was an open question what special consideration the weeklong sexual partner of a murder victim should receive.

Rebecca, with a longer claim to friendship, hadn't come to work. Only when I'd been there a few hours did it dawn on me that people might see me as callous for showing up the day after finding her dead.

This realization came as a shock and was my first sign that my internal calibrations were disturbed, my self-assessments not to be trusted. But my dread of going home and being alone outweighed my worries about what my coworkers might think.

I sat at my desk staring at a document open on my screen, completely unable to work or to think of anything but Jordan. If I let them, the images of our relationship bowled me over. There was much to remember and I was afraid of losing the immediacy of the nights we'd spent together. I e-mailed the court reporter and ordered the transcript from Rodriguez's trial. Never mind the expense; I could find a justification later for needing it.

As for the rest, we might as well have been writing on water. And now the universe had sucked Jordan away.

I sat at my desk all morning, forgetting lunch, until a piercing headache reminded me I'd had no coffee. When I came out of my office, I realized it was late afternoon. Instead of pouring myself a cup I went outside and walked, following Embarcadero around the city until I was lightheaded with hunger, my heels sore. I meant to find food but instead I walked home through downtown, climbed the stairs to my room, and fell into bed.

Jordan's funeral took place Friday afternoon. The burial would come later, when the medical examiner released the body. But the family had decided to hold the ceremony now.

Dozens of lawyers were in attendance, including Rebecca and Gabriela, who'd given a rousing speech to the troops at the office. *There are those who say we couldn't do the work we do if we knew how it felt to be victims. But the truth is none of us is immune, and we're not indifferent. The crucial thing is not to let anger overwhelm us. What Jordan would want, what any of us would want, is that we go out with renewed purpose and fight all the harder for the clients she'd hoped to spend the rest of her career defending.* To Gabriela, Jordan was a martyr to be exploited in the service of our mission, not the warm-blooded woman who'd slept in my arms.

At the funeral, by contrast, the emphasis was on a reconstructed, sanitized version of a life that to me bore little connection with the Jordan I'd known, the passionate lover, the hard-nosed lawyer. It was as if her adult self, including her professional persona, had been carefully set aside. The priest recalled memories of her as a teenager. Then her best friend from high school talked of trouble they'd gotten themselves into during a trip to Europe before college. The facts that she'd been murdered, most likely by one of her own clients, and that she'd suffered terribly before dying, weren't mentioned at all. By the end, the effect was nauseating to me. I couldn't take seriously a religion that wouldn't call the devil out.

A large contingent was present from Baker Benton. I recognized Tom Benton, the named partner, from his profile on their website. I'd looked him up when Jordan and I first teamed up, after she told me about the case they'd tried together just before she took her leave of absence. Benton was all vertical lines, as if carved from a slab of wood, with hair precisely chiseled and fixed in place. He wore a black suit and a red tie over a cream-colored shirt. The lawyers with him seemed to form their own tribe, set apart by their awareness of their superior gifts.

Jordan's father, by contrast, was weak chinned and narrow shouldered. Standing between wife and daughter, he seemed not to know where he was, or why. His wife had to prod him to stand for the hymns. Both men wept openly: Walker's head dipped as if in shame, Benton's high. By the end of the service, I disliked the latter without having exchanged a word with him.

In the receiving line afterward, Benton ended up next to Gabriela. Each evinced a similar aura of charisma held carefully in check. They appeared to know one another, but that was hardly surprising.

Gabriela was required to stand for election every four years, which meant she had to seek campaign donations from those with the means to give, and to ingratiate herself with the power structures that made her lesser power accessible.

I waited my turn, then shook hands with Jordan's father, sister, and mother, introducing myself by reference to the case we'd just tried. When I mentioned Rodriguez's name, Hiram Walker just nodded. He was glassy-eyed, undoubtedly unused to whatever sedative had been urged on him. His silver-haired wife stared at me with the sharpness her husband lacked. The receiving line behind me couldn't move until I walked on, and I couldn't do that until her eyes released me.

"Jordan was very proud of your accomplishment," she said, tilting her head back for emphasis. "I asked, 'What if he's guilty and goes out and rapes someone else?' 'Mother,' she said, 'I can't worry about that.' It wasn't all principle. She believed he was innocent. She and her father argued terribly about it before the trial."

Her gaze went instantly cold, as if suddenly she'd remembered who I was and what I'd done to cause her daughter's death. I had an urge to tell her how I'd felt about Jordan. Yet if my throat hadn't choked up, such a declaration was the last thing she or anyone in her position could want to hear. Meanwhile the line was moving forward, pressing me on.

~ ~ ~

Monday morning I was seated at the back of the courtroom when the deputies led Rodriguez in. He'd been arrested over the weekend and according to news reports had immediately confessed. Several of us from the office had managed to find places in the crowded gallery. Gabriela and her deputies were there, as was Rebecca. I'd walked over with the others, but there wasn't enough room for us all to sit together. So I'd found a spot near the back, wedging myself in between family members waiting for their loved ones' cases to be called on the felony arraignments calendar. It felt strange to be sitting on the DA's side of the courtroom. Jordan's family was near the front. They still had the look of people who'd been pulled alive from rubble. Because there was no room left in the gallery, the deputies had allowed reporters to sit in the jury box.

Seven arraignments were scheduled for Department 22 this morning, but the crowd was only here for one of them, and the judge called Rodriguez's case first. When my former client was led in between three deputies I felt a wave of déjà vu. He wore the same county orange he'd worn when he was arraigned for the rape of Janelle Fitzpatrick. He looked just the same as he'd looked then, as he shuffled in shackles between the deputies from the holding cell to the well of the courtroom. He was over six feet tall, with tree limbs for legs and arms, his addict's wrists knotted with scar tissue and showing the faded blue of amateur tattoos. His beard was matted and tangled. Despite his size he seemed to cower as the deputies led him forward, presenting the same pitiful aspect that had struck me so powerfully the first time I saw him.

Rodriguez had experienced only a week of freedom since his initial arraignment over a year ago. At that time, of course, Jordan had still been with Baker Benton, preparing for that big trial with her mentor. I'd been the sole lawyer defending the case. He wasn't represented by the PD's office today, of course. His appointed lawyer, a private attorney paid hourly to handle cases where our office had a conflict of interest, stepped to the well of the courtroom to take his place beside him. He said a few words and touched Randall's arm. Instead of Harold Cole, Mark Chen was the lead investigator at the DA's table beside Saenz.

Judge Ransom addressed the defendant and read a summary of his rights, including the right to remain silent and to have an attorney. Then he read the charges, which included sexual assault and first-degree murder, and asked Rodriguez if he understood.

Possibly Rodriguez was still high. His tone was assertive and sharp, like someone voicing a grievance. "That's right, judge. I did it. I'm guilty just like you said."

A stir passed through the gallery. Rodriguez tried to turn, blinking as if he'd just noticed the crowd. Walker bowed his head and his wife stared at the man who'd just spoken. The lawyer bent and whispered furiously in Rodriguez's ear, seeming to get his attention for the first time. He nodded. The lawyer stepped forward. "Alex Ripley for the defendant. The public defender's office has declared a conflict of interest."

"You're appointed."

"I'd like to raise a doubt as to the competency of my client to stand trial or enter a plea, and I'd like to request a mental examination."

Rodriguez's lawyer may not have realized this—I hoped he did, because any competent lawyer ought to have known it—but he was repeating word for word the request I'd made at Rodriguez's initial arraignment.

Rodriguez raised his hand, like a kid in school asking permission to speak, but again the lawyer silenced him with a tight grip on his arm, whispering into his ear. The judge studied him with a frown, then said, "Let's take this up in my chambers."

A recess ensued. The bailiffs returned Rodriguez to the holding cell. Ripley and Saenz followed the judge out the back of the courtroom to his chambers. At the DA's table, Chen turned and went to the rail to speak to Jordan's family, crouching low to put himself at their level. I hadn't noticed before, but now I saw that Janelle Fitzpatrick's father was in the courtroom. He sat beside Mrs. Walker.

After twenty minutes, the judge and the lawyers returned, and Judge Ransom declared he had no doubt Rodriguez was competent to stand trial under California law. Perhaps fearing another spontaneous outburst, Ripley immediately asked for a continuance before entering a plea. The judge granted this. Ripley didn't bother to ask for bail.

Next, the judge called a recess so the spectators could clear the courtroom and allow the remaining arraignments to proceed in peace. I ought to have been prepared for what happened when I stepped into the hallway. I'd been screening my calls and deleting phone messages from reporters all week, and I'd just barely managed to avoid being cornered after Jordan's funeral. This time, however, the crowd coming out of the courtroom propelled me straight into the mouth of the beast.

Turning away from one camera crew, I found myself with another lens in my face. A blond woman holding a logoed microphone appeared. "I'm here with Leo Maxwell, who along with cocounsel Jordan Walker pulled off the acquittal in the rape trial of Randall Rodriguez last week. In a shocking twist, Mr. Rodriguez today confessed in open court that he murdered Ms. Walker. Mr. Maxwell, you were at the funeral Friday. What words did you have for Jordan's family?"

"Their loss is beyond words," I said, because this was undoubtedly true. "Jordan was a lovely woman and a fine attorney. She didn't deserve to have her life brutally cut short."

"We understand from police sources that you've admitted to a sexual relationship with Ms. Walker, and were with her just hours before her death. Did your personal involvement with your cocounsel compromise your handling of Mr. Rodriguez's case in any way?"

The question did what it was supposed to do: anger me into saying something foolish. "That's an incredibly stupid question, given that Mr. Rodriguez was unanimously acquitted of that crime by a jury of his peers. We presented overwhelming evidence that in spite of having confessed to rape, he was innocent. The jury obviously agreed with us that our client's confession was false." I stopped, took a deep breath, then said, "Now if you'll excuse me."

Chapter 8

No matter what else happens, the machinery of criminal justice will always grind on. The day after Rodriguez's arraignment was my first back in court after the murder. I had a preliminary hearing. I'd thought I was prepared, but when my chance to cross-examine came I was like a sleepwalker. During my argument, the judge twice had to prod me to finish sentences. Being in better command wouldn't have changed the outcome, as it was a foregone conclusion my client would be held over for trial. Nonetheless, the experience disturbed me. I'd walked into that courtroom believing I was fine when I wasn't.

Back at the office, I found a message from Rebecca asking me to call her right away. "Jordan's father's at my house," she reported, picking up, her voice just above a whisper. "I don't know what to do with him. He wants the *details* of the crime scene."

"How long's he been there?"

"Twenty minutes. He went to the office first, but neither of us was there. They called me from the desk, and I gave the okay to send him over. I've been able to put him off so far. You're the one he really wants to talk to."

I wasn't surprised. My ten-second sound bite had undoubtedly been seen by half the Bay Area's TV audience.

"The thing is, he's feeling very confused. This is a sheltered man we're talking about, Leo."

A shiver went through me as I was visited by a bodily memory of Jordan on my lap, my hands on her hips, her hands on my shoulders gripping hard for leverage, my palms alternately thrusting and pulling her back. "Oh, Jesus Christ."

"Just tell me you'll be here."

I assured her I was on my way.

Rebecca and her girlfriend, a banker, lived a few blocks from Dolores Park, in what had become one of San Francisco's most desirable neighborhoods. She nodded toward the big corner living room and I went in ahead of her, crossing a wide expanse of rug to where Hiram Walker hunched in a corner chair.

I had to speak his name twice, his eyes finding me as if from a long way off. Then he shook my hand. I perched on the footstool across from him, noting that his eyes, though inflamed and dark shadowed, were clear, the pupils not dilated as they'd been at the funeral.

When he spoke, his tone was more commanding than I'd expected, drawing Rebecca in from the hall. "Is it true you and Jordan were in a relationship?"

"I don't know if you could call it that." I was determined to give him the truth and nothing but—whether or not it might be painful, or not what he wanted to hear. "And we never had the chance to find out what it was."

Rebecca stood leaning in the threshold. It was her house but we were both prisoners to the man in the wing chair, waiting to hear what he wanted.

"I saw you on the news last night," he said after a pause. "Even after what happened, you still seem to think you were right. That takes pigheadedness. I suppose it's no different from these district attorneys, the true believers who refuse on principle to accept the possibility they might have convicted an innocent man. The flip side of that is the defense lawyer who believes all his clients are innocent. Is that what you are—a true believer?"

"I'm able to admit when I'm wrong. All I was saying is that we did our jobs. The DA's supposed to convict the guilty and not charge the innocent. My job is simpler. No matter what a client's done, I'll try to get him off. I did that. Jordan and I did it. We did it together. And we did it well."

"I'm sure she did. She was on her way to becoming a brilliant attorney. I never understood why she wanted to throw it all away on the public defender's office." He looked around, his gaze again seeming to return from an immense distance. "No offense, it's just how I feel. I'm angry, you see. Very angry. So I need someone or something to blame. You, your office, the whole shitty system. Just not my daughter."

"I see," I told him, even though I couldn't imagine the pain of losing a child the way he'd lost Jordan.

"Jordan liked to talk to me about her cases. The Kairos case, for instance. They knew for months it was going to trial. She'd come home on the weekends and we'd sit at the kitchen table, share a bottle of wine, talk through whatever problem she was working on. Tom gave her the plum assignments. No one was more surprised than I was when Jordan first decided on law school. She'd always been so independent. I never thought she'd want to follow in my footsteps. I was very proud. It's a wonderful thing to share one's profession with one's child, to discuss important matters as equals."

He cleared his throat. "After the verdict, those talks stopped. I didn't hear anything more about her work for months. Then the last time she was home, we spoke about your case. It was the first time Claire and I'd seen her in months, since she'd taken that sudden leave of absence from Baker. I was feeling left out of the loop.

I needed to understand what was going on with her—why she'd been shutting me out. I suppose bringing home the Rodriguez case was her way of making amends.

"I didn't think much of your theory of defense when I first heard it. Why would the man confess if he was innocent? I've spent a substantial portion of my career representing police officers against allegations of misconduct. I'd built up a professional wall of skepticism, and she wasn't prepared for that. We fell into an argument after too much wine. It ended with her telling me she thought Rodriguez was innocent and me laughing at her."

He winced and closed his eyes tightly, waiting for that painful memory to pass. "She walked out. Her last words to me were, 'Daddy, the problem with you is you always have to be right.'

"I tried to call her after the verdict to congratulate her, but she didn't pick up. She probably knew I wasn't ready to make a real apology, that I was going to rain on her parade by saying I hoped nothing bad would come of it, that sort of thing. Of course, it turns out I *was* right. Now, for the first time my life, I find I don't want to be."

"Would you rather the killer was still at large?"

He ignored my question. "Can Rodriguez even be made to suffer? I don't think he can. It's at least an open question whether a man who wants to confess, who wants to be locked up, as the two of you argued, can experience punishment, whether you can even call it that. How do you go about punishing a masochist? You can only reward him."

"So you want someone who can be made to suffer to be responsible for this crime?"

He shook his head as if I were missing the point of what he was saying. "*Jordan* suffered terribly. How long do you think she was alive in that bathroom, half-suffocating before she died? They won't tell me. It must have been at least an entire day, maybe as much as forty-eight hours. She was strong. She wouldn't have given in. She'd have held out as long as possible, hoping someone would come."

Someone like me, I thought. But, clearly, her father had cast himself in the role. "I can't tell you how long she might have lived," I said. "The position she was in could have constrained her breathing, leading to rapid suffocation. I'd like to believe she didn't suffer."

He was shaking his head, refusing to accept this cold comfort. "I know she was alive, waiting for help, because I know my daughter. You were the last one to see her alive. The last one except the killer. Tell me what happened between you that night."

I took a deep breath and told him the truth, or rather the facts, leaving out how I'd felt about them. I told him that we'd gone back to her apartment after dinner, that it was the first time she'd taken me there, and that we'd been in bed when she'd received an e-mail or a text on her phone. I told him about what she'd said, her refusal to explain, and the cab ride we'd taken together, with Jordan dropping me off before continuing to a destination she hadn't disclosed. Also, I told him about the gun.

He seemed to take it all in. "And then she ended up back at her apartment, and someone was waiting there," he said. "Someone who'd committed a crime like this before."

"Someone like Rodriguez."

"Someone who knew about Rodriguez's trial and was following it," he said. "What I think is that it was someone who had a special interest in following that trial, enough of an interest to know who Rodriguez's lawyer was, and enough vicious imagination to pick her out as his next victim, knowing Rodriguez would stand up and confess. You might also hypothesize this was a crime of opportunity, but the steps the killer took are too deliberate. The man who did this had done it at least once before."

"A serial rapist."

"A serial killer," Walker said. "Listen, for once in my life I want to have been wrong where my daughter was concerned. I don't want to live knowing I won the last argument we ever had. What I need is for someone to agree with me on this."

Rebecca had taken a step back from the doorway but was still there, listening.

"About Rodriguez being innocent, you mean." I lowered my voice. "He'll have to plead guilty this time, or stand trial and be convicted. The defense we used won't work a second time. All the DA has to say is look what happened last time he got out."

"Meaning?"

"Meaning, the police have their man, and this time the DA's going to obtain a conviction for sure, or more likely force a plea. The case is closed. I'm not agreeing that Rodriguez is innocent, but either way, it's going to happen now just how it happened before, except this time they're going to seal the holes. After all, we showed them how."

Rodriguez's confession was the easy answer, a thoughtless balm, and I'd wanted it to be true. Until now I'd accepted it, though it didn't sit right. But I knew Jordan wouldn't have given in so easily. She'd have gone on fighting for her client.

Though I'd been relieved of that responsibility, didn't I owe it to Jordan, at least, to find out where she'd gone in that cab? Walker didn't ask me to do anything. His desire was to understand what had happened, without resort to the easy answers the press and the police had seized on. It didn't seem the moment to mention that if Rodriguez were eliminated as a suspect in Jordan's death, the police would just try another easy answer.

When he stood to leave, I realized I didn't actually want him to go. Talking to him had cleared my head.

~   ~   ~

"It's magical thinking," Rebecca insisted when the door had shut behind him. "I don't want any part of it. He thinks he can somehow bring her back by believing the man who confessed is innocent. He's not. Jordan was wrong. We almost always are in this business, and that's how it should be—even though we fool ourselves with every case, or, at least, we try to. Rodriguez is guilty."

"Jordan didn't think so. Her father's right that this new confession wouldn't have changed her views. A confession is what you'd expect if our theory of defense is correct."

"Yeah, but Jordan doesn't get to decide, and you don't get to win arguments by saying what she would have thought. She's not here to speak for herself and she didn't nominate you to speak for her. So don't tell me what Jordan would want."

"She'd want whoever did this brought to justice. She wouldn't want her client blamed because blaming him is the most expedient solution."

"How do you know Rodriguez isn't telling the truth? Leave it to the police."

"I'd certainly like to know the identity of whomever she was planning to meet when she left me. That message could have been a trick, or a trap. Maybe someone was trying to lure her away from her apartment."

"Or maybe there was no text. Maybe there was no cab ride." Rebecca faced me across the room. She held my gaze long enough to make clear she'd said more than she intended, but that the words, irretrievable now, would not be called back.

"I'm sorry," she said, her jaw trembling. "Or, rather, I'm not. Anything could've happened. Anyone could have done this if Rodriguez didn't. My loyalty is to Jordan. You were the last person with her. Who knows if you had a motive? Or if you needed one. I don't know you. Why should I believe you?"

I stood shocked in front of her.

Rebecca walked past me, opened the door, and held it open for me to leave.

Chapter 9

Even though I'd faced Chen's suspicion in the interview room, that had been cop suspicion, unthinking and reflexive and utterly familiar. A Maxwell family birthright, you might call it. Rebecca's words, by contrast, had entered me like a sword, the wound remaining fresh. Falsely accused, I found myself missing my father. No doubt he could have told me a thing or two about the little death that premature judgment brings.

Later that evening my phone chimed with a text from Rebecca. *Sorry*, it said. *I miss my friend and I'm scared. Call me when you know where the cab driver went.*

~ ~ ~

When I'd explained the situation, the man on the phone began apologizing, telling me the company's policy of not giving out information about employees or customers. And anyway, he said, the police had already talked to the driver a week ago. I cut him off. "Your driver was the last person I saw with my friend the night she was murdered. He picked her up around twelve thirty, made one stop in the Tenderloin, and continued to a second destination." I gave him first Jordan's address, then my own.

It finally ended with him promising to give my number to the driver, with no promises I'd be called back. Part of me hoped this would be the end of it. Rebecca's mistrust had made me wary of further involvement in what, after all, was a police matter. Two hours later, however, a phone call summoned me from bed and I rose with a sigh and went down to the street.

It was the same guy—heavyset, white with a dark goatee—who'd driven the cab we took that night. I got in the back and he pulled away. "Meter's been running since dispatch called."

I didn't say anything, and he simply drove. His eyes kept checking me in the mirror. It suddenly seemed too great an effort even to open my mouth, let alone make words come. I wondered what was wrong with me. Instead of feeling energized by taking the first concrete steps I'd taken since Jordan's death, I felt pinned down. I suppose it was the futility of it that depressed me. No matter what the answers to my questions were, they couldn't bring Jordan back, and I'd long since quit believing in the usual idea of justice.

"Where we going, man?" the guy finally said when the meter hit fifteen dollars. We were somewhere in the Sunset.

Instead of answering, I asked if he'd been watching the news.

"I used to listen to the radio all through my shift. I had to give it up. You follow the world too closely, you start to care too much, and sooner or later you end up talking back to these assholes. Started cutting into my tips."

It was silent as the grave in the cab. I finally gave him Jordan's address and told him to drive there. When we arrived outside the building I said, "You picked up a double fare a week ago last Saturday night at this address. One of them was me. You took us to the Seward, and dropped me off there. The young woman who was with me stayed in the cab when I got out. She had you drive her to another destination."

"I remember. I was wondering what the fuck she was doing going to a shitty SRO like the place I dropped you off."

"I need to know where you took her after you left me."

His fingers drummed a quick riff on the steering wheel. He seemed to be debating with himself. Finally he said, "You're lucky I got an easygoing boss. What you did was, you called him up, after he'd already got through dealing with the cops, and evidently you made a very inflammatory comment about me being the last person to see your murdered friend alive. I'm just the cabbie, man. You can't blame me for what happens to people after I drop them off wherever they want to go."

"I'm sorry about that, but I *had* to find you."

"I already talked to the cops. I told them what I know. They already arrested the guy who killed her. He confessed, right? So why should I talk to you? You're probably working for the guy's lawyer, trying to get him off."

"Get him off *again*," I corrected. "Believe me, that's not going to happen."

"Then what do you care?"

"Because I have to know. Please, just take me where you took her."

"We're already there," he told me. "I drove her right back here."

I sank lower into the well-worn seat, turning my head to gaze out the grimy window at her building, which I'd been inside exactly twice. So she'd lied to me about the meeting; it was just a ruse to get me out of her bed. Or maybe someone was coming over, someone she'd wanted to be with that night more than she wanted to be with me.

Or someone she was afraid of, whom she didn't want to know about me.

"Did you notice anything? Anyone lurking around inside?"

"Normally, if it's a woman alone I'll watch until she's through the door, but that night I didn't. I'm telling you, man. I didn't see anything, and she didn't say a word to me." He glanced in the mirror. "You want to go somewhere else?"

I told him to take me home. Up in my room again, I reviewed what I'd learned. The story I'd just heard was consistent with Rodriguez's confession. I had no reason to believe the driver was lying, though it'd seemed to me that at the last minute, parked in front of Jordan's place, he'd been about to tell me something important. In any case, nothing he said had made me fear the cops had arrested the wrong man.

I wondered if the police had even gotten a warrant for Jordan's phone records. With the goal of finding out, my first stop the next morning was Gabriela's office. She was writing longhand on a yellow legal pad. I stood there, waiting.

"Leo. Just the man I wanted to see. Come in and close the door."

I did as she asked. "What'd you want to see me for?"

"Why do you think?" She paused. Then she looked at me. "You're new here. Unlike most of our lawyers, you came in with experience trying felony cases. We took a chance that you'd be able to mesh with our system."

"I appreciate that."

"On the plus side, you're not afraid to bring a hopeless case to trial. You've proved you can win against the odds. Don't get a big head about that. Any lawyer who can't work miracles won't last long."

"Okay." I didn't say that I wasn't planning to last any longer than I had to. It was moments such as this that made me determined to be my own boss.

"So you're over the first hurdle. You've got talent. But do you have judgment?"

I tried to play off the question, but my response fell flat. "No one's ever accused me of that."

"With your backstory, I imagine you've learned a lesson or two."

I remembered Jordan examining my scars, the light touch of her fingers on my belly. "I never learn. If I'd learned anything, I'd be sitting in some cubicle downtown, reviewing documents for fifty bucks an hour. I'm here because I try criminal cases and you've got a steady supply."

"You're all messed up by Jordan's death. I can see it in your eyes. You're here, but you're not here."

"I'm all right."

"No, you're not. I heard about what happened in Department Eighteen yesterday. You think that's competent representation, a lawyer who drifts off midsentence?"

I'd thought I'd gotten away with the mess I'd made of the prelim. I'd convinced myself it didn't matter. "I wasn't as prepared as I should have been."

"You weren't a lot of things you should have been."

"Jordan and I won the case together. If our relationship is the problem . . ."

"I'm trying to figure out what the problem is. A lawyer on my staff is dead and her client will soon be going to prison for it. Obviously, something went very wrong."

"Very wrong or very right. Either we were wrong about Rodriguez or we were right about him—that the police arrested and charged the wrong man. And now it's happening again, except this time the real killer planned that Rodriguez would confess."

Gabriela studied me for a moment. "I want you to take leave. You'll need to see a doctor, bring me a medical certification. You're not thinking clearly and I don't want you representing clients in this state."

I thought I'd argue but I was ready to go. "Fine."

"You're not Rodriguez's lawyer anymore. Now we're on the other side. I'm sure you can think of half a dozen theories why he might not be guilty, or why he shouldn't be held criminally responsible, but that's not your job." A different concern passed through her eyes. "Have you been in contact with Rodriguez's new lawyer about this?"

"All she has to do is read the file. All my theories are there."

"She'd have to get it first."

"She hasn't requested it?"

"Everything but the evidence is our work product. We don't give up work product without a court order. So far, no court has ordered me to turn it over."

"She'll get it from the DA, won't she?"

"No warrant has been served. The minute one is, we'll file a motion to quash it. We have the papers ready to file. I doubt it'll come to that."

"I'm sure Chen and Cole would love to sift back through our file and figure out what we were hiding from him. But you're telling me they're too lazy to serve the warrant?"

Her eyes narrowed. "I've earned a lot of credit at the DA's office. Not just for winning cases, going toe-to-toe and getting up every time they knock me down, but for straight shooting. I've reviewed every piece of paper in that file, and I've scanned every document the two of you saved on the shared drive. There's nothing there that could possibly assist the prosecution. I called the DA and told her that myself."

"And she's taking your word for it."

"Keep in mind that Rodriguez's acquittal and Jordan's murder were every cop's worst nightmare. The first tendency is to blame the defense lawyers, and we'll have our share of that. But among those whose opinions matter, it's understood you and Jordan couldn't have won the trial if Cole and Saenz hadn't lost it first."

This was basically what I'd told Chen as I was leaving our interview after I'd discovered Jordan's body. Hearing it from Gabriela was powerful reassurance. But I couldn't ignore the fact that she was trying to play me in the hope of keeping me from becoming an obstacle to Rodriguez's speedy conviction.

"She was one of us," Gabriela now said. "I'm going to do everything I can to bury the son of a bitch who killed her, and right now the odds are on Rodriguez."

Whatever my doubts, I had no desire to assist in Rodriguez's defense. I wanted him right where he was, behind bars until further notice, and I told Gabriela as much. "I just want the same thing her father wants, which is to make sure the police are right about Rodriguez this time." I then corrected myself: "Or to make sure Jordan was wrong."

Gabriela shook her head. "You need to worry about yourself, about getting your head on straight. We're bystanders. We watch and wait. And we trust in the workings of our justice system. As of now, you're on leave. If I see you in the office before Rodriguez pleads guilty, you won't have to worry about bringing me a doctor's note. You'll be fired."

I couldn't believe what I was hearing, but her attitude made it clear she didn't want any more questions or opposition from me. She began writing at the top of a fresh page. I rose to leave.

Chapter 10

I had no intention of giving Rodriguez's lawyer our case file, and was dismayed Gabriela might suspect me of wanting to do so. The actual physical file was no longer in my possession, but all the documents, exhibits, and notes were still on my hard drive. In about ten minutes I could have put together a complete packet for Alex Ripley, including a number of points that hadn't seen the light of the courtroom. After my meeting with Gabriela, I went to my office and burned all the documents from the Rodriguez case onto a CD. She could force me to take leave but she couldn't stop me from looking into Jordan's murder.

In every trial, there are pieces that don't get used, leftover trial exhibits that never emerge from our box behind the defense table. Then there's the other stuff that doesn't even make it into that box, ideas that never advance past the stage of brainstorming and perfunctory Google-search fact-checking. In the Rodriguez case, one of these was our theory that a serial rapist was at work in San Francisco.

We'd played on this possibility at trial, though we hadn't presented any evidence to back it up. Rather, we simply argued that if Rodriguez was innocent, the guilty man must still be out there, waiting to strike again. Originally, I'd toyed with the more ambitious plan of taking the jurors on a tour of unsolved sexual assaults. My idea had been to identify crimes similar to the Janelle Fitzpatrick rape, then call the investigating detectives as witnesses.

I still had the notes I'd made during my first weeks on the case, before Jordan had brought a second set of eyes to bear on the problem of Rodriguez's confession. Initially I'd seized on indications the rapist wasn't new to sexual violence. Making the victim shower to eliminate physical evidence struck me as the act of someone with foresight and experience. Rather than reacting impulsively, he'd followed a plan. Same with the way he'd stripped Janelle's bed and taken away the sheets, blankets, pillows, and clothing on which he might have left any fluid or hair. The only mistake he'd made was turning the light on when he forced her to shower, allowing her to believe she'd gotten a good look at his face.

Feeling certain the person who'd raped her had done it before, I'd started looking for crimes that seemed similar to her case, where the description of the suspects was consistent with the description Janelle had initially given of Rodriguez—before the botched lineup—as a large man who could have been either white or Hispanic. None was an exact match. Those that had been closed by arrest were no use to me, because those rapists were in prison when this latest assault had occurred. Also, I needed a crime for which my client had an airtight alibi, preferably one that had taken place while he was locked up.

The best match had been a police report from two years ago. The incident it described was another home-invasion rape that had never been solved. I'd seized on this crime not only because of certain similarities to the Fitzpatrick case, but also because on the night of this earlier event, Rodriguez unquestionably had been in jail.

Just as in the Fitzpatrick case, the assailant had followed the victim to her door, waited until she unlocked it, then charged forward and grabbed her. The rape had happened not in the bedroom, but in the front hallway, from where the rapist had dragged her into the bathroom, forced her to strip, and made her wash. Then he'd stuffed her clothes and the washcloth into a kitchen garbage bag and fled. This evidence had never been found.

There were differences, of course. The victim in the previous rape was a waitress and part-time student who lived with roommates near Balboa Park. The roommates hadn't been home at the time of the assault, but one had arrived barely twenty minutes after the rapist fled and found her roommate locked in the bathroom naked. However, the timing here suggested the crime had been impulsive and opportunistic rather than planned. In my imagined narrative, this was one of the first completed stranger rapes by a perpetrator who'd become more methodical with experience. By the time Janelle Fitzpatrick entered his sights, he'd honed his plan, and followed it to the letter.

Jordan had convinced me to drop this theory. "The crimes aren't similar enough," she'd pointed out. "Also, there aren't enough data points. Between any two events you can draw a trend, but unless there's a third point to test your theory on, it's just coincidence. You need at least three similar crimes to form a convincing pattern."

I'd spent several days sifting through police reports, but every similar rape I'd found had been committed by a man who was convicted and sent to prison and who was still behind bars at the time of the Fitzpatrick rape and thus could be eliminated as a suspect.

Now, with Jordan's rape and murder, we had the third data point we'd lacked. But I also remembered another caution from Jordan: the imagination can create a pattern out of anything.

I'd never developed the theory beyond my notes and the documents. If I had, my next step would have been to track down the victim of that first crime and talk to her, see if she'd have had any value as a witness. I'd gone so far as to print search results from the usual databases, yet I'd held back from making the initial contact—both because around then Jordan had hit the jackpot with the investigators of Rodriguez's previous confessions, and because my gut told me the jury was unlikely to buy the idea of a serial rapist on the prowl. Would anyone be any more likely to buy it now, when Rodriguez was so much more obviously guilty?

Her name was Britney Yarmouth. A list of possible cell phone numbers from the LexisNexis database was in the file. The first two numbers I tried were no longer in service. The third connected and, just when the call seemed about ready to go to voice mail, a woman said hello, with an urgent challenge in her voice. I told her I was a lawyer and what office I worked for and that I wanted to talk to her about a crime she'd been involved in as a victim a few years before. Then I waited, expecting the silence that signaled she'd ended the call.

Instead her words came in a rush, tumbling out so fast I could hardly keep up. "I've been going around for days wondering what the hell is going on: should I call the police, should I call *you*, or should I just forget about it. Like, for my own safety. But I can't just *forget*. I'm too scared. Even in the middle of the day, I can't walk down the street without looking over my shoulder. The cat was making noise last night and I nearly put a bullet through my bedroom door. Jordan told me we were safe but obviously she was wrong."

My heart rate spiked. "You knew Jordan?"

"She first called wanting me to be a witness in that trial. I told her I didn't think I could. In the end, she said I didn't have to. I asked her to keep me posted on how it was going, and she said she would. I didn't expect her to follow through, but during the trial she called me every single night. Even if it was just a few words, she always called."

I hadn't realized Jordan had actually spoken with Britney before our focus shifted to discrediting Rodriguez's confession by reference to his history of interactions with the police. I was even more surprised to learn they'd kept in close contact months after Britney ceased to be a potentially useful witness in Rodriguez's trial.

"What did she want you to testify about?"

"What happened, of course. The rape. She said it couldn't have been your client. After I saw a picture of him, I knew she was right. She was sure that the guy who'd attacked me must also have attacked other women." The urgency came back into her voice. "We discussed it again the night she died."

I couldn't believe what I was hearing. "Discussed what?"

"About how the police had long since given up investigating the rape. She had this idea, after Rodriguez was acquitted, that now they'd have no choice but to start looking into the possibility that the guy who'd attacked me was still out there, that I hadn't been his first or his last, that he'd been attacking other women and getting away with it. She wasn't going to just walk away after the case was over. In her mind, the jury's verdict was only the beginning. She wanted to get the real guy. I believed in her. I wanted to get him, too."

"And then she turned up murdered."

"*He* killed her. Because he knew she was gunning for him." Her voice rose, becoming almost manic. "I've never been more sure of anything in my life. And now they've got Rodriguez behind bars for the crime, so that means the real killer can do whatever he wants. As far as the police are concerned, *he* doesn't exist. And that means he never did."

"What did you mean before about Jordan saying the two of you were safe?" I wondered if there'd been threats, or some other indication that they might *not* be safe, that the rapist had one or both of them in his sights nearly two years after Britney had been attacked.

"She said he wouldn't dare come after me again. His whole MO is watching, waiting in the shadows. Like a panther in a tree. That's what we started calling him during the trial. The Panther. I'd ask her: 'Do you think the Panther's following this?' Meaning the trial. And she'd say 'I'm sure he is.' She wanted to send him a message. 'We're coming for you' is what she wanted him to think. 'You can't hide much longer.'"

I steered the conversation back to the part that kept ringing in my ears. "You talked to Jordan the night she died?"

She confirmed that she had. Then, suddenly, she needed to cut the conversation short. "I have to go to class," she said, and asked what time would be good for her to call back.

I told her I wanted to meet in person, that what we had to talk about was too important for the phone. She reluctantly agreed. I was about to suggest my office, but the memory of my conversation with Gabriela made me backtrack. I was on leave, which meant I shouldn't show my face during business hours.

"The flower conservatory," I suggested, figuring she'd prefer somewhere public.

"Fine," she said, and we made plans to meet at four o'clock that day.

~ ~ ~

She'd seen my ten seconds of fame on the evening news and knew what I looked like. The idea was for me to wait outside the front entrance of the Conservatory of Flowers, near the east end of Golden Gate Park, and she'd find me.

At ten past four I was standing at the top of the steps, chilled by a frigid Pacific wind, the first fluttering of panic beginning to stir in me as the fog turned August into December. I worried she'd decided not to come.

Then a voice spoke behind me. "Mr. Maxwell?" I turned and saw a slight young woman in jeans and an oversized sweatshirt.

Inside the conservatory, the air was humid, thick with the scent of greenery and soil. The light was the same as outside yet seemingly illuminated a different planet.

"You're still in school?" I asked as we moved along an aisle between overhanging palms.

"I stopped taking classes for a while after the attack. I quit my job. But I have another one now, waitressing again. In a few years I'll be a nurse. You do what you need to do, and you learn to shut out the rest."

I could sense she was trying to convince herself. "You've had to shut out a lot."

"You go on living," she said. "You can't spend your life behind a locked door." She paused, gazing at a bird of paradise. She reached out as if to touch the exotic bloom, then seemed to remember it wasn't permitted and yanked her hand back.

"Jordan never said anything about being in contact with you."

"Why should she? Jordan talking to me had nothing to do with the case you two were working, not after we decided I wasn't going to testify. We were just . . . friends."

Each time we paused she turned away from me and moved on. As the minutes passed, I became increasingly aware of an almost unbearable turbulence in her. "Jordan and I shared a lot of things outside of work, near the end."

"Okay, I get it." At last she turned to me. As our eyes made contact, her gaze began to melt. "What happened to her, I just can't bear to think about it. All I can think about is how it was for me. I've been reliving that ever since she called me the first time. For a while, I thought it was helping. I thought we were moving toward a solution, that one of these days I'd see the bastard locked up forever. Then I could stop being afraid."

"What did you talk about the night she died?"

"She wanted me to go public, to give an interview with this reporter she knew. She figured that if there was a big story in the papers, if people started believing there was a serial rapist on the loose, the police would have to reopen their investigation. That's what we talked about the night she died. She knew I got off work late. A lot of times she'd call at two, three AM."

"Is that when you talked to her that night?"

She took out her phone and opened the call log. "She called me just before three."

I did the math. She'd have been back at her place by then, no sign of an intruder. "What did she say?"

"Nothing, really. She said she was sure that I was safe. I didn't need to worry about the publicity of the trial stirring things up. She kept repeating I was safe, until finally I just said, 'Okay, I believe you.' That was it."

"Did you text or e-mail her earlier that night?"

"No. We always just talked."

"Has anyone from the police contacted you, asked you questions about her death?"

"I've been waiting, but you're the first person I've heard from. I'm scared. I'd have gone to the police, but they've already proved they can't protect anyone. All they care about is showing that Rodriguez was guilty all along."

"I don't know how much Jordan told you, but it does look as if he killed her." I said this as gently as I was able to. "If he did this, he probably raped Janelle Fitzpatrick, too. He confessed to both crimes. The facts of your case are superficially similar, but what Jordan told me when we first considered you as a witness was that they weren't similar enough. I agreed with her at the time, and I still do. We could never prove it was the same guy."

Britney shook her head, still clinging to the hope Jordan had kindled. "Rodriguez was innocent of that rape. He'd confess to any notorious crime. Isn't that what the psychologist said when she testified? Jordan was too smart to be fooled by someone like that."

"But even if Rodriguez is innocent, that still doesn't mean the same person committed all three of these crimes. I know you're hungry for answers, but it's a huge leap to conclude that just because you were raped and Janelle Fitzpatrick was raped and Jordan was raped, the same person's responsible. There're a lot of bad people out there."

"But if I am right, that means I'm in danger, right? Jordan said we weren't in danger, but I think she was scared."

"Tell me everything she said to you the last time you talked."

We'd stopped under a huge date palm. "Like I said, right after the verdict she'd mentioned the idea of getting the *Chronicle* to do a story about me. You know: 'rape victim still waiting for justice,' that kind of thing. She said she'd suggested it to her reporter friend, who seemed interested. She wasn't committing to doing a story yet, but she wanted to set up a meeting. Jordan was going to call me in the morning with the place and time."

"What was this reporter's name?" This could have been the person who'd texted Jordan.

"Rachel Stone. She wrote about your verdict, and she did a story about Jordan's death. I expected her to contact me but she never did."

I asked her what else Jordan had said to her the night of her death. "Just that we didn't have to be afraid," she repeated as we circled back toward the entrance. "She said that at least twice. 'He won't come after you, and he won't come after me.' But he must already have been nearby when she told me that." She shut her eyes. "Maybe even outside her door."

I gave her my card, and encouraged her to keep in touch. But I still couldn't bring myself to believe in a panther with no face, no name. If Jordan hadn't deemed this theory good enough for the jury, why had she picked it up again after the verdict? What had kept her from discussing it further with me?

Most troubling of all, why had she given Britney false hope that her attacker might be brought to justice?

Chapter 11

I'd picked up a used Yamaha motorcycle a few months before, regarding it as a suitable compromise between the demands of living in the city and my occasional need for escape. A parking slot in a building not far from my hotel had been included with the bike at a grandfathered rate. On the Friday of my first week of medical leave, I rode across the bay to Teddy's house, knowing the ride would be a good chance to think.

In contrast with his former agility of mind, the new Teddy was painfully clumsy, his old confidence having given way to self-consciousness. He was prone to lapses in memory and confusion, and he was incapable of making quick judgments. Physically he looked the same, except for the bright dimple of the scar on his brow, the scar usually kept hidden by a wide-brimmed hat. He carried his regained weight easily on his bearlike, six-foot frame.

"We've missed you," Tamara said at dinner.

"It's just that I've been busy with work. There was the trial, then, after that, I was two weeks behind on everything else. Now I'm on leave." I explained about Gabriela telling me I wasn't mentally fit to represent clients. I didn't tell them that I'd concluded my "leave" was, in fact, a pretext for keeping me out of sight and discrediting me while the state built its case against Randall Rodriguez.

"You're tearing yourself to pieces about that girl," Teddy said.

I shook my head. I couldn't put into words the tumult of conflicting emotions I felt each night when I lay down to toss and turn on my thin mattress. Needing to change the subject, I said, "Heard from Dad?"

"He seems to be staying put, according to the last postcard he sent Carly."

With a possible murder charge hanging over his head, I doubted he'd be back. Lawrence had Bo Wilder to thank for that, as surely as Teddy and I had him to thank for the burning of our office.

Carly and I played in the backyard while Teddy and Tamara cleaned up after dinner, one of their typical one-pot concoctions that required neither recipe nor forethought, just open the fridge and see what's there.

Carly ran up and down on the grass, making a game of bringing me all the toys from her playhouse back by the fence under the persimmon. "Unk-ah 'eo!" she called out to me, screaming with laughter. I wondered if she missed Lawrence, gone now for nearly three months on his travels, having absented himself from her life almost as abruptly as he'd reentered ours. I tried not to blame him, but I knew Teddy did.

Lawrence had had the good fortune to be acquitted in his retrial. He'd be a fool to put his head on the block again.

Tamara came out to the patio table with a glass of lemonade, leaving Teddy to finish up inside. I stayed on the grass playing with Carly. But when she began to seem bored with me, I went to sit with my sister-in-law. Tamara gave me a wan smile, but the fatigue showed around her eyes, and she wouldn't meet my gaze. Ever since the fire, nothing was the same.

"We have a gun in the house now. Did he tell you that?" she asked, proving our thoughts were on the same wavelength.

Her acuity had improved drastically over the years. Every once in a while, like now, it was possible to hold a normal conversation without her spacing out, especially when, as now, she was consulting the notebook she always kept close at hand, where she wrote down everything of importance. It appeared she had a list of topics ready to bring up with me.

My last lunch with Teddy a few weeks ago seemed a different lifetime. "He told me."

"It doesn't make me feel safer. It makes me think that before this is over, he's going to end up shooting himself or me."

"My feeling is the fire was probably the end of it. If Bo wanted us dead, we would be. But I'll talk to Teddy about it."

"What about this coworker of yours who got murdered?"

This leap gave me a start. "The police have the guy in jail. He confessed, evidently. Bo didn't have anything to do with what happened to Jordan."

"I'm sorry to sound this way," she said. "But we're seeing bogeymen here, every night. Meanwhile, your father, the cause of it all, gets to live happily ever after thousands of miles away. The least he could have done was write a check from some of those settlement funds. The fire cut off Teddy's income. Even if he goes back on disability, there's not enough."

"I feel responsible. From now on, I should be able to help more."

She shook her head. "That's not what I was saying. I know it's wrong to be afraid all the time. But I'd never have thought they'd go as far as they did."

Tamara's gaze remained fixed on Carly, sitting under the lemon tree beside the neighbor's calico cat, its tail flicking as Carly experimentally stroked its fur. Then, as if at some unheard signal, the cat's tail went straight up. It shot toward the fence and was over it in a bound.

At dinner we covered our awkwardness with one another by focusing our shared attention on the child. A natural show-off, and fortunately still too young to pick up on the undercurrents between adults, Carly drank up our attention, running through her whole routine of faces and repeating the few words she knew.

I read a bedtime story; then Tamara put her to bed. Teddy and I took our beers to the patio. A long silence was followed by this revelation: "Bo Wilder's been calling me. Late at night, from prison, on a contraband cell."

I digested this. Finally I said, "You don't have to answer when he calls."

"We can't live in fear anymore. I need to earn a living. Bo knows I can't afford to walk away." *The way you could*, his tone seemed to add. "I have a family to think about."

"So what are you saying?"

He seemed to have trouble getting it out, gazing off toward the persimmon tree, his face twisting before he answered. "You and me, we never really talked about my work. The summer I got shot, when you were working for me, I always meant to sit you down and ask you if this was really what you wanted to do with your life, defend guys like Ricky Santorez. Guys like Bo Wilder. But next thing I knew I was lying in a hospital bed. And now you're the alpha dog and I'm the one who runs behind picking up scraps."

I nodded for him to go on. I owed it to him to hear him out, even if it was years too late for what he was saying to make any difference.

"What I would have told you if we'd ever had that heart-to-heart talk is this: being my brother, certain people are going to expect things from you that they don't have any earthly right to expect. Brilliance, for one. At least, back in the day, that's what I'd have said. Nowadays, not so much."

The old brilliance still showed in sparks, as well as the ego that went with it. But there was no way to fan that near-dead coal back into flame.

"The fact is," he continued, "being in your line of work, Bo Wilder has the right to expect that certain arrangements I had with certain people—Santorez being one—are still in effect, only with you standing in my shoes."

"Because of what he did for Dad." I was speaking of the murder of Russell Bell, the snitch who otherwise would have testified against my father and put him back in prison.

Teddy nodded and shrugged. "And if they're not, he'll feel that someone owes him. Because in this world that he runs in, no privilege ever dies. Everything that's worth anything gets handed on, like rights of inheritance. That goes for people, too, everyone who's ever played a useful role. There's no such thing as an unowned man."

"I don't accept that, and neither should you."

"You wanted to follow in my footsteps. Look, I'm sorry if I never explained what that meant. I figured, a smart kid like you, people'd talk, you'd listen, and you'd figure out pretty quick what you were getting into and chart a different path."

Kid. Five years ago, that description had sounded natural. "I always believed in you. Even when all the signs pointed to you being dirty, even when you'd been shot in the head, everyone saying you deserved it, I told them they were full of shit." Once, these words would have come with the heat of my disappointment behind them. These days, I'd long since come to terms with who my brother was, what he'd done, the price he'd paid.

"What was I supposed to do? Come out and tell you I was a crook? I didn't want to shatter your expectations, Leo. On the other hand, I could have given you Jeanie's old desk, since you were dying for a chance like that. But I kept you at arm's length. I definitely wanted to teach you a few survival skills, but when the time came, I was gonna push you out of the nest. Then . . ." He made a gun with two fingers and shot himself in the head.

"So the next thing you're going to tell me is you knew this day would come."

"It seemed for a while you were in the clear. You probably were in the clear as long as Santorez stayed alive. I didn't count on Bo reopening accounts Santorez had considered closed. And I certainly didn't count on anything like that fire. What I mean to say is, I'm sorry."

I just nodded. I felt so tired. Whatever Teddy had been before, he'd changed, or so I'd thought. But now he was telling me he was going back to working beyond the pale of the law, or at least with one foot over the edge.

~ ~ ~

Monday I left a message for Rachel Stone, the *Chronicle* reporter, mentioning Jordan's name and Britney's. I gave her my cell number and asked her to phone back. Her most recent piece had been written the day after Jordan's murder. She'd portrayed Jordan as an idealist whose liberal intentions had opened a Pandora's box. The story was structured in three parts. First came a recitation of the circumstances of the attack, ending with the moment when Jordan must have recognized her assailant as the man whose freedom she'd won in the courtroom just one week before.

Next there was a summary of Jordan's courtroom performance, with a quote from an interview after the verdict expressing her absolute confidence in our client's innocence.

Finally, the article concluded with a description of the crime scene at Jordan's apartment, the details of broken glass, splattered blood, and duct tape supplying the moral it would have been tasteless of Stone to spell out. I hated her as I read it, but I couldn't help crediting the lawyerly skill with which she'd let her narrative present her argument.

I also read the two previous pieces she'd done on the Rodriguez case. Britney had called her Jordan's friend, and in the story covering the verdict she'd placed the fault for Rodriguez's acquittal squarely on the police department and the DA's office, cataloging their missteps. In these pieces, the PD's office came in for a more favorable portrayal than was usual from Stone. As a matter of principle, she liked to draw attention to the constitutional "technicalities" that freed our clients, the evidence we managed to suppress, and all the other tactics by which we persuaded jurors to embrace gauzy doubt and abandon common sense.

Just before noon, my phone buzzed. I answered it and agreed to Stone's brusque suggestion that we meet in a half hour at the tearoom on top of Yerba Buena Gardens.

"Sit," she said when I approached her table on the outdoor patio. Her voice had the raspy note of a former smoker, contrasting with her aura of athletic fitness and health. She had a sharp, alert face and short silver hair that curled at the tips.

"There's a minimum charge, so you may as well order something," she said, eyeing me up and down as if she disapproved of my cargo shorts and hoodie. In all fairness, I *was* underdressed, but I'd come as I was.

She requested the "Moorish tea service," which the menu described as vegetable kebobs over kale salad and a pot of mint tea. I ordered a grilled cheese, which nearly brought me to the mandatory minimum, and also a coffee, which the waitress informed me they didn't have. Black tea, then, I told her. Stone observed this exchange like a professor watching an unprepared student fail an entry-level test.

Evidently her restrained view of Rodriguez's defense team hadn't survived Jordan's death. "I have to say, I was hoping Jordan would have had better taste in men."

"Like Tom Benton?" It was a shot in the dark.

She studied me for a moment as if to gauge how much I knew, then looked away. "Poor Tommy" was all she said.

I was intrigued to learn that apparently she knew Tom Benton, but I let it pass for now. "I hear Jordan, before she died, was trying to talk you into writing about a serial rapist. I need to ask you about that."

"The 'Panther,'" she said, both mocking the sensationalist tone and taking pleasure in it.

"It was an idea we'd thrown around, brainstorming Rodriguez's defense, but we never had anything to support it. I was surprised to hear she was pursuing it again."

"You're surprised any defense lawyer cared. Isn't that it? What you normally do is put on your big show in the courtroom, then forget about it the minute the trial's over. Well, Jordan actually seemed to believe Rodriguez was innocent. Apparently, she felt an obligation to act on that belief. A true believer, isn't that what you'd call her in your business?"

"That label diminishes her and you know it."

"Only a defense lawyer would think it's a character flaw to believe what comes out of your own mouth. I'm not saying she was a bad lawyer. I was in the courtroom. I saw how the jury responded to her. You think you'd have won the case without her?"

Maybe I would've won it alone; maybe I wouldn't have. But Jordan had been instrumental to our victory and now she was gone. "Your piece didn't say anything about Jordan's belief this so-called Panther was responsible for Fitzpatrick's rape."

"I had the piece written, but it took some convincing before my editor would sign off on it. We ran into the same problem you had, which was how do you look at a series of unsolved crimes and find the pattern. We couldn't come up with anything conclusive, only enough to raise the question. It was set to run the Wednesday after the murder."

"And now you've changed plans."

"What Jordan believed is no longer the story. The story is what happened to her because of that belief. Your client confessed. *He's* the Panther, if there ever was one."

"It's a good thing you didn't run the piece before her murder. Then you'd have had no choice but to double down. 'The Panther strikes again.' In retrospect, it would have looked like a dare. You might even have felt responsible."

"So because you were fucking her you get to be self-righteous?"

I ignored this. "You believed her before she was killed. Why not afterward?"

She poured more tea for herself and gave a shrug. "Rodriguez confessed."

"Exactly. And then almost immediately, he confessed again."

I watched her eat. We both were thinking. Finally she said, "When Jordan was still alive, I was willing to accept that a jury might arrive at 'not guilty.' That *could* mean he's innocent. It could also mean he did it—but that for whatever reason the state didn't bring enough proof to convict.

"I was willing to explore both scenarios. My piece immediately after the verdict suggested the DA had fucked up and lost a case it should have won. Out of fairness, and because Jordan was a convincing advocate for what she believed, I was willing to give that possibility serious treatment. What if Rodriguez *was* innocent? Britney was going to be the centerpiece of my Panther story. Not out of choice, but because there was no way Janelle Fitzpatrick was going to talk to me about her case.

"But then Jordan was murdered and Rodriguez confessed. You and I both want Jordan to be right, but look at it from my point of view. My reputation's at stake with every story, and so is my newspaper's. When Rodriguez confessed to Jordan's murder, do you think the odds he was guilty of raping Fitzpatrick got better or worse?"

She was trying to spin me and I didn't like it. "*You* don't want her to be right. You just want the most sensational story you can possibly write. You wanted to use the Rodriguez case to make a moral example out of someone. At first, you could make your little lesson out of the DA's failure to present a compelling case and the cops' failure to investigate thoroughly. Then, after Jordan was killed, you had a more sensational story to tell, with a much simpler takeaway. 'Naïve liberal defense lawyer gets what she deserves.' What we all deserve. Isn't that the effect you're going for in your latest piece?"

Her voice was icy. "I make a point of writing the facts and letting readers draw their own conclusions."

"How'd you know her?" I asked.

"Tommy introduced us."

"Benton?"

"He and I go way back." There was an opening there but her tone indicated she intended to guard it.

Not accustomed to prying into other people's lives—at least when I didn't have the people in question on the witness stand under oath—I left it alone. Just for the moment. "Did you talk to her the night of her death?"

"Know something? You're the first person to ask me that question."

It didn't surprise me. "Did you send her a text message or an e-mail that night?"

"No. I didn't talk to her, didn't text her. No e-mails. You can cross me off the suspect list."

"I'd like to see her phone records, and, better yet, I'd like to know if the police have gotten them. Otherwise, it seems to me you may have a chance to revisit that story you wrote after the verdict. There's more at stake now than simple laziness. If Chen doesn't nail Rodriguez this time around, Cole's ass is on the street because of what happened with the Fitzpatrick trial. This is their one shot at redemption."

"I'd agree with you there," she said.

"What you said before, about exploring the alternative possibilities—why can't you still run with that? You've been down the first road. Idealistic public defender gets a fatal reality check. That's the official version. But what about the possibility Jordan was right and Rodriguez gave another false confession, just like he did in the Fitzpatrick case?"

Stone shook her head. "No one tells me what to write."

"You were talking to Jordan about writing a column on Britney. The what-if piece: 'Panther stalks the city' and all that. Obviously, you can't do it the same way after what happened, but the premise you were working from hasn't fundamentally changed."

"If I'd realized you were coming here to lobby me for a story I'd have told you not to waste your time. Jordan and I had a lot in common. You're just another man trying to tell me how I should do my job. I don't tell you how to try your cases—though since I've probably spent more time in courtrooms than you have, I could give you a few pointers."

"Let's stay on topic. You liked Jordan. So did I. So did Tom Benton. So did her father, who, by the way, is convinced she was right. I'm not so sure." I needed to keep her attention and achieve something approaching trust. That's what I was here for. "Part of me thinks you and the police are right about Rodriguez killing her. But I'm sure the police, the DA, even Gabriela at the PD's office are railroading Rodriguez straight to a guilty plea and the rest of his life in prison. It's too fast, and no one is asking the questions that need to be asked. I've even been told I'll lose my job if I stir the pot. What do you think of that?"

"I'm still sitting here and my tea is gone. That should tell you something."

"Rushing to judgment was wrong before and even more wrong now. You wrote what you wrote then, so I know you agree with me now. No one's asking you to be inconsistent."

She studied me for a moment, then said, "While we're conducting these little thought experiments, let's say there's a third option. Someone on the inside, someone who knew Rodriguez and how he'd react. Someone with access to Jordan, someone she trusted to let in the door of her apartment. Someone with a personal motive to want her dead. She wasn't 'into' you the way you were into her, is what I hear."

Stone meant Rebecca and Cole, I guessed. Contact between them was not unthinkable. Cole's survival depended on his acquittal in the court of public opinion, a court over which Stone and the *Chronicle* presided. "Write whatever you have to write."

"If I dive back into this I intend to look at all the angles. But I need a source, and until a better one comes along, you're my man. I want your promise, Leo, that no matter where this leads, you'll talk to me. On the record, too. That's my precondition."

"You want a blank check."

She smiled grimly. "If you've done nothing wrong, you've nothing to fear."

Chapter 12

The piece ran three days later, appearing online in the middle of the night. It was long, running to six full pages in the digital version, and it presented a powerful and comprehensive indictment of the police investigation into Jordan's death. It summarized and built on all the evidence of incompetence we'd presented, as detailed in previous articles focusing on the Fitzpatrick rape. Yet I clearly hadn't been Stone's only source. Inside the police department there'd been somebody able to confirm that no additional warrants had been issued since Rodriguez's latest confession, that the police hadn't yet obtained Jordan's phone records, and that her e-mails had been searched not by the police but by the IT people at the PD's office.

As before, no physical evidence linked Rodriguez to the crime scene, Stone's article noted. Once again, the only apparent indication of his guilt was his own confession. The first section of the story included a quote from the police department spokesperson, to the effect the police had closed the case with Rodriguez's arrest and weren't presently pursuing additional suspects. But Stone wasn't done yet.

Next, despite her seeming resistance to my ideas, she went on to basically follow the script I'd suggested. Reporting Jordan's belief that Janelle Fitzpatrick had been the victim of a sexual predator who was still at large, Stone dwelled on the coverage of the Rodriguez trial, inviting the readers to imagine the reaction of the "Panther's" to seeing another man confess and be tried for that rape.

Furthermore, Fitzpatrick's wasn't the first unsolved rape. Other assaults had appeared on the blotter sheets over the years, with characteristics that might be viewed as forming a pattern. The victims left alive but bound and confined. The sheets, clothing, and other possible repositories of physical evidence meticulously removed—carried away by the perpetrator and never recovered. Across the city, Stone wrote, women were waiting for justice. Waiting, and wondering where the Panther was now.

Reading the piece, I felt a mixture of satisfaction and dread. I'd used Stone as my proxy to stick my thumb in Cole's eye. But there was no telling how the police might react. The only certainty was the authorities couldn't now go on ignoring the possibility a serial rapist was stalking women in San Francisco.

Not surprisingly, the story kicked off a minor media frenzy. Each story confirmed that as far as anyone knew, I'd been the last person other than the killer to see Jordan alive.

At six thirty Saturday morning, a pair of cops knocked on my door. They had no warrant, they informed me, only a strongly worded request that I voluntarily accompany them to Southern Station to resume my interview with Detective Chen. Evidently I'd succeeded in stirring up the hornet's nest. I made them wait in the hallway while I showered, shaved, and dressed. Soon enough, I once again found myself sitting in a cramped interview room facing Chen across a table.

"We'd like you to provide a biological sample," he said. "A cheek swab. It's not invasive. We know you had intercourse with Jordan the night of her death. We need a sample from you to identify whether a third party's genetic material may also be present." His tone was carefully neutral, but I knew he hadn't dragged me out of bed on a Saturday morning merely for such a routine request.

On the surface, this was a reasonable appeal. Jordan had been on the pill, and we hadn't used a condom. My semen was undoubtedly present in her body at the time of her death, and providing a sample of genetic material from my cheek lining would enable the police to confirm what they already knew by virtue of my own statements. On the other hand, if no one else's genetic material was present, the inevitable DNA match would help the DA seal a case against me. Still, I couldn't really believe they'd make me their target—especially not with Rodriguez's confession in hand.

After quickly weighing these calculations, I did as he asked, leaning forward to let him swab the inside of my cheek. "You haven't checked the sample against Rodriguez yet? Or didn't you get a match?" I asked as he screwed the sample into its sterile case.

"I'm not expecting a match with Rodriguez. We didn't have one in the Fitzpatrick case. This is to eliminate the possibility of a third party at the scene."

He sealed the sample case in a manila envelope.

"What about Jordan's cell phone records? Come on," I said, seeing his reluctance. "Haven't you gotten them yet?"

"They just came in. The only message that night came from a prepaid."

"What did the text say?"

"I can't discuss that."

"That's all right," I told him. "I'll just wait and read it in tomorrow's paper. It must be frustrating to have a leak in your investigation and not know who it is."

Chen refused to take the bait. "Last time we were discussing your reasons for possessing an unregistered handgun. You said Jordan had recommended you get rid of it. Remember that discussion?"

I met his stare. "I do criminal defense for a living. You'd have me on a misdemeanor. I'd get pretrial diversion and the charge would go away."

"Normally ballistics takes about a month, but I was able to put a rush on this job. That gun killed a man named Russell Bell."

I blinked.

"You know the name, I take it. The chief witness in the prosecution of Lawrence Maxwell. Who, of course, happens to be your father. Russell Bell turning up shot to death was the only reason your father ended up being acquitted."

I blinked again.

"Now do you want to give me your story about how you came by that weapon? Or do you need some more time to think about it?"

If he was bluffing, it was a pretty cheap bluff, certain to kill his credibility with me when the truth came out.

I decided he wasn't bluffing.

I thought back to how I'd gotten that gun.

Shortly after the fire, when I was still recovering from being shot and trying to sell my condo and get out of Oakland, a former client had come to see me, and, after hearing about my troubles, offered to give me a clean gun, no charge. The guy's name was Roland McEwan, and he'd just gotten out of prison after serving a two-year term that should have been ten, given the facts. He owed me a favor for my unpaid fee and, in a moment of weakness, I'd taken him up on the offer. A week later he'd called and told me he had the piece. I'd taken it and felt better for a few days, but it spooked me to carry a felony in my pocket. When I moved to the city, I put the weapon in the drawer for good.

Only now, over a year later, did I understand that Bo Wilder most likely had set me up. It was the only possibility that made any sense. But I couldn't tell Chen that. Revealing the truth would be the equivalent of admitting I knew who'd killed Russell Bell, and who was to say I hadn't known it before the deed was done?

"I'm asserting my right to silence. If you intend to keep questioning me, I want a lawyer present."

"You're going to need one," Chen said as he rose.

~ ~ ~

It was six o'clock when the booking process was finished and I was finally allowed to call Jeanie Napolitano, my brother's ex-wife and my first boss, a criminal defense lawyer in Contra Costa County.

"It's me," I said when she picked up.

She knew from caller ID that I was calling from jail at 850 Bryant. "What'd you do?" was all she asked, her voice more amused than anything.

"Nothing. But that doesn't matter. They haven't charged me yet."

"With what?"

"Russell Bell's murder."

"That's just perfect." Jeanie was angry now and immediately on my side. "We'll have you out of there first thing tomorrow morning. Unfortunately there's nothing I can do tonight."

I thanked her and hung up. I hadn't told her close to everything she needed to know, but no client ever does. They—we—always hold the worst facts back. Jeanie would learn the whole story soon enough. It'd almost be a relief to finally be able to come clean with her.

I went back to my dorm unit and stretched out on my lower bunk, then closed my eyes and waited for sleep to come, but all I could see was the leering smile of a man I'd never met.

Bo Wilder.

The next morning I had to spend a few hours in the holding tank before Jeanie came back to retrieve me. "No charges today," she announced. But her attitude was different now from the instant solidarity of the previous evening. She was curt, as if she needed to be somewhere else. In fairness, I'm sure she did.

She wouldn't meet my eyes. "You didn't tell me your gun was at the scene."

"See if you can get a copy of the ballistics report. I don't trust the police."

"For now, there aren't any charges. That means they aren't giving you or me jack shit because they don't have to until there's actually a case. Do you really think the police would jerk you around that way?"

"If they're not setting me up, then Wilder did."

"I don't want to hear about it. We're not going to have a big attorney-client-privilege come to Jesus. When you called last night, I thought this was going to be a simple thing. Obviously, you forgot to mention a few important details, such as the fact that you'd asked your girlfriend to get rid of the murder weapon that was found at the scene of her death."

She uttered these words with the kind of disgust that implied a complete loss of faith in Teddy, Lawrence, and me. What other conclusion could she come to except that we'd been lying to her and to everyone else since the day Bell had been gunned down? "I'm not going to be sucked back into the Maxwell family dirt," she continued angrily. "I'm just not. You'll have to find another lawyer, one who doesn't mind getting her hands dirty, operating blindfolded and with one hand tied—the whole works."

I knew Jeanie too well to buy must of what she was saying. She was only venting. She didn't really believe we were crooked, or if she did, found it easy enough to overlook. She'd been married to Teddy during the period when he was working for Santorez, after all.

"A former client gave me that gun after Bo burned my office," I told her. "This is payback."

"Payback for what?"

"For refusing to work for Bo, refusing to pay off the favor he thinks he did us. The trouble is, no one asked him to kill Russell Bell. None of us knew it was going to happen before it did. Bo's counting on me not being able to tell the police the truth. Plus, he knows there's no reasonable explanation I can possibly give for having that gun."

"So you think we can expect more of these little hidden bombs to go off?"

"Probably not. He just wants to make it impossible for me to work for anyone other than him. This was the whole point of coming to work at the PD's office."

Jeanie just nodded, like this was what she'd expected. Still, her expression was concerned, wary. "You may think they don't have enough to establish probable cause for murder, but the DA's office can do what it wants. If they think you've got information, they won't hesitate to use the gun as leverage."

She was telling me the obvious. It was hard for her not to assume I was as much of a novice as I'd been when I first worked for her.

"I'll keep that in mind," I said.

"And, Leo? Next time call someone else."

Chapter 13

My arrest was quickly reported, probably as a result of the very leak I'd needled Chen about. The press was similarly forewarned of my release, and Rachel Stone had positioned herself to be the first person I saw when I emerged from the jail into the clear September morning. It was a rare hot day foreshadowing the beginning of San Francisco's only true summer.

"Leo, do you expect to be charged with Jordan Walker's murder?" shouted one reporter.

"Is it true the charges against Rodriguez are being dropped?" This, from another.

"Did you invoke your right to remain silent?" A reasonable question.

"Mr. Maxwell, turn this way, please." A semblance of courtesy.

However, getting answers wasn't the point. The real meaning of this scene was that the tide had turned, and public opinion, knowing nothing of the true facts, had now labeled me a murder suspect. As I fielded the flurry of questions, I noticed Stone watching and listening and occasionally making a note on her pad. By remaining silent, she made me think she expected to glean her information through other means.

I had a long walk back to the Seward, with a pair of reporters trailing me for over a block. I didn't hear a single question about Russell Bell or the gun in my apartment. As far as these escorts were concerned, I'd been detained because I was a suspect in Jordan's murder. I could set them straight, but that'd be like jumping out of the path of one train and landing in front of another. The last thing I wanted was for the murder of Russell Bell to be news again, when it had finally started to seem as if my family was going to live it down.

Once inside my room, I showered off the jail, then opened my laptop and checked the usual news sites. None of the articles reporting my detention went so far as to name me as a suspect in Jordan's murder. Rather, each simply stated the fact of my arrest, the reason being unknown. Every story identified me as the last person to see Jordan alive, and stated that it was known we'd had a sexual relationship, and that as Jordan's cocounsel I'd of course been aware of Rodriguez's alleged tendency to make false confessions.

Connect the dots.

No one as yet was calling for Rodriguez to be freed. The idea of a serial rapist seizing the opportunity to strike again, anticipating that Jordan's client would take the blame, remained far-fetched. I wondered again about that text she'd received. From what Chen had told me, it appeared the police hadn't yet identified the sender. On the other hand, if Rodriguez was innocent and the Panther didn't exist, then a lover—a category that included me—was the best candidate for another suspect.

I bought lunch, then retreated to my rented room to eat it, preferring to remain in the Tenderloin, where no one gave a shit that I'd been arrested and might have killed my girlfriend. In the TL, such notoriety was irrelevant to the more immediate business of hustling to get laid or high, or else making a living off those appetites in others. The squalor of the place was like a cloak that I could pull around me at will, and I suspected this quality was why, despite having the opportunity to leave, I'd remained.

I called Nina Schuyler, my father's former court-appointed attorney, who, like Jeanie, had sworn off further involvement with him or with me. But that was before the jury acquitted him, and I had good reason to think victory had softened her aversion. I explained the situation and gave her the name of Roland McEwan, the former client who'd passed me the gun. "If we can find him and get a statement from him, that should be enough to take the DA off my back."

"You want your guy to handle the investigation or you want me to subcontract it?"

I thought for a moment. My brother's former investigator, Car, could have dredged up this man in a heartbeat, but I owed Car too many favors—and, besides, if I was charged with Bell's murder, Car would be in the thick of it.

"Let your guy handle this. If he draws a blank, I'll put Car on the job, but I'd prefer to keep this one out of the family if possible."

She agreed, saying she'd represent me for a small retainer of one thousand dollars, plus her investigator's expenses. "If you're charged, though," she warned, "I'll need five figures to try it."

I promised to put the check in the mail. Around four thirty, my phone rang. It was too early for Nina's investigator to have produced any results, but, still, I grabbed the phone with a surge of hope. Rachel Stone's name, not Nina's, appeared on the screen. I pressed Talk anyway. I couldn't just hide in my room, letting accusations and innuendo swirl around me.

"Don't worry. I'm not expecting a quote," Stone said, sounding almost jubilant. "You'd be crazy, anyway, to comment on any of this ridiculous mess while the feeding frenzy's still going on. I'm not saying I'm stopping you from talking, but I'm not holding my breath, either. The real reason I'm calling is I have the answer to the question you asked me the other day."

My mind had traveled so far since my breakfast with the reporter I couldn't think what I'd asked.

"The phone," she reminded me. "Remember, you asked me whether the police had found Jordan's phone at the crime scene or whether the killer might have taken it away with him. Well, the answer is the phone hasn't been found. The wireless provider can't trace it."

I knew she must want something from me, that this information was merely the bait. But it was good bait. "Taking the phone suggests the phone contains evidence the killer wanted to conceal," I said.

"A safe bet. What kind of evidence? A picture, do you think?"

"I was thinking more along the lines of the text or e-mail she'd gotten when she was with me. But I don't see Rodriguez taking the phone and being smart enough to deactivate it. It's more likely he'd have tried to unload it for quick cash. You can't print that, though."

"Doesn't help you."

"I'm not worried about myself. You mind me asking you something?"

"I'll tell you that after you've asked me."

"How well do you know Tom Benton?"

The idea had been swirling in my mind for some time. Jordan's abrupt departure from the firm remained unexplained, especially after the triumph of the Kairos trial, and I'd never fully accepted her explanation that the trial had burned her out. In fact, remembering it had seemed to energize her. I'd suspected her of the opposite of burnout, sensed that she'd loved trying cases and craved more trial experience than civil litigation could provide. Still, she was ambitious, and a jump to the public defender's office wasn't in the game plan. What I figured was that something must have happened at Baker that made Jordan feel she needed to put distance between her mentor and herself.

The pause before Stone answered was a long one. "Like I said, we go a long way back," she finally said. "I know Tommy very well. If you want the sordid details, I'm afraid you'll have to get them from someone else."

"He was Jordan's mentor at Baker." I chose my words carefully. "He advanced her much faster than any of his other associates. Special treatment, special attention. She tried the Kairos case with him. I understand you covered it. Yet after they'd won that huge verdict, Jordan suddenly up and left to be a volunteer at the PD's office. You probably know that, too. She talked about all her cases with her father, and even he doesn't know why she made the move. I'm just wondering what it was that might have left a bad taste in her mouth. Was it the firm, or Tom Benton in particular?"

"Well, Gary Cho committed suicide after he lost the case," Stone said. "That would leave a bad taste in anyone's mouth. Tommy and Jordan helped Jacob Mauldin destroy him."

Mauldin owned Kairos, a local subcontractor on a huge, in part publically funded project to develop the site of the ballpark formerly known as Candlestick. The plan, which had undergone many iterations and was still in its early stages, was to redevelop the peninsula and the old shipyard that adjoined it as the centerpiece of a massive new retail- and housing-development.

Cho's construction company, Lizhi, had been awarded a minor subcontract, but had missed out on the more lucrative aspects of the deal. Cho's suit had alleged that Kairos was engaged in a conspiracy to defraud the public by submitting false invoices, overbilling the city, and falsifying its employment records.

"Kairos's defense," Stone continued, "was that Cho had dreamed up the suit for the purpose of knocking Kairos out of the picture so that his connected cronies could move in and take over the project. They implied Cho was connected with organized crime in Chinatown, and backed up their accusations with a sex tape of him with a teenage boy in a bathhouse run by a notorious Chinatown gangster.

"Not that it was Jordan's fault, or Tom's, that Gary committed suicide. But I've noticed that lawyers, young ones especially, tend to forget there are human beings on the other side of cases. Benton's ploy was probably the most devastating counterclaim I've ever seen."

I remembered hearing about the death but for some reason hadn't connected it to Jordan's case. "The bathhouse tape was entrapment, I thought."

"That's what Cho claimed, but Benton's point was that entrapment or not, Cho was in a position to take the bait. After that, he was facing ten years in prison and lifetime registration as a sex offender. Benton basically prosecuted the man for racketeering and sodomy before the judge put a stop to it. Still, the jury had heard enough. They ruled against Cho and in favor of Kairos, and awarded a huge verdict on their unfair business practices counterclaim. Cho's entire net worth was wiped out. Two weeks later, his car was found at the parking area of the Golden Gate Bridge. It's presumed he jumped to his death."

Jordan had never mentioned Cho's death, but it potentially explained a lot. "Was there anything else? Anything that happened in the courtroom?"

Her tone turned defensive. "I wasn't in the courtroom every day. It lasted four weeks, and I gave it a total of five days. Opening statements, key witnesses, closing statements, and the verdict. That's a lot more time than I'd normally spend. This was a rare public view of the feeding frenzy San Francisco politics has become."

"Sounds like Benton was the alpha shark. Those are some pretty heavy tactics."

"I wasn't focused on the lawyers. They were doing their jobs. Tommy's ruthless, of course, but he's the kind of attorney who never raises his voice. A gentleman. From what I remember, Jordan started in third chair but leapfrogged over the other associate to second chair by the end of the trial. That doesn't mean Tommy let her say a word in front of the jury, of course. The point is their team did their jobs, and fought hard but honorably."

This fit with the idea that Jordan had come to the public defender's office to try cases rather than watch older men take all the speaking roles. I just didn't think she'd have lost patience so easily. Another few years and she'd have been first-chairing her own trials.

"Did you notice anything that suggested a personal relationship between Jordan and Benton?"

"It'd be unthinkable if anything personal showed between them in public, if that's what you're suggesting. Are you implying they may've had an affair?"

"I'm not sure. I'm just thinking aloud." Even as I said this I remembered what Jordan had said to me the night of her murder, about commitments she couldn't throw off, ones that kept her from being able to walk away from Baker for good.

"Did you suspect her of seeing someone else?"

"I didn't suspect anything. We didn't talk about it. But, like I said, that message on her phone the night she was killed ... She said it was from a client but also that it had nothing to do with any of our PD cases."

"I doubt she'd have been communicating directly with clients from Baker."

I'd reached the same conclusion. "So if it wasn't a client, it had to be someone else who felt justified in demanding her attention in the middle of the night."

"And she accepted that demand. Threw you out because of it."

"Not exactly. She ordered a cab and first took me back to my room. What I thought was that she was going to meet whoever it was at another location. But I was wrong."

Of course, I had to wonder if the cab driver had been honest with me about where he'd taken her. He had no reason to lie, not unless someone had gotten to him before I did.

I realized I was edging over into paranoia.

"So you think I should take a closer look at my old friend Tommy," Stone now said.

"If I were you, I'd want to understand why she left the firm. And, at the same time, why she felt she had no choice other than to return there."

"Okay, I hear you."

"And I'd like to hear what you find out." I could only hope, though, that she'd keep me in the loop. It was also important to me that Jordan's dad not read the truth for the first time in the paper. Trying to prevent that was something I could do for her.

Stone made no promises, but I sensed a bit of give in her tone as we said good-bye. I realized I'd given far more information than I'd gotten, but I understood that I had little choice if I hoped to learn the truth.

The next step, I decided—sitting for a few moments after hanging up—was to talk with someone who'd spent more time observing the Kairos trial than Stone had.

I went into the LexisNexis database and pulled up the Kairos case docket, which had swelled to 543 entries. Many of the filings were sealed.

The lawyers were listed: Tom Benton, Jordan Walker, a second associate appearing on behalf of Kairos, and a single lawyer, Brian Ma, for Cho, the owner of the construction company Lizhi, who'd committed suicide after trial. It was Ma with whom I now got in touch.

I gave Ma's secretary a perfunctory hint of why I wanted to see him, and she scheduled the appointment for that afternoon. When I arrived she seated me in a small conference room with a spectacular bay view. Her boss, shorter than me but with a weight lifter's build, came in a moment later and gripped my hand in a shoulder-loosening handshake. We sat down on either side of the table, San Francisco arrayed like an architectural model at our feet.

"Until a few weeks ago, I worked with Jordan Walker," I began. "She left Baker to work for the PD shortly after the Kairos trial. We tried a single case together. And of course everyone knows what happened to her after that."

He nodded. His expression was cordial, revealing curiosity and wariness.

"Rodriguez confessed, but I'm afraid that's not quite good enough for me." I briefly recapped the evidence we'd presented at trial about Rodriguez's history of making false confessions. "From what I understand, there's again no physical evidence connecting him to the crime."

"So you're playing detective," Ma said.

"Jordan was important to me. I feel that her death deserves a more careful investigation than it's gotten."

"I read about your arrest." He paused, appraising me with sober interest. "For what it's worth, you don't seem to me like a murderer. Then again, I wouldn't know what one's supposed to look like."

"But you probably know there's no love lost between the San Francisco police and my family. Now I've humiliated the investigating detective in court. There's a measure of self-interest involved, sure, but even if there wasn't I'd be here asking you these questions. I need answers. Jordan's family deserves to know what really happened."

"I'm not sure how I can help you. If you're suggesting my client may have done this in a fit of revenge, you're not as intelligent as your trial work makes you seem. The stakes were high, but they weren't that high. Anyway, Jordan wasn't the one he'd have gone for."

"More importantly, Cho was dead by the time she was murdered," I reminded him, puzzled by his mention of the man.

"If you say so. The body hasn't been found. Just the car. Like you said, that's not good enough for me. If I were Cho, I'd have considered faking my death. Not least to avoid paying the hundred and fifty thousand dollars he still owes me."

"Wasn't there the possibility of his being prosecuted for under-age sex?"

"That, too." Ma shook his head.

"Was the charge legit?"

"They sprung it on us. It was clearly a setup. It made Cho look like he was connected to criminal enterprises in Chinatown. But come on, bathhouses? This is the twenty-first century. The old stereotyped ideas of Chinatown as this exotic place filled with opium dens and gambling halls is laughable. Nothing could be further from the truth."

"I thought there was a video showing the encounter."

"There's a video showing two men having sex. And they brought in a witness who claimed to be one of the two, and he testified the other person was my client. The idea was to show he was receiving illegal favors from Chinatown bosses, but the purpose and effect were to distract from the real issues in the suit—Kairos's fraudulent practices."

"You have any specific reason to believe he's still alive?"

Ma suddenly had lost his appetite for speculation. "He left a note in the car saying he intended to jump and apologizing. It was his handwriting. I'm told it's not uncommon for the bodies of bridge jumpers never to be recovered, and his wasn't. So, odds are he's dead."

"No one seems to know why Jordan left Baker. Maybe Cho's suicide threw her for a loop, but I'm not sure I can see her blaming herself. She took her leave right after the Kairos trial, which leads me to suspect something happened. That is, other than Cho's death. I guess it seems to me that if I knew why she'd left the firm I might have a better understanding of who wanted her dead."

"I thought Kairos's tactics in that trial were underhanded and even sanctionable, but killing . . ." He flushed. "People willing to manufacture evidence and lie brazenly don't need to commit murder to get what they want."

I sensed he had more to say, but didn't want to come right out with it. Evidently I was meant to extract it from him. "By people, you mean Jacob Mauldin?"

"He's the owner of Kairos, and the person with the most to gain by discrediting Gary. You tell me who else. But we're not in court now. I can't take advantage of the litigation privilege to make reckless accusations and expect to be shielded from a libel suit. So if you tell anyone I said any of this, I'll deny it. Mauldin will have to get his satisfaction from you."

"Did Cho have a family?"

"A wife. I think she's still in Portola Valley. Look, Gary's dead, okay? He was going to be prosecuted and locked up for a decade at least. I'd like him to be around still, because then I might get paid. But he's not, okay? And much as I'd like to stick it to Kairos, it's true that Gary's business would have benefited if he'd won the case. Clients insist all the time the other side's evidence is fabricated, but never once in my career have I been able to prove it. I think that, probably, it doesn't ever really happen. Tom Benton doesn't strike me as *that* dishonest."

"What about the dynamics between the lawyers on the other side? Did you notice anything out of the ordinary?"

"Between Jordan and Tom Benton, you mean?" He looked at me pointedly. "Like, was he fucking her?"

"You said it, not me."

He shrugged. I realized he was still simmering with rage six months after the verdict. "They kept their clothes on in the courtroom. But it wouldn't surprise me. It wouldn't surprise me if he screws all his associates. Nothing about the man would surprise me, except that he'd knowingly be party to a fraud on the court. I can't imagine any lawyer of his stature risking his career for any client."

"You mentioned manufacturing evidence. What did you mean?"

He looked at me across the conference table as if gauging how much to say. "I can't prove it."

"I imagine the trial would have turned out differently if you could."

"Cho insisted the video was fake, of course. Even after we saw the evidence, he continued to tell me it was all fabricated, that the witness was lying, possibly bought by Jacob Mauldin. We took that position during the trial. You saw how well that turned out."

I nodded, hoping he'd keep talking.

"He also insisted that the books were cooked, that all the evidence they'd turned over was contrived to screen their fraud from view. We couldn't prove it, of course. Anyway, I'm sure it didn't happen." He looked away. "It doesn't matter now. I'm off the case. In fact, being sued by Gary's wife for malpractice."

"The expert report you tried to submit after the deadline?"

"It shouldn't surprise me you've been looking up my docket."

"What kind of expert? Whatever you filed was sealed."

"A forensic accountant. We had two theories. The first was that Kairos was failing to live up to the terms of its contract that required it to hire locally, from the Bayview Hunters Point area. Theoretically, if we prove that, it would have invalidated the entire contract. Gary promised me he'd be able to produce witnesses who would testify that they'd never done a day's work for Kairos, even though the company's payroll shows a full complement of unskilled labor from the projects being paid for forty hours per week.

"To prove the second theory, which was overbilling for labor and materials, we needed a forensic accountant. Gary was against it. Cash flow problems. He promised me he'd be able to show the jury how the fraud worked. He was the whistle-blower, so it made sense to me that he'd understand. Then he gives his deposition and the house of cards falls. He couldn't point to a single clear instance of fraud, other than Kairos supposedly refusing to hire the local workers who were supposed to be filling its payroll. Like I said, he believed the records we were relying on in the lawsuit were fraudulent, cooked up by the defense. He also couldn't give the name of a single witness with firsthand knowledge of the fraud or a single person whose name was on the payroll who hadn't done work on the project."

Ma, seeming to realize he was violating client confidences, took a breath and went on: "Before that deposition, I was still drinking Gary's Kool-Aid. After the deposition he changed his mind. He started telling me we needed an expert after all, to show that the books were cooked, and that the numbers couldn't possibly be correct. But it was too late then. Now his wife is claiming it was my fault we didn't submit the report on time."

He rose and went to stand at the immense window. "The bottom line for me is, I didn't vet the case carefully enough. I believed my client, and worse, I trusted him. I bet you never made that mistake."

"You've got insurance."

"I've got insurance."

"But it rankles, having the wife blame the trial's outcome on you. After you fought for her husband, after his problems had kept you awake at night. Suddenly, you're the bad guy."

"It wouldn't have made a difference anyway." Ma was staring down at the street with intense focus. It was as if Gary Cho himself were crossing the plaza below. "What difference could a forensic accountant make when the other side's got you on video with a fourteen-year-old kid in the sauna of some gym controlled by the Chinese mafia? What the hell was he thinking? There's always surprises in litigation, but this takes the cake."

"What was the Chinatown mafia's interest, according to Benton?"

"They had three theories of their own. First, Mauldin testified he'd been approached by representatives of a Chinatown civic organization with a strongly worded demand for 'charitable contributions.' Kickbacks, in other words. It's clear Chinatown interests had bought up large amounts of residential property around Candlestick. Benton argued that Gary and Lizhi were a front. That if Kairos was knocked out, and its contract instead awarded to Lizhi, money would have flowed straight out of the public coffers and into the pockets of the Chinatown bosses. They would've been in a position to siphon off a fortune."

"If the evidence was manufactured, do you think Benton knew about it?"

"I think Tom Benton would've believed what he needed to believe to win. Like any lawyer would."

"What about Jordan? Do you think she knew?"

"No," he said after a pause. "She shared Benton's ruthlessness. He'd taught her, after all. But from what I saw, she had an integrity he lacked. I was impressed. She seemed to have her own compass. Most young lawyers don't. Especially not ones mentored by Tom Benton."

"Her compass led her right out the door as soon as the trial was done."

He nodded. "They were probably having an affair. Long hours, the heat of trial. By the third day out of seven, they knew they were going to win. After that, they were just running up the score. I tried to negotiate a settlement before closing arguments, a deal that would let Gary save face. Tom just laughed at me. He wanted scorched earth, and they got it. Gary was left with nothing."

"And how much was the result worth to Kairos?"

"Sky's the limit. The verdict on the counterclaim was four million dollars, plus civil penalties, based on the project delays caused by the allegations Gary made that the jury decided were false and malicious. That basically meant Mauldin owns Lizhi now. But that's really the tip of the iceberg. If Gary had won, Kairos would have been debarred, removed from the contract and prohibited from bidding on such projects in the future. Jacob Mauldin would have been left begging for scraps."

"No wonder Gary's wife wishes you'd gotten that expert."

Ma took it in stride. "That's how it always is with clients. They decide to draw a line, but they pick the wrong one to draw. To repeat myself, it wouldn't have mattered. After that video surfaced, his credibility was shot."

He walked me out. "So who do you think killed her?"

I shrugged. "Maybe it was Rodriguez after all. A truly innocent client is a rare thing. Jordan and I thought we had one. We were probably fooling ourselves."

As the elevator doors began to close, Ma stuck his hand in front of the door. "If Gary was right—and I don't think he is—then these are some heavy people you're dealing with. You might want to keep that in mind if you plan on asking others these same questions."

Chapter 14

It'd been a long day. Since getting out of jail that morning, I hadn't had a minute's rest, but I'd wanted to act immediately because I knew Chen could have me picked up again at any time. While I was still a free man, I needed to make as much headway in my investigation as I could. I didn't trust anyone else to interview these witnesses, because it seemed to me no one else could care the way I cared. I recognized the possibility that my personal involvement with Jordan might cloud my judgment, but at the same time it meant I was entirely dedicated to my task in a way no hired investigator could ever be.

That said, family business came first. Although the gun that killed Russell Bell had been found in my possession, I wasn't alone in facing the risk of prosecution. The police would assume what they'd always believed: the plot to kill Bell had been a conspiracy among the three of us Maxwells. Especially after Teddy's revelation about being in contact with Bo Wilder—which if known, would further suggest we were in on the conspiracy—I considered it essential that my brother know the true reason for my arrest. He needed at once to break off all contact with the man who'd orchestrated Russell Bell's murder.

I called Teddy to tell him I was on my way over. He instantly began quizzing me about my arrest—which of course he'd seen in the news—but I simply said we'd talk in person. If nothing else, the gun was probable cause for a wiretap on our phones, and I guessed now that my conversation with the reporter this morning probably had been recorded. It was possible Chen's hope in releasing me was that Teddy or I would say something stupid on tape, providing direct evidence that would tie us to Bell's murder.

Soon I was explaining it all to him face-to-face, sitting on his back patio with a beer, listening to the sounds of traffic a few blocks away. "They think they've got us now," I told him. "They're just waiting for us to make a blunder."

"But I still don't understand how the gun ended up in Jordan's apartment."

"Because I gave it to her," I said. "Bo set me up perfectly. He used a former client to do it, a guy I had no reason to distrust." Seeing Teddy's face tighten in anger, I shook my head, holding up a hand. "I'm sure when he gave me the gun he had no clue what he was doing, or that it would come back on me. He was just trying to make a buck. I had no business with an unregistered gun. When I came to my senses and realized it was too risky to carry it, I should have made it disappear. But I didn't. I kept it in a drawer."

"You're not telling me Bo could have planned this."

"He couldn't." Not unless he was behind Jordan's murder. But that possibility was too horrifying even to consider. "Planting the gun on me was probably just a hole card, something he could play if he needed it. All it'd take would be an anonymous tip. At the same time, I doubt he minds what happened. As far as he's concerned, he has unfinished business with me, and he knows that no matter how much heat I get, I can't roll over on him without worse trouble. That's because I've got no actual proof he was behind Bell's murder, and trying to hang it on him would be admitting too much. We can't let them establish any connection between us and Bo."

"Hopefully, they can't tie the cell phone he's been using to him," he said. "Otherwise, the calls are right there in my phone records."

"I know. But from now on, you've got to assume your phone is bugged. No more late-night chats. If Bo calls, don't pick up. Any contact with him now offers them the chance to make the case that we were in contact before Bell's murder, that we hired the job through Wilder. If they can tie Wilder to the hit, then any association with him can hang us."

"But now they don't even need to tie Wilder to it. They found the murder weapon in your room."

"If I were guilty, it makes no sense that I'd hang on to the gun."

My brother slumped in his chair. "It doesn't have to make sense, does it? It just has to stick."

Seeing Teddy's fear, I tasted my own, like metal in my mouth. For most of the day, I'd been able to fool myself, passing off the discovery of the gun as simply a show of power from a police force with a personal vendetta against my family and me, but this was different. We had a clear motive, and Teddy's ongoing contact with Bo meant the police could put together enough evidence to charge us with murder.

"We need to let Dad know what's happened," Teddy said.

"Why? So he can come home and be arrested with us?"

"That's right." He turned vehement. "He ought to be here. For a while there it was like he was trying to make up for all the lost years, spending every minute with Carly. Then, after the fire, he was suddenly out of Dodge, leaving us to wonder what's next."

The heat in my brother's voice surprised me. In the past it'd always been me judging our father and Teddy defending him. Now our roles were reversed.

"I don't think he can take going through another trial, or face the chance of being returned to prison now that he's out. If he'd stayed, sooner or later they'd have charged him with Bell's murder. No, I don't blame him for getting out while he had the chance. One false conviction's enough."

"If you believe this one would be false," Teddy shot back.

"Watch what you're saying," I reminded him, suddenly aware of the night pressing in, the nearness of the neighboring houses, dark corners where listeners might be lurking. If the police had tapped Teddy's phones and mine, they certainly could have made the additional effort to conceal a bug in his patio table. I was becoming paranoid again, I realized.

"I don't mean it." Teddy shut his eyes. "I'm just tired. I thought this was over but evidently it's only just beginning again."

"Nothing's ever over," I said. "You know that."

"I still think Lawrence should know what's going on."

He was right, I knew. "Do you have a phone number for him?"

My brother went inside and came out with a sheet of paper with a string of digits on it. "They've got a place in this little beach town in Croatia. Zadar. He was talking about trying to find a bed-and-breakfast to buy last time I talked to him. Can you imagine it?"

I couldn't. The idea of my father, the freed convict, going into the hospitality business was a serious stretch. I folded the sheet of paper into my pocket. "I need to pick up a prepaid phone. I'll buy one tonight, then call him in the morning. In the meantime, try not to worry. We've had our backs against the wall before."

We went into the house. I said good-bye to Tamara, accepting a kiss on the cheek after she'd held me at arm's length—as if she was trying to divine what new trouble her husband and I'd been discussing. I'd leave it to Teddy to decide how much, if anything, to tell her about our predicament. She deserved to know, but on the other hand, I'd already resolved that if one of us had to go down for Bell's murder, it would be me, not Teddy.

On my way out the door I ducked into Carly's room, straight-ened the covers, and bent to kiss her sleeping cheek, promising silently that I'd do everything in my power to make sure she didn't grow up the way I had, fatherless and alone in the world.

~   ~ · ~

In the morning I bought a prepaid cell phone and used it to call our father as I walked along the Embarcadero. It was nine hours later in Zadar, the coastal city where Teddy had placed him. When he answered, I heard street sounds in the background.

"It's Leo."

A pause. "Hey, we were just talking about you." He said some-thing, but not to me. "Wait a minute," he told me.

The ambulatory sounds grew dimmer and then I knew I had him to myself. The sense of missing him came back, and I was just as surprised by it as I'd been the first time it swept over me, when Rebecca had all but accused me of Jordan's murder after we'd talked to Hiram Walker in her apartment.

After the fire last summer, he and Dot had flown to Amster-dam, bought a pair of used motorcycles, and worked their way southwest through France, Spain, and Portugal. They'd crossed to Morocco and spent a dusty week traveling Algeria and Tunisia before returning on the ferry to Genoa. They'd toured the length of the Italian peninsula and back up the opposite side. Now I was hearing about Zadar, where they'd settled for the winter in an off-season rental while scouting for a more permanent home. They had a half-formed idea of starting a bed-and-breakfast after my father identified Croatia as a country having no extradition treaty with the United States and a place where Bo Wilder was unlikely to trouble him. They'd been up in the mountains most of the summer but were back in Zadar now, trying to decide whether to stay or move on.

"I can't imagine you in the hotel business," I said.

I heard him snort. "I looked into it enough to see that an honest man can't possibly get ahead. A country like this, every official you deal with has got his hand out. Seems the bureaucracy's there for no other purpose than to let the bureaucrats squeeze you. And these European tourists . . . Leo, you've never seen such trash."

I didn't know what to reply. And anyway, I knew he wasn't expecting a comment.

"It's hard to settle down," he went on. "It just doesn't seem right. I feel like I ran away, left you two in the lurch when the going got rough. I'm always checking the news, waiting for the next terrible thing to happen. When, all along, I was the one who has to answer about the fire. I mean, I'm the one with the unpaid debt to Bo."

"I don't think he's too particular about who pays," I told him. Then I added, "But, in fact, it's the reason I called." Having heard him admit to paternal anxiety on our behalf made it easier, somehow, to give him the bad news.

I started with Bo's late-night calls to Teddy, identifying these overtures as paving the way for a relationship like the one Teddy'd had with Ricky Santorez. Except I knew, even if Wilder didn't, that my brother was no longer up to the task. All his cunning and guile had been left in that restaurant when he was shot in the head.

My father just listened. Next I explained about Jordan, our working together and how it led to our too-brief affair. None of this was easy, but I made myself keep talking, moving on to her rape and death, and finally, to the cops finding at the scene the gun they believed had been used to kill Russell Bell.

Despite his claim of having kept tabs on the local news, my father hadn't heard any of this. "You're not saying Bo had your friend killed?"

"No. Bo's style's a little more direct. If he'd done it, he'd have made sure we knew."

"A good point." As he said this, my father no doubt remembered the message Bo had sent us after he'd had Santorez murdered in prison. We'd received Ricky's ears in the mail one morning at our office, a message of ownership we'd refused to heed. The fire that followed had also been a message, equally unmistakable.

"I'd better come home," he said.

"That isn't why I called. We just thought you deserved to know."

"We'd already half decided. It's just not possible to keep moving all the time. We're drinking too much, with too little to do. Starting to feel the strain."

Hearing this made me think about my father's failed marriage to my mother, whose death had sent him—wrongly—to prison. Everything in my life stemmed from that sad, grim chain of events, and neither of us could ever put it behind us.

I realized he was still talking. "Dot's tired of living like a fugitive, she says. She keeps reminding me I was acquitted, wasn't I? She's made up her mind. We're coming back."

"I worry that you're playing into their hands if you do."

He knew I meant the cops. But his take was different. "It wasn't the police I was running away from. It's Bo. He's held the key all along. That's what the gun means. It's another message, letting us know he's still running the show, just the way he always has been."

"*I'm* concerned about the police."

"That's because you've closed your mind to certain possibilities. Bo wouldn't have passed that gun to you if he hadn't planned a way out. The point of the gun is to remind us all of our obligations." He paused, then said, "After all, none of us has shed any tears over Russell Bell."

"So you've decided to go to work for Bo, after all."

"It's you or me or Teddy—and we both know it's not going to be you."

"How much longer will the settlement money last?"

"Depends whether I have any income coming in."

"And you're hoping that Bo Wilder will help you with that."

"You tell me what other kind of work there is for an ex-con, even one who's been exonerated. Everyone in the state knows the only reason I was acquitted is Bo had Bell killed to keep him from testifying. The DA and the cops made sure the newspapers got their fill of that. What else am I supposed to do? Flip burgers?"

I let a moment pass, then tried for a conciliatory tone. "Carly asks about you every time I'm there. It's pretty clear she'd love having her grandpa back."

"There've been many nights when I think freedom's not worth it if it means being away from her. These years aren't ever going to come again."

We'd talked through all my prepaid minutes. "Just don't make any hasty decisions," I reminded him.

"I'll let you know what our plans are. I need to make a few contacts first, but don't worry. Nothing I do will be traceable. One way or the other, Bo and I are going to straighten this mess out. I don't intend for my sons to pay my debts."

"It won't do us any good if you end up back in prison."

"You're exactly right. That's what I mean to tell Bo."

Chapter 15

A hiatus ensued in the news cycle, but I understood it was merely temporary. I used part of this time to find out everything I could about Jacob Mauldin.

He'd been around a long time, running Kairos out of his home base in Stockton. He'd ridden the cresting wave of the tech boom, made millions putting up housing tracts—along with the super conglomerations of retail outlets that went with them—in Cupertino and San Jose. Recently, however, with the collapse in the tech market, he'd been left holding the bag on a massive development south of Sacramento, where two hundred unsold houses stood like a ghost town. The Candlestick project and the public money that went with it were all that stood between future prosperity and bankruptcy.

I thought of trying to contact the man, but guessed he wouldn't speak to me. In any case, I knew for a fact he had a lawyer—Tom Benton. Ethical rules prohibited me from contacting Mauldin directly, meaning that to get to him, I had to go through Benton.

I wasn't yet ready to make that approach however. First I needed to know more.

Meanwhile, the police continued to maintain that Rodriguez was guilty and unofficially leaked that my overnight detention had been for an unrelated violation. Rodriguez remained in custody, no follow-up stories from Stone appeared, and it might have seemed safe to assume the idea of a predator stalking the young women of San Francisco had faded into the background unease of city life. However, on the first Friday in October an event occurred that seemed to bring the Panther into every dark stairwell from Balboa Park to the Sunset.

A woman was raped. She'd just entered her apartment in the Mission District when she was grabbed from behind. After her assailant was finished, he required her to shower, took her bedding, and left her bound in the bath. Though roped hand to foot, she was able, eventually, to free her hands and call 911. He was a large white or Hispanic man, matching the description Fitzpatrick and his other victims had provided. It was the crime Jordan and I had been looking for when we first theorized the existence of the Panther, an attack for which Rodriguez, in jail ever since Jordan's death, had an unshakable alibi.

Inevitably, the media visited old crime scenes and interviewed the detectives who'd investigated all the unsolved rapes they could dig up. They also got accounts from as many victims as they could convince to talk, seeking to reexamine the evidence under the theory that all had been attacked by the same unknown man. The effect was to create the sensation that somewhere out there, a predator was lurking, a definite personality, nebulous but real.

Not surprisingly, the official reticence had the effect of fanning the publicity into a whirlwind. After three days of this I received a flustered call from Rachel Stone. "My source tells me this most recent vic is definitely making it up. I'd only been making a theoretical case. Now it's taken on a life of its own. It wasn't supposed to, is the problem."

"You're a reporter. You know how it works once you put something out there. Just ask Rodriguez."

She cut to the chase. "Remember how we talked about the three possible scenarios? I'm working on the third one now. The last article in the promised series of three. You care to tell me if it's true what I've heard about you and Jordan having a disagreement the night she was murdered, that she asked you to leave?"

"You've got your source. Talk to him."

She seemed impatient with her own questions. "I also hear you gave a genetic sample, and your sperm was found at the scene. So, I have to ask you. Was your face the last one Jordan saw?"

I didn't have to play along. "No match with Rodriguez?"

She grudgingly acknowledged her sources had told her there was still no physical evidence definitively tying Rodriguez to the scene. Officially, he remained the only suspect.

"Were any other DNA samples recovered?"

"Know one thing reporters and lawyers have in common? We're the ones who ask the questions. I called you, remember? That makes it my turf." She paused before again relenting. "Rodriguez's lawyer would probably have the complete test results. But he's not talking to anyone from the press. Still, there's the chance he might talk to you."

I hadn't had any contact with Rodriguez's new lawyer—first, because of Gabriela's warning, and, second, because I knew Ripley wouldn't tell me anything. Though I believed Rodriguez was possibly innocent, I didn't want to give his lawyer any ammunition to defend him until I knew for sure. This made Stone my best source of information.

I confirmed her information about me, then tried to change the subject and earn some quid pro quo. "I remember you telling me you were old friends with Tom Benton. Talked to him lately?"

Stone wasn't finished yet. "Is it true that you'd confessed to Jordan that you and your family were behind the murder of Russell Bell? That she'd offered to get rid of the murder weapon for you? And that it was found in her apartment after her death?"

I made no answer. There was nothing I could say. The silence deepened, but I couldn't bring myself to end the call.

"I'll note your denial in my story," Stone finally said. "Check it out later today."

~ ~ ~

Stone's first story had depicted Jordan as a young attorney whose idealistic impulses had overshot her judgment with tragic results. Her second had spun out the portrait of the bogeyman we'd conjured together, turning a critical eye on the SFPD. Her third, imminent now, was the piece she'd been building toward all along.

Maybe I'd given her the idea—or maybe I'd just picked up on where her thoughts were already going—but what appeared online that night was nothing less than a full-scale assault on the criminal defense profession, offering me as exhibit A.

She didn't accuse me—not of Jordan's murder. Instead, she'd stumbled on a more sensational prize—my family's probable involvement in the murder of Russell Bell. The presence of the murder weapon raised the question of a possible connection between Russell Bell's death and Jordan's. My denial of any such connection was the first sentence of her story, and it had the effect of tainting all that followed.

I thought about our conversation. I'd gotten the feeling someone had been whispering in her ear all along—someone besides me. Benton, maybe. After all, Jordan had known Rachel through him. Maybe he'd worked at planting the idea I was the killer. Before I could approach him, however, I needed to know more about Kairos and the Candlestick project. Given the increasingly tight spot I was finding myself in, it was important I judge for myself what kinds of people I was dealing with.

I decided to contact a former client, Walter Hayes, who worked for the city and preached on the weekends. Hayes, who'd lived all his life in Bayview-Hunters Point, had become something of a community activist, a go-to information source for any reporter covering this part of town. Though he'd initially supported the Candlestick development, Hayes had become a vocal opponent, and in a recent news article had been quoted as labeling the project a scheme to drive up property values and squeeze out his constituency.

I called his cell phone and reached the man himself. When he heard I wanted to talk about Kairos, he seemed almost eager to meet me. "Not downtown, though," he said. "You want to understand where I'm coming from, you got to see where I come from. And that's Double Rock. Meet me at the entrance to the Alice Griffith homes at four PM."

On a peninsula strung from San Francisco's extreme southeastern edge, isolated from the rest of the city by geography and the freeways, Bayview-Hunters Point was the city's poorest and most African American district. I knew it as the focus of stop-and-frisk policing tactics and zero-tolerance prosecution, a hotbed of poverty and poor health. Double Rock was the unofficial name for the neighborhood between Third Street to the west and Candlestick Park to the south. A gated road was the only access point for the sprawling Alice Griffith public housing development, a collection of two-story townhouses separated by barren lots occupied by broken-down cars, strewn with trash and broken glass. On weekend nights, dealers manned the gate, taking orders from the parade of cars off the freeway. I was reminded of my visits to my father at San Quentin. A sign spelled WELCOME TO ALICE GRIFFITH, but the message seemed perverse.

Hayes told me to leave my bike and promised a kid twenty bucks to watch our rides until we returned. What first struck my eye as we walked in was the blackened, melted ruins of a playground behind a waist-high fence. Hayes gave a slow shake of his head.

Not many people were around—and those who were seemed to have little to do other than watch us with hostile mistrust.

"It may not look like much, but we've got an active neighborhood center, a Boys and Girls Club, even a community garden. Underneath all the drugs and violence, these are good people trying to live their lives."

His sales pitch might have been more effective if the stark reality of the landscape hadn't intruded on every word.

"In six months, Kairos will knock it all down. When the bulldozers move in, everyone who's still here gets to relocate, according to the terms of the deal, right alongside yuppies paying six or seven hundred thou. Public housing's supposed to be integrated with market rate. But anyone who's evicted before then, or leaves on their own, tough luck."

As far as I knew, just about everyone agreed that Alice Griffith needed to come down. "You make that sound like a bad deal."

"Don't get me wrong. These people deserve homes that aren't filled with mold. They need safe neighborhoods and an end to the open-air drug market. I don't doubt the bulldozers will show up on time. But what is there to make me think the developers intend to keep their promise to relocate these people according to plan?"

"What makes you believe they won't?"

"Simple economics, man. Why bring down everyone's property values when it's so much simpler just to rebuild the ghetto with a smaller footprint, build an old-school high-rise and thereby create more room for the *really* valuable real estate?"

I waited for him to explain. Instead, he shifted directions. "You must have noticed the press this place has been getting lately. About a dozen shootings in the last three weeks alone. Eight dead, including that four-year-old kid shot through his bedroom wall. People outside the projects are starting to wonder how this integrated housing idea is going to work. Are middle-class white people going to have to live in a war zone?"

"What's it got to do with Kairos?"

He had a ready answer. "Simple. They're behind it. With the SFPD's blessing, Kairos's private security force started patrolling Double Rock and the other projects six months ago. The idea was to run an aggressive campaign of arrests and evictions, make sure the worst aspects of Alice Griffith aren't relocated to the new projects. What's happened, though, from what my people tell me, is these ex-military types are turning the projects, after dark, into a kind of free-fire zone. And, of course, the dealers and gangbangers shoot back."

My first reaction was to doubt that such brutality could take place in this most liberal-minded of cities.

"But why would anyone want to provoke more violence?"

"To influence public opinion. What else? The tide's already starting to turn. You may have noticed, the press never misses a chance to piss on Double Rock. Once the clamor reaches a critical level, the city will allow Kairos to reduce the number of affordable housing units mixed in with the market-rate properties—maybe all the way to zero.

"You see, the beauty of 'market rate' is context. If you're selling condos in a building where every other unit is Section 8, the market's going to set the price at a certain level. If you're catering entirely to young urban professionals, on the other hand, the market will set a very different price."

Again expressing skepticism, I wondered aloud why none of this had come out in Cho's lawsuit.

"Some of it did," Hayes answered. "The phantom payroll, for instance. That money's going to pay these security guys. Has to be. Ex-military doesn't come cheap, and you couldn't justify the expense on the face of the contract. But if Cho's company were awarded the contract, it'd be the same. Probably worse, because the gangsters would have been pushing their own dope on these corners instead of simply killing off the competition."

We stood surveying the bleak landscape as I pondered what he intended me to do with this information. A trio of young men had appeared in a patch of dirt in front of one of the nearby townhouses. Hayes turned, and we started back toward the entrance.

"People need to know what's going on," Hayes said, getting to the point. "Lately I've sat in a lot of meetings where rich white people from downtown talked about what's best for the city, but no one's down here asking what's best for Double Rock. As long as that's the case, people are never going to trust that the city has their best interests at heart."

"If what you're telling me about these security patrols is true, it's a real scandal. Before it can reach that level, however, we're going to need proof. Witnesses who are willing to talk."

"A defense lawyer like yourself ought to know better. Ain't no witnesses in Alice Griffith."

"Not even for something like this? Get me a cell phone video. I have connections at the newspaper. My boss is on good terms with the DA."

I held back from mentioning my suspicion that the senseless violence he'd described might be connected somehow with Jordan's death.

As if sensing my concealed self-interest, Hayes now—for the first time—alluded to my recent troubles. "From what I hear, your connections aren't doing you much good lately. But maybe you could pass the word to some of your attorney friends at the PD's office."

I agreed to do as he'd asked, telling myself there was nothing personal in his rebuff. We shook hands, and I climbed on my bike and rode home.

Chapter 16

I phoned Benton's office. To my surprise, his secretary forwarded the call to his cell, apparently according to his instructions. He immediately answered, saying that if I wanted to talk, I should be at the Sausalito sailing docks in half an hour. He'd been planning to go out single-handed this afternoon, but the gusting winds were more than he cared to handle alone. He'd resigned himself to an afternoon of dock work, but if I could listen and follow directions maybe the day wasn't lost after all.

I'd experienced it as a warm day so far, but on the bay the cold wind cut right through the thin jacket I was wearing. I would have been freezing even without the spray that kept flinging itself in fine needles over the bow. With the marina behind us, Benton cut the motor and raised the sail, nodding for me to haul on the rope that controlled the front sail.

Without the engine noise, the boat suddenly became a living creature, like a powerful, leashed animal as opposed to the dead, clumsy weight it had seemed when the outboard was rocking us out of the harbor. A thrumming vibration came from below, and the boat leaned over farther—alarmingly so.

"It's all right," Benton assured me. "We've got a two-ton keel. It'd take a lot more wind than this to turtle her. Besides, if that rail ever does go under, the boat just swings into the wind and stops dead. A built-in braking mechanism. Now that we can hear one another, I'm ready to listen to you."

He'd been unreadable when I arrived, not looking me in the eye. Now, at the tiller, he was alert and precise. He wore nylon shorts, an ancient windbreaker, and a baseball hat with a marine-supplies store logo. He sat erect and peered forward as he tugged on the line to adjust the sail. With his other hand he steered, speaking only to instruct me to crank in the jib or let it out.

"Jordan mentioned she used to go sailing with you," I said. Benton had taken all the associates together, I knew, but she'd also gone with him alone at other times. When I'd come on board, I'd noticed a spacious cabin below decks. "She told me how much she loved it."

"Tacking," he said. And when I gave him a questioning look he said, "Uncleat it. Let go that end of the line and cross over. Watch the boom. Go." He pushed the tiller hard, making the bow swing as I ducked just in time, the metal bar at the bottom of the sail suddenly cleaving through the air like a club swung at my head. I fell with the roll of the deck, rose to my knees, and grabbed the jib as the big sail caught the wind again, tilting the cockpit the other way. The boat surged through the waves at the opposite angle into the wind with barely a hitch in its forward momentum.

A shadow fell across us, and then the Golden Gate Bridge was up above, the traffic sounds eerily remote. The bow began to plunge and surge as we entered the ocean swell.

"Not seasick, are you?" Benton asked.

I wasn't sure. It was glorious to see the coastline stretching away in both directions, the waves smashing into foam on the rocks, but as always the open ocean filled me with foreboding.

"I hear you're friends with Rachel Stone," I tried out.

"Friends? No one who wrote what she wrote about Jordan would still be a friend of mine. We were never 'friends,' in any case. It was both more and less than that."

He'd let the tiller swing around so we were heading north, following the coast but slanting out to sea, the bow pointing toward where Point Reyes was just visible in the haze. I felt we were leaving safety behind.

"What part of what she wrote bothered you?" I asked. "The part where it seemed Jordan deserved what she got?"

At first, he seemed not to want to answer. Finally, he said, "I didn't think she had any right to editorialize. She didn't know Jordan. She was using her death to make a point. And, also, to settle old accounts with me. Though I shouldn't blame her for that part of it, I guess."

"I'm bothered by the first piece, but of course even more by the last," I said. "The first, because Jordan was only doing her job, and doing it well. But Stone prefers to paint her as naïve, as a 'true believer.' That's crap. She was a lawyer, and a damn good one."

"And she was just getting started," Benton said. The two of us could find common ground here. Although I knew he was in his late fifties, his persona seemed to project boundless youth.

"The middle story was the only one Jordan would have wanted her to write."

"Exciting stuff. Killer stalking the city. But you don't really believe that, do you?"

"No, I guess I don't."

"Good. Because this girl from Friday night is lying. From what I've heard, she broke down and admitted it in the third round of questioning. There was no rape, which means there is no Panther."

"The press hasn't reported that yet." I didn't say I'd heard it from Rachel Stone.

"I have high-level contacts in the DA's office. They consider it a delicate situation. No one seems to know quite how to handle this mess."

"Nothing's what it seems in this case, is it? On the one hand, there's Rodriguez, who seems addicted to confessing. On the other, we've got media hysteria and, if what you say is true, this woman inventing a claim of rape for the same reasons Rodriguez confessed. To get attention."

"Makes you wonder what the world's coming to, doesn't it?"

I kept waiting for him to turn the boat around, but his eyes remained fixed ahead, as if he were set on leaving the city behind and taking me with him, never once looking back or adjusting course. We weren't heading for the land, I saw, but past it, on a point that would carry us offshore from Point Reyes and on into the vast unknown. "So, what did you want to talk to me about?" Benton said.

"Jordan was planning to go back to your firm. She told me so the night she died."

"I didn't know that." He paused as if mistrusting himself to go on. When he did, his tone was rough. "She hadn't said anything to me about coming back. We'd always talked about the stint at the PD's office as if it were temporary. But that was just talk. Of course, I'd have welcomed her back in a second. Most associates, we wouldn't have dreamed of leaving things so open-ended, but Jordan was different." He paused again. "As you know."

"She seemed unhappy about the decision to go back, talking about commitments she couldn't walk away from. I asked her what she meant, but she wouldn't say."

"We have civil cases that last for years. Maybe one of those was what she was referring to."

"Why'd she leave?" It was the question I'd come here intending to ask him.

"I don't know. She wanted to spend time just trying cases, is what she told me. She was tired of being bogged down with document review, letters between attorneys confirming this or that under-standing of what was discussed on such and such a call. You can spend a whole career in civil litigation and never set foot in the courtroom. For a good many attorneys, that's a relief. For others, it's a necessary evil, a compromise they accept in exchange for the privilege of billing six hundred an hour." He took a deep breath. "The thing is, Jordan was hungry for experience. I admired her tremendously for that. I still do."

"Then why on earth would she be intending to return to civil practice?"

"I don't know. Maybe she decided money was a necessary evil. Making it can be quite an experience in itself, if you do it right. And with the skills she possessed, Jordan could have made a boatload. Even in civil litigation, there are always cases to try for those who know how to win. And Jordan did. She knew because I taught her."

"Is that so?"

"I'm not being arrogant. Or at least not *only* arrogant. She found the right teacher, but she was an exceptional student, picking up in about two years the skills it had taken me two decades to master, stuff most of these fatuous assholes with bar cards never figure out."

"I think we both recognize that money had nothing to do with her going back."

"Or maybe she felt she owed me something. It was abrupt, her leaving. At first, I didn't take it well. I felt like she'd pulled the rug out from under my feet, and I told her so. I reminded her of all the opportunities I'd given her, all she had to look forward to. She swore she'd come back after her volunteer stint was over. I knew better. I said I thought she was throwing away her career." Benton shrugged, eyes fixed on the horizon, where a line of fog was discernible. "She was loyal. Maybe she just wanted to keep her word."

"Some people looking at the situation might guess she left because you were sleeping together."

"Some people meaning *you*." We stared at each other, our personal agendas now between us like a wall. "Jordan never told you that," he said calmly. "So you're guessing. Based on what? Jealousy? Or what Rachel Stone told you?"

"No one told me. It just felt like there was someone else." I held his gaze, more certain than ever he'd been the one. "Let me guess. She was sleeping with the boss and she didn't like it. It wasn't how she wanted to advance her career. Her idea was that she'd leave for a while, cool off at the PD's office. You two'd stop seeing each other, then it would be over for good and she could come back."

I was aware, of course, that such a scenario would cast my relationship with Jordan in an unfavorable light. It turned me simply into the man she'd chosen to rebound with.

His gaze had hardened, his attention drawn to something behind me. "Grab that line, will you?" he said, pointing to a trailing rope dancing in the wind just over my head, threatening to catch in the waves. I stood and reached for it, leaning out while keeping one hand on the lifeline wire that ran between metal posts. At the exact moment that my fingertips brushed the rope, the deck pitched beneath me, launching me over the lifeline into the sea.

I plunged deep. The cold stabbed like a thousand knives in my chest, and I made a great surprised gasp, my lungs expanding against the rigid muscles of my chest and back, filling with frigid seawater. My body stiffened, a spasm like an electric shock spreading from between my shoulder blades. I fought for the surface and burst into the trough of a wave, where I coughed again and again without effect, struggling to keep my head above water. The horizon briefly appeared, then my clothes were dragging me down, the pain of the cold already fading as numbness set in.

A speck in the enormity of the Pacific Ocean, I turned and turned, catching glimpses of land between the swells, and was finally rewarded with a brief vision of the sailboat idling into the wind a hundred yards off. Benton was standing in the cockpit hauling

down great armfuls of sail. Then I heard the marine engine kick
to life.

He had a long, hooklike device on an aluminum handle that he
threw to me as he went past. One end of it was tied to a rope. It
floated, and I was able to grab it, still coughing so hard it felt like
my chest would split. He killed the engine, and as the boat swayed,
the mast tip tracing crazy figure eights against the clouds, he hauled
me to the ladder at the back of the boat. Then, with a strong grip
under my arms, he heaved me into the cockpit.

"Three points of contact," he said. "That's the golden rule, and
you broke it."

The shivering had begun. I sat on the fiberglass bench, trying
not to move inside the cement weight of my clothes. "No one
told me that rule." My teeth chattered so violently I could hardly
get the words out.

Benton stood watching me with a frown of satisfaction. "That's
life, isn't it? You don't know the rules until you break them. And
sometimes you don't get a second chance."

"You asked me to fetch the rope, then jerked the tiller as I was
reaching for it."

"Would I have dumped you into the water just to swing around
and pick you up?" He seemed less sure of himself now, though, as if
it'd hit home to him what he'd done. "Come on. Let's get you below.
I have some foul-weather gear and a sweatshirt you can borrow."

The cabin was roomy, with a couch and banquette table on one
side and a galley kitchen on the other, most of the bow taken up
by a large, apparently custom-made bed. Watery light was coming through its portholes. "My home away from home," Benton
told me.

He found me clothes and I put them on. I was still shivering
and didn't want to go back up. I realized Benton was waiting for
me, that he didn't want to leave me down here alone. I wondered
how far from shore we were, where the boat was drifting. Even as

my anxiety increased, I sensed something was down here below decks that he didn't want me to see.

On impulse I stepped through the narrow door into the cabin at the bow. First I grabbed one pillow, then the other. Beneath the second I found a set of women's pajamas, neatly folded.

I didn't need to say a word, just looked at Benton, who'd come to stand beside me. Even if I'd wanted to speak, I couldn't have. There was no way to know if they were Jordan's. She'd never left pajamas under *my* pillow, and I'd never seen her in sleeping garb. But I was certain these were hers.

Benton came forward, carefully took the pillow from me, set it on the pajamas, and closed the door. "That's a private place," he said with surprising kindness. "These are private things."

The swell seemed to be increasing, the boat seesawing wildly from side to side, gathering greater momentum with each swing. Still neither of us moved to mount the steps to the deck. My companion was watching me as if waiting to see what I'd do, as if he were expecting violence and was fatalistically prepared to meet it with the same.

"You planning to let us wash onto the rocks?" I asked.

He seemed to consider the idea, then slowly shook his head. He motioned toward the ladder, and we went back up. The boat was startlingly close to shore, the waves breaking just a hundred yards away, yet he seemed unconcerned. He started the engine, motored the boat into the wind, and pulled the mainsail back up. In a few more minutes, we were tacking back south toward the Golden Gate as the fog pressed in.

Still shivering, I felt I'd never be warm again. "Do the police know?"

"What do they care? They've got the man who did this."

If the police knew about Jordan and Benton, they apparently weren't even investigating the possibility that he might have been involved in her death. "Someone sent her a text message the night she died. Was it you?"

"I didn't see her that evening. I didn't talk to her. We didn't *text*."

"That text is what made her decide we shouldn't spend the night together. Maybe it didn't have anything to do with her death. But whoever sent that message, it meant I wasn't there whenever the man who killed her showed up."

"And what would you have done if you had been there?" It seemed to me a question without an answer, yet he apparently expected one. "She didn't need protecting," he went on after a pointed pause. "She wouldn't have opened the door to a stranger. She certainly wouldn't have opened it to Rodriguez."

"So who sent her that text message, if you didn't?"

"My connections in the police department tell me the number was from a prepaid cell phone. All they know is what it said."

"And what was that?"

Benton seemed to take satisfaction from the answer. "'Get rid of him.' According to you, that's exactly what she did."

Chapter 17

The trip back seemed to take much longer than the trip out, probably because we'd said all we were going to and there was no more drama to distract us. Or maybe it was just that the wind had died as the fog rolled in.

We came under the bridge just ahead of the fog. It was then I chose to break the silence in which we'd sailed for twenty minutes, a quiet broken only by Benton's brusque instructions. "Was Cho really having sex with a kid in a Chinatown bathhouse or was that a lie cooked up by Jacob Mauldin?"

Benton looked startled. The shadow of the bridge fell across his face and he looked upward like part of him hadn't realized where he was. Then the fog obscured the sun. He rubbed his face with his free hand, suddenly fatigued. "I ought to have left you out there."

"He committed suicide," I pressed on. "They never found his body, right?"

"Just the car, parked on the Marin side. But you already know that."

"It's strange how little coverage his disappearance received. There was a story right after the car was found, quoting his wife to the effect her husband would never have killed himself."

"They always say that. Besides, he left a note."

"Evidently it didn't convince her."

"Gary Cho was a disturbed man. He hid a great many things from a great many people, and he was clearly under immense strain that no one else knew about. It's not easy to keep up a secret life, especially when those secrets jeopardize everything you care about. Sometimes a person seems strong, but all it takes is one strong gust to bring him down."

"Then, a few weeks after the death, his wife suddenly pulls a switch. Now she's even begun a memorial fund in his name, to support suicide prevention. They've got cameras there, you know. If he'd jumped, one of them should have caught it on video—but none did. And yeah, I know there are a few blind spots."

"He was thorough. That was his character. He'd have done his research. Such a man wouldn't have wanted to leave a video of his suicide behind. He'd have known Lydia might see it someday. There's websites for all sorts of sickos these days. There's actually one devoted just to bridge jumpers."

We were tacking past Alcatraz now, the sail flapping in the fickle winds. I'd started to warm up slightly, but as the fog increased the chill settled deeper, soaking into my bones. I dreaded having to get on my motorcycle and ride back across. "You've checked out that theory pretty carefully. Was it because you felt responsible?"

"As you said, there wasn't video evidence and it seemed as if there should have been. Clearly he killed himself because of the dirt that came out in the trial. It had been his decision to sell out to organized crime, not anyone else's. The law, at times, requires us to inflict suffering. That doesn't mean we're meant to enjoy it. So yes, as I implied, I checked it out."

"So you found the website telling the would-be bridge jumpers about the blind spots where they can jump without being caught on videotape, and you figured it was at least plausible he was dead."

"As opposed to what?" Benton's voice was utterly calm.

"Alive, obviously," I said. All at once, I recognized another possibility. "Or murdered."

I realized Benton was the kind of man, the kind of lawyer, who was at his calmest in his moments of deepest anger—and he was angry now. "Why would anyone want to kill him?"

"I talked to your opposing counsel. He seems to think the deck was stacked, that the sex tape and the kid's testimony were fabrications, along with most of the rest of your client's evidence. Maybe Cho didn't consider himself beaten. Or maybe someone miscalculated and left him with nothing left to lose."

Benton found this laughable. "If Ma said that, then he's an incredibly bad loser. It's remarkable he'd think so, and even more remarkable he'd speak the thought aloud. He's being sued, so I suppose he has to have some excuse. Lawyers will tell themselves—tell their clients—anything to avoid taking responsibility for their own mistakes."

We were a few hundred yards from the marina, in a patch of still water. He brought the boat into the wind and started the engine, uncleated the mainsail and let it drop, gathering the slack and binding the sail around the boom with bungee cords. A seal surfaced a few yards from the boat, regarded me with black eyes beneath long lashes, then disappeared in a swirl of foam, slapping the water with one flipper as it went.

"Have you mentioned this theory of yours to anyone else?" he now asked.

I brushed the question aside. "So, Jordan and Cho. That's two deaths associated with the Kairos trial. Clearly, there was a lot at stake. We're talking public money, enormous contracts, the development of what could be the most expensive real estate in the country."

Benton had to raise his voice over the rumble of the engine as he guided us into the marina. "Are you accusing my client of murder? Because if you make those kinds of accusations, you'd better be ready to back them up with proof. I don't think you'd enjoy having to defend yourself from a slander suit."

"I'm sure Jordan would admire your continued loyalty to your client. When I make that accusation, I'll be ready to back it up. Don't worry."

He tucked the boat into the slip, throwing the engine into reverse at just the right moment to swing the bow against the dock. I was ready with the line as he instructed me, hopping down and wrapping it around a cleat. Then I did the same at the stern.

He tossed my sodden clothes at my feet. "You'll have to find your own way out."

~ ~ ~

Still wearing Benton's borrowed clothes, gritting my teeth against the rush of cold air that cut into my flesh even beneath the fabric, I accelerated onto the bridge, thinking only of a hot shower back in my room.

As I rode along in the left lane—which was separated from the opposing ones by a series of widely spaced plastic pylons, nothing more—I glanced to my right. An SUV was drawing even with me in the middle lane. I gave it no more interest than I'd have given any large vehicle speeding along at sixty-five miles per hour. Its only slightly unusual feature was that its windows were tinted so darkly I couldn't see inside. It stayed beside me for a moment, then began to draw ahead. But before its rear wheels had advanced past my front wheel, it abruptly swerved into my lane. At the same time the driver hit the brakes.

I reacted instinctively, tugging the left handlebar to steer past the SUV's bumper. My bike skidded and to keep from laying it down I had to veer between two flimsy pylons into oncoming traffic. I made it across the first lane without being touched, feeling the buffeting shock waves of cars shooting past front and back. Horns blared and brakes squealed as the truck to my left swerved and sideswiped another car. At the same time, the car approaching on my right began knocking down pylons as it crossed into the eastbound lanes I'd vacated.

I saw a gap and gave the throttle a quick surge, crossing the remaining lane and driving the bike up next to the wall separating the pedestrian walkway from oncoming traffic. A truck was coming fast in my lane. Without room between the truck and the railing, I squeezed the front brake, slowing as much as possible, then bailed off and slid along the railing before flipping over it. I landed on my left shoulder on the cement walkway and kept rolling, hearing the crunch of chrome and metal as my bike was smashed, the semi's horn blaring as I continued tumbling, only one-inch metal bars separated me from the white-streaked bay far below. A red post was suddenly in my field of view through my helmet visor. I felt a tuning-fork jerk, then my body whirled—and seemed to keep on whirling forever.

~ ~ ~

"A crossover motorcycle accident on the Golden Gate Bridge? It's a miracle you survived," Teddy said the next morning upon arriving at the hospital. Jeanie had brought him by but had stepped out, leaving us in the false privacy of my curtained-off bed.

I had a concussion, badly bruised ribs, and road rash on my shoulder and back. Even with a narcotic drip in my IV, the slightest movement was agony. Lying still was only marginally better, because then all my attention was on my splitting head.

"Feels more like a curse," I told him.

"At least you've still got all your brains on the inside of your skull."

He had a point there. Last time we were here together, he'd been a patient in the traumatic brain injury ward after being shot in the head.

"How's it feel to be back?" I couldn't help asking.

"It wasn't easy walking in those doors. The smell, for one thing . . ."

I knew exactly what he meant: that distinctive odor of human sickness overlaid with antiseptic fluids and decaying flowers. Those had been long, very difficult weeks when first he'd hovered between life and death, and next slowly had to face the dawning reality of his diminishment. I knew my brother and understood he'd rather die than live in a dependent state. Yet, though his impairments remained significant, he'd managed to achieve a recovery beyond all medical expectation, and he was now grateful for each new day.

"You get to walk out of here," I said. "Just keep reminding yourself of that."

"I told you you were going to kill yourself on that bike. Jesus, an accident like that!" He shook his head again in disbelief.

"It *wasn't* an accident."

That got his attention. "You're not saying . . ."

"No. My God. You think I'm going to kill myself after all we've been through? Somebody tried to kill *me*. A black SUV with tinted windows came up behind me, then deliberately cut me off. I had no choice but to go over into the opposing lane."

Now his face was dark with fury. "Wilder. He's been having you followed?"

"I don't think so." And it was true. I didn't.

Instead, I explained to him as well as I could about my meeting with Benton and the theory I was developing that Jordan had been murdered not by Rodriguez, and not because her defense of him had attracted the attention of a psychopath, but because of what she'd inadvertently learned during the course of the Kairos trial. I added that Gary Cho might have been murdered, too.

"By whom?" Teddy asked, his voice sharp.

I had to admit I didn't know. "Benton's client, I guess."

"What about Benton? You're saying he and Jordan were having an affair?"

"It's likely he tipped someone off in advance about our outing today, but that'd be the extent of his involvement. I doubt he was behind it. He's just a lawyer working for a client, keeping himself useful and therefore employed. My sense is he's as distraught about what happened to Jordan as I am but doesn't see a way out."

"See no evil, hear no evil, you mean."

"It's not so different from what we do, is it?"

He shook his head, making a face.

"It's not so different from what *you* used to do," I said, making my point clear.

Teddy looked away. "But I don't have any blood on my hands," he said unconvincingly.

"That's probably what Benton tells himself. Promise me you won't go to work for Bo Wilder. You've got to promise."

"Okay," he answered. "I won't." But he wasn't convincing now, either.

Lying there, however, I lacked the energy to press the point, and so changed the subject instead. "I may need Car's help," I told him. Car'd been my brother's investigator originally. Since I hadn't heard from Nina, having hired her and given her the information her guy should have been able to use by now to find Roland McEwan, it looked like time to try a different approach.

"Car's not going to want to get within ten miles of this problem again. Anyway, it's not just finding your old client. It's getting the dude to talk. If Wilder put him up to passing that gun to you, then he isn't going to say a word unless Bo gives him the order."

"I don't want to hear that." I closed my eyes tight as the spike in my blood pressure made the pain in my head grow suddenly piercing, followed by a wave of nausea that left me in a cold sweat.

"Look, you need to rest. I'll have a talk with Car. Try not to worry. You need to get well again before you can even start to think about taking care of business."

I gave Teddy all the information he needed, telling him where to find the contact information for the former client in the files in my storage unit in Berkeley. He carefully wrote down Roland McEwan's name, the number of the locker, and the combination for the lock.

Talking had worn me out. I kept flashing back to my hospitalization after the shooting last summer, when time itself had seemed to expand and contract with the cycles of pain and narcosis. I tried to keep my eyes open for Teddy's sake, wanting to show him I was still in control, but the next time they opened, he was gone.

~ ~ ~

I was released after two days. Still suffering bouts of dizziness, I wore a compression bandage around my ribs, had a sling over my shoulder, and was provided with a vial of Percocet. Somehow, armed in this manner, I was expected to face the world.

Look on the bright side, I told myself. *No one's tried to kill you in the last twenty-four hours.*

I took a cab to the Seward. When the weekend guy saw me his face lit up, seemingly as if in approval of my battered condition. Previously, he'd made it clear he viewed me as an unwelcome harbinger of gentrification—which, no doubt, I was.

On my floor, the hallway bulbs nearest my room were burned out, allowing me to see a glimmer of light beneath my door. I went rigid. It'd been three days since I was home. Maybe I'd left the light on and forgotten, I told myself, but I knew better.

I considered backing away and leaving, calling the police, but I suddenly felt so tired. If they wanted me, they were going to find me eventually. It might as well be here. Moving gingerly to spare my ribs, I fit the key into the lock and quickly turned it. I stepped to one side so I wouldn't be silhouetted in the door when it opened, then peeked around the jamb.

"Hey there, kid." My father lay on my bed, hands behind his head, wide awake. Before I'd come in he must have been staring at the ceiling the way he'd spent innumerable long nights in prison. Now he'd turned and was gazing at me.

"So you're the reason the guy downstairs was smiling," I said, trying not to breathe too hard because of my ribs. "How much did you give him to let you in here?"

"A hundred bucks."

"I thought somebody was waiting up here to kick my ass." I came in and closed the door. "How long have you been back?"

"A couple of hours." He rose, seeming about to clasp me by the shoulder, then seemed to consider my damaged condition and held back. I stepped to the dresser to empty my pockets of keys and phone. Lawrence sat again on the bed.

"So at least the police didn't pick you up at the airport."

"Maybe my return caught them by surprise. I came here because I heard you were in the hospital again. A motorcycle accident? I called Teddy as soon as I landed, and he said you were being released today. I figured I'd wait here instead of showing up at the hospital. Just in case the cops *are* looking for me."

"Someone cut me off on the Golden Gate Bridge. I ended up in oncoming traffic."

"A black SUV with dark windows, I hear." He'd been studying me and now announced his verdict. "Recent injuries aside, you look *almost* yourself. A hell of a lot better than last time I saw you. Though that's not saying much."

I'd still been fifteen pounds underweight when he left the country after the fire. Since then, I'd gained back ten. "I'm fine," I told him. "We're all fine." I was so glad to see him I could have wept, but my eyes were dry, as always. The many things that couldn't be said seemed to expand to fill the room, leaving not enough air.

"Look, I haven't been able to get in touch with Bo yet. Now that I'm back in the country, it shouldn't be so complicated. At least if I'm here I'm the one who'll be in danger—"

"I don't want you to get in touch with him on my behalf," I said, cutting him off. "This wasn't about him. This is something else I'm mixed up in."

"Something else," my father repeated.

"A friend of mine was murdered."

"I heard about that. By your client, I thought."

I slowly shook my head. "Dad, it was a setup. I think Jordan was killed by a client, just not one from the public defender's office. You ever hear of a company called Kairos?"

Predictably, he hadn't. Realizing I had no choice but to talk about it, I told my father everything I knew, concluding with my suspicions regarding Jordan's death. I also told him about Cho going missing after the trial, evidently a suicide.

"Tomorrow I'm thinking about paying a visit to his wife."

"If what you say is true, they'll likely be watching her. What can I do?"

I told him the most helpful thing would be for him to assist Car in finding Roland McEwan. His agenda in providing me with the gun hadn't occurred to me at the time, and now it was too late. Still, it was a piece of the puzzle I needed to have.

"Is Dot with you?" I asked, changing the subject.

"She's back on home soil, yes," he replied tersely. Then, himself switching subjects, said, "Buy you a drink?"

His tone made clear that he didn't want to talk about it. I swallowed a Percocet and we went out for beers.

Chapter 18

Lawrence's Harley, kept in storage during his absence and now retrieved, was the tangible symbol of his freedom. After we'd had a few drinks he talked me into accompanying him to the garage where he'd left the bike for the evening, on the pretext that I was newly in need of a replacement and ought to consider springing for a hog like his. After he gunned it down the ramp, leaving me to hobble home alone, I went back up to my room and spent a long night lying with gritted teeth, the bands of pain tightening around me every time I breathed, fire spreading from my battered ribs and abraded skin.

I spent the next two days mostly in bed washing Percocets down with beer. Still, I had time to make a few calls. My first was to Rebecca at the PD's office, letting her know what I'd learned from Walter Hayes. I asked her to check around, to see if any public defenders had cases out of Double Rock involving private security guards. She also promised to check with a few housing attorneys she knew.

The next morning Rebecca called me back. In a tone of surprise, she told me that the story I'd heard appeared to check out. She'd talked to two lawyers handling felony charges for clients who claimed to have been attacked by private security guards who'd shot first, engaging them in gun battles before the SFPD showed up. She'd also managed to confirm that in the housing projects scheduled for demolition, evictions and citations were through the roof.

I called Hayes and reported what I'd learned, passing on the names of the defendants and the phone numbers of the PDs handling their cases.

The following morning, I flushed the rest of the Percocets down the toilet and resolved to make contact with Cho's wife.

A woman's voice answered when I tried the number I'd managed to unearth. She was breathless, as if she'd run to grab the phone.

"This is Leo Maxwell," I said.

"What! Don't ever call this number again."

The line went dead.

The database where I'd found her gave me a Portola Valley address. It's a mountainside community on the peninsula, per capita one of the richest places around. I'd often ridden my road bike along the byways that wound across and along the peninsula's spine: Skyline Boulevard, Alpine Road. Many of the most scenic segments were through Portola Valley and its environs. After my wreck I was in no shape to ride my bicycle, which would have been my preferred means of approach—spandex being a universal badge of harmlessness—so I had no choice but to rent a car if I wanted a closer look.

I picked up a Ford Focus, the cheapest no-frills option at any of the rental agencies near the Seward. One of these days soon I'd have to settle on a new set of wheels, and also a real apartment. On the other hand, I saw no point in forking over first and last months' rent until I was reasonably certain of living through a one-year lease.

When I reached Portola Valley, forty minutes south of San Francisco, I located the Cho house without much trouble. Lydia had declared bankruptcy, and the house was on the market, I knew from my research, though no realtor's sign marred the view. Above its flat roof the wooded foothills rose to gentle heights. It was Thursday afternoon, and there didn't seem to be anyone around other than the perennial landscape crews.

I couldn't expect to sit for any length of time in such a neighborhood without attracting unwanted attention. In addition to Lydia's phone number and addresses, LexisNexis had given me the make and license numbers of the couple's vehicles—a BMW 5 Series sedan and a Volvo station wagon. I made one slow pass around the cul-de-sac, saw the carport with only one car, the Volvo, sitting in it, and drove back out the way I'd come.

On the way in I'd noticed that a hiking trail crossed the hillside just above the road where the Chos' house was. I parked my car at the Portola Café Deli and hiked back to a spot with the right vantage point. Lounging on the path like a hiker taking a rest, I didn't have to wait long before a BMW with the correct license number appeared, a woman at the wheel.

I didn't immediately get up. I didn't want to frighten her or put her on the defensive, at least no more than was necessary. Rather, I wanted her to talk to me about what she really believed had happened to her husband. As I'd mentioned to Benton, the news stories I'd read had reported that in the week after Cho's disappearance, she'd told the police and anyone else who'd listen that Gary couldn't have committed suicide, that he wouldn't have voluntarily written the note found in his abandoned car. Within a few short weeks, however, she'd changed her tune and begun pressing for a court ruling declaring her husband legally dead.

Something or someone had changed her mind, and I didn't believe it was the Kübler-Ross model I'd learned in Psych 101, i.e., denial transformed into acceptance. If there was bargaining involved, it wasn't of the metaphysical kind. It seemed to me, rather, that a very real person had either made her a threat or a promise she'd had no choice but to accept.

These were the thoughts running through my mind as I pondered how to make my approach. Then another car turned in to the cul-de-sac after Lydia's BMW—a black SUV with tinted windows. Just like the one that had run me down. A wave of fear ran through my guts as I remembered my all-too-recent terrifying encounter on the bridge.

I couldn't be sure it was the same car. There's probably no more common or nondescript vehicle in America than the armored tanks half the populace outside urban centers like San Francisco prefers to ride around in. There was an oddness about this one, though. Maybe the way its dark paint shone without a trace of dust or wear, or the utter blackness of its windows, which gave no glimpse even in silhouette of the occupants inside.

My mind replayed the sound of fear in Lydia's voice when I'd spoken my name.

I took off running down the grassy slope, this movement delivering jarring pain. I landed on my heels in the ditch beside the road, sending a concussion through bones that deserved no further battering. Still, I managed to keep going, across the road and down the middle of the street into the peaceful neighborhood Lydia Cho had just returned to.

I could see the black SUV at the curb in front of her house, pointed back in the direction it'd come. It was a Yukon, I saw. I faltered as I came into view of it, wondering if from inside it or the house I was being watched. I slowed to a walk, keeping to the other side of the street, ready to run if any of the windows started inching down.

With no sign of life from the Yukon, I cautiously cut across the street toward the house. Because it was uphill from the road and surrounded by scrub oak and cypress, I couldn't see inside. The BMW was parked next to the Volvo in the carport. Keeping one eye on the windows, I went up the drive. I reached the safety of the carport and paused there, out of view of anyone in the house. I still saw no movement or other sign of observation. I listened and heard nothing, scanned the street, and was reassured to see that my prowling hadn't been noticed by any of the neighbors. Or not that I could tell. Finally I gathered myself, ducked behind the bushes at the front of the house, and eased along beneath the windows.

The visitor, or visitors, had come in an SUV like a million others, I told myself again. They might not even be in this house, where nothing seemed amiss. I kept going, even at the risk of being picked up as a vagrant who had no business there.

The rooms I could peer into—a study and a formal living area—were empty. I kept going around the corner, following the slope up half a level. Now what I was seeing undoubtedly was the master bedroom. It was ringed by a deck that extended along the back of the house, with a massive buckeye growing through a hole. Wide picture windows provided a multimillion-dollar view. In a corner, a Jacuzzi was barely shielded by a partial screen. I stared in shock at what I now saw: a kneeling man trying to drown a woman in it.

He had her wrists pinned behind her. Catching a glint of metal, I realized she was handcuffed. Using the cuffs to control her, he was, with his other hand, pressing her head under the surface as she kicked and struggled. The attacker was tall and lean, with a military-style haircut, short on top and even shorter on the sides. His wide brow narrowed to a tapering chin, giving his face a wedgelike appearance. Dressed in a clean white T-shirt, jeans, and cowboy boots, he had a handgun secured beneath one arm in a shoulder holster.

I circled the deck, fumbling in my pocket for my cell phone, then realized I'd left it in the car. Suddenly the man let go of her head and yanked her from the water by her hair. She seemed to get her feet underneath her but lost her balance, gasping and choking. Then he grabbed her under the arm before she could slip beneath the surface again, a great wave washing over the edge of the tub and splashing beneath the deck.

The woman was shivering, coughing and retching, her workout clothes stuck to her body, water streaming down her head. She sagged over weak knees, held up by her tormentor. She was slight of build, and at around thirty or thirty-five years old, a good deal younger than her husband must have been.

Finally he decided to speak. "What was that lawyer doing calling your number?" His voice was calm, completely detached.

My stomach fell as I again remembered the fear I'd heard in her voice over the phone. Suddenly a radio crackled with a disembodied voice. He immediately silenced it, but, upon hearing the sound, my view of the situation hideously shifted, a single word reverberating in my mind.

Cop.

"What lawyer?" she gasped, and, as fast as a stone dropping, she went down again, her feet kicking wildly until he got one hand around both her wrists and used the other like a boat hook to sweep her legs completely out of the water, plunging her head beneath it.

I began to move away from the more private bedroom section of the deck. Moments later, I came to four wide steps not visible from the hot tub nook, concealed from this vantage point by the living room's protruding angle. I crossed the five feet of open space and reached the cover of the Jacuzzi's privacy screen. Once there, I eased along the wall, my heart racing as the splashes continued for longer than it seemed anyone could hold her breath. Then all was still, followed by a momentous thrash as, presumably, she was again yanked from the water.

With my back to a picture window, I inched toward the screen and peered through the lattice just as Lydia Cho, once more being held above the surface only by the hands that had been forcing her down, gave a retching cough. She appeared unconscious, her eyes rolled back.

"Where's your husband?" he asked.

"He's dead," she gasped, in a voice so hoarse the words were hardly intelligible.

"Too bad." Her attacker hooked the neck of her shirt with one finger and pulled it away from her chest. As he ogled her, I rushed around the screen and grabbed for the gun holstered beneath his arm. If it'd been loose in the holster I would've had it, but it was fastened down.

In an instant his hand was locked around my wrist, his eyes inches from mine, filled with outrage and surprise. I tightened my hand around the gun and with a tremendous heave used the shoulder holster to lift him and shove him backward over the rim of the hot tub. He held on to me as he fell, sending us both over into the water. I had to keep my hand around the gun—and the gun in its holster—or I was a dead man.

The water was cold. He was beneath me, but the tub was deep and for a moment my hand slipped and I thought I was going to lose him. Then I lunged and closed my hand over the gun again, finding my feet. He came up and tried to roll me over but suddenly Lydia was behind him.

Deftly, she'd flipped her legs through the loop of arms and handcuffs, wrapped the chain around his neck and pulled it taut under his chin, simultaneously strangling him and forcing his head underwater. He kicked and flailed, his neck muscles straining as he tried to free himself, raise his head, and breathe. He had a choice. Either he could let go my wrists and grab her arms, or he could win the struggle for the gun. He chose to continue fighting. The trouble was, I had both hands on the weapon now. His fingernails clawed more and more desperately at my wrists, his legs kicking, knees bucking. I was practically kneeling on top of him, my own face just inches from the water.

His hands flew up to Lydia's wrists. I found the snap and was about to yank the weapon from its holster when he let go of her wrists and went for the gun again, but she was quicker than he was, reaching down and taking the weapon from me as I tugged it from the holster.

"Move," she said, pointing it.

As I fell back, I heard a muffled thump and saw bubbles surface. A pink stain billowed in the water. Waves lapped the sides of the tub.

For a shocked moment, we sat facing each other, Lydia's hair streamed down either side of her face. One cowboy boot surfaced. She pushed it aside and fished underwater, ransacking the man's pockets until she came out with a set of keys, which she used to unlock the cuffs. She dropped them in the water, keeping the gun and keys. Then, holding the weapon down at her hip, she went like a sleepwalker across the deck and through the sliding glass door without a word to me.

As the adrenaline trickled out, pain set in, the muscles tightening over my wounded, now reinjured ribs. Each intake of breath brought tears to my eyes and sent spasms shooting through me. I was afraid for a moment that I wouldn't be able to climb out of the tub unassisted, but finally I managed it by rolling over the edge. I lay on my back for a few moments, then maneuvered onto my side and got to my knees, then at last to my feet.

I followed the trail of drips, including spots of blood, and found Lydia in the bedroom. She crouched there, filling a large suitcase from the bureau drawers, wincing in pain as she moved. A bruise was forming on her jaw. A clump of her hair had been torn out, I saw, and blood dripped from the raw patch on her scalp.

"There's an SUV out front. I didn't see anyone in it but couldn't be sure."

"Don't you think they'd be in here by now if there was?" She glanced over her shoulder but didn't pause, grabbing garments out of a drawer and pressing them down tightly into the suitcase to make them fit. By the size of the bag and the amount of clothing she was squeezing into it she didn't plan to return to the house for a long time. If ever.

The place was perfectly quiet. I'd been listening for sirens and heard nothing, but I couldn't shake the feeling that we were already being encircled by silent forces.

I could barely talk, and felt like my legs would give out. "Who was he?"

She shrugged helplessly. "The man who's been looking for Gary. He never bothered to introduce himself or show ID. So not a cop. Anyway, who are *you* and what do you want?"

I told her my name. "We've got to report this." I also thought it was possible that one or both of us needed to be in the hospital.

"No, we don't. Once you went for his gun, it was the only thing we could do."

We. What was I doing now? Helping her? In any case, I hadn't yet called the police. "I went for his gun because I thought he was going to drown you. You shot him in self-defense. The thing is, it's not going to seem that way if you run away now without calling it in."

She let the comment pass. "Bring the suitcase, please. You have your car?"

I could phone the cops and explain what had happened—the man drowning the woman in the hot tub when I arrived, my reasonable fear for her life . . .

"Do I need to say I'll shoot you if you don't do as I ask?"

I didn't believe she would. On the other hand, she seemed remarkably unfazed, considering she'd just killed a man.

"It's not here. I left it at the Café Deli off Alpine Road." I figured she was probably in shock.

"Forget it, then. Put the bags in the trunk of the Beemer."

It was simplest to do as she asked. She had his keys and we went out to the Yukon on the street.

It was empty, as bare as a rental inside. There was a cell phone on the center console. After making sure it was deactivated, she pocketed it. She'd done a fast change in the bedroom, slipping on dry clothes, but I was still sopping wet. I heard no sirens, saw no faces at any of the neighbors' windows as she backed out of the driveway.

"Your hands are shaking," she said, glancing over at me as she drove.

"Yours aren't?"

"I've worn out my nerves, waiting for the earth to crack open and swallow me. Now that it has, all I feel is relief. And resolve."

"Where will you go?"

"To Gary," she said, and with a leaping sensation in my stomach, I glanced over at her, confirming that in fact he was alive.

Neither of us spoke for a while after that. She kept the car pointed north. Night had fallen before she told me where we were going. We were on Interstate 5, tucked into the ceaseless anonymous flow of traffic, mostly long-haul truckers.

"Before Gary disappeared, he mentioned once that if we were ever in danger, there's a cabin in the mountains we could hide at. A friend from a long time ago owns it, he said, a person no one would ever connect him with. He had me memorize the directions. It seemed strange at the time, but he must have known this day was coming. That's where we're going now."

"Have you talked to him?"

"A week or so after they found the car, I got a call from a number I didn't recognize. A throwaway phone, obviously. It was Gary. He was furious at me for trying to persuade everyone he was still alive. I was going to ruin everything, he said. Yesterday he called again and told me where he was. He knew I understood which place he meant; otherwise, they'd have gone straight to him instead of trying to make me tell them how to find him."

We stopped for gas. Lydia went in to use the toilet and buy us something to eat while I filled the tank. She gave me a doubtful glance as she was getting out, like she knew better than to trust me by leaving me alone, but felt she had no alternative. She couldn't very well march me at gunpoint into the women's restroom with her. Or maybe she guessed that my ribs had tightened so badly there was no way I could stand on my own.

I was a lawyer. Though most of my clients were criminals, I believed in the rule of law. What had happened at the house had been self-defense, but the longer we went without reporting it, the more it looked like murder. If so, I'd be judged an accessory as of the moment Lydia came out and we drove on, any pretense of my being an unwilling hostage fading further with every mile in which I turned down the opportunity for escape.

On the other hand, if Gary Cho was at the end of this long drive, I didn't want our trip to end here before we reached him. I was convinced he knew who'd killed Jordan and why.

I was still in the car when Lydia climbed back in behind the wheel. She'd bought several packets of Motrin and some sodas for us to share. I watched the rearview mirror the rest of the way, but no police car had appeared by the time we reached the end of a gravel road in the Shasta-Trinity National Forest late that night.

Chapter 19

The headlights shone on a fairly primitive log cabin. Behind it, mountains blocked out the stars. There didn't appear to be anyone home, though the air was tinged with wood smoke. Beneath a rough overhang on one side of the house, wood was stacked. An axe stuck out from the chopping block out front, which was surrounded by split logs. A mountain bike hung upside down over the board porch beneath the overreaching eaves.

I needed help from Lydia to get out of the car. She was surprisingly strong for her size. On my feet, I found I was able to walk—haltingly at first, but better after a few steps. With the added exercise, however, breathing once again became a painful problem.

Inside, the place was a surprisingly large single room holding a queen bed, a table, a woodstove, and a basin. From the looks of it, the inhabitant had vacated, seemingly in haste. Flames still crackled in the woodstove. I found a battery-operated lantern and turned it on. "What now?"

"We wait." Lydia went through the cabin discovering what she recognized as signs of her husband: a pair of running shoes, an Italian-style stovetop coffee percolator, a bottle of Knob Creek.

We'd been there half an hour when, without warning, the door was flung open and Cho came in. I jumped, earning another excruciating spasm from my ribs, but Lydia seemed unsurprised. I recognized him from online photos. He was a very tall, thin man with graying hair and a disparaging gaze. He wore ski pants, hiking boots, a hooded sweatshirt, and a waterproof jacket. He seemed to make no differentiation between his wife and me.

"What are you doing here?" he demanded.

"We weren't followed," she assured him, answering an entirely different question from the one he'd asked.

"How can you be sure?"

"The one who's been following me is dead. That's how."

Concern deepened in his eyes. Surprise yielded to tenderness, and he stepped forward, gathered her to his chest, and hugged her.

Self-conscious, I turned away, but they'd already parted, Cho turning his back.

At the stove, he opened the door and added a few hunks of split wood, then stabbed at the embers with a poker until the flames leapt up. He seemed to be studying them as if the solution to their problems might be found in that fiery belly. He closed the stove door again.

"Who are you?" he wanted to know.

I told him my name. Cho shared a look with his wife I couldn't read, an intense wordless communication. Then he said, "Leo and I are going to step outside."

Lydia nodded. He held out his hand and she passed him the gun. I felt a shock like an electric charge as I realized the danger I might be in.

The night air was crisp, the temperature just above freezing. The scent of pines was overpowering, intoxicating. The moon had risen above the mountains, making them seem almost near enough to touch, though they must have been miles away. The fissures and furrows of their stark topography remained in shadow, presenting a study in contrasts, like Japanese woodcut prints I'd seen.

He wanted to know: "Did you kill the guy or did she?"

I told him briefly what had happened. "It was self-defense, though the law may not see it that way," I concluded.

"What were *you* doing there?"

"Jordan Walker," I said simply.

The name seemed to have nearly as much of an effect on Cho as the news of his wife's lethal deed. He leaned his shoulder against the rough post that held up the roof of the porch and looked off toward the mountains. "I know who you are now. You're the boy-friend at the public defender's office. The one who was with her the night she died."

"You mean the night she was *murdered*."

Lydia chose this moment to join us. She'd changed into jeans and a sweatshirt from the suitcase we'd brought. I, on the other hand, was shivering.

I expected her presence to silence Cho, but he went on. "I was dead by then," he said. The comment might have been flippant but his voice was mournful, nostalgic for a life to which he could never return.

"If you're implying I had something to do with her murder, I didn't," he added.

"You were there, though, weren't you? You were the 'client' she had to meet. 'Get rid of him.' Isn't that what your text said?"

"*I* was never her client. I was the guy Jacob Mauldin cheated out of his life's work, then out of his life, with the help of Tom Benton and a crew of lawyers. Including your girlfriend," he said bitterly. "Or should I say Tom Benton's girlfriend. But yes, I was in San Francisco that night. And you're correct that I spoke with her after you left."

I wondered why Jordan had made the comment about attorney-client privilege. Maybe in her mind she'd switched sides by that point, never mind that the most inviolable rule of our profession is that no lawyer ever gets to switch sides.

Perhaps, for Jordan, this fundamental lesson had come too late.

"Did she know the reason you'd faked your death?"

"She knew I'd have been arrested and charged with a sex crime, and that the evidence against me was completely fabricated. At least, I *hope* I made her understand that."

"Why'd you tell your secrets to Jordan?"

"Who else? Getting *someone* to turn was my only chance at being able to come home someday. She was in a position to obtain evidence showing the case against me was a straight-up fraud. And, unlike the rest of them, she seemed to have a conscience."

"I talked to your lawyer, Ma. He told me you maintained throughout the trial that the video was false, that the kid's testimony was bought. What made you think she'd believe you now, let alone betray her client, when you hadn't convinced her or anyone else the first time?"

"Because she'd left the firm. It seemed to me she wouldn't have done it the way she did, right after her big success, unless she knew what had happened wasn't right. The fact that she left told me she was a person who might well put her principles into action. If she knew the full scope of what Kairos had done, how Mauldin and Benton perpetrated a fraud on the court and now were using the same false evidence to try to get me arrested and thrown in prison, I thought she might feel obligated to blow the whistle." He grimaced, indicating his awareness of his own role in Jordan's elimination.

"She was going back to the law firm so that she could try to satisfy herself one way or another about the truth of what you'd told her. Is that basically it?"

Cho nodded. "She couldn't take my word for it any more than she did at the trial. Also, she wasn't going to turn against her client without solid proof. But she sensed there was truth in what I was telling her. I think she already knew."

"Sounds to me like you did a pretty good job of manipulating her." I felt a sudden, irrational anger at the way this man—Jordan's former opponent—had been willing to put her at such risk in service of his own interests. "If you were innocent, you could have stayed to stand trial. Instead, you convinced Jordan to be brave in your place."

Lydia, watching silently up to now, joined the conversation. "When a civil litigant rigs a trial with perjured testimony and manufactured evidence," she said, "it's a fraud on the court and a federal crime. When business interests conspire with gangsters to siphon public money for private profit, it's a national headline. *If* anyone finds out. The stakes were too high. He'd have been found dead in his cell."

"What conspiracy?" I was skeptical. It still seemed possible to me it could have been Cho who'd killed her.

"Mauldin and the Chinatown mafia," Cho said. "How do you think Mauldin got the contract in the first place? *He's* the one who's connected."

"So you're telling me they rigged the trial. But why go to the trouble?"

"If the jury believed me, they'd have been out of the project. I was meant to play ball and keep my mouth shut, but I wouldn't, and they decided to set me up. And because I'm Chinese, the jury bought it."

I drew his attention to what I felt his self-justifications sought to hide. "Nothing you're telling me changes the fact that it's your fault she's dead."

Lydia slipped her arms around her husband's waist. The gun was in his hand, resting on the deck rail. Jordan was dead but they were alive, her protective embrace seemed to say. No doubt to her it was a trade worth making, or it would have been if Jordan had lived long enough to exonerate her husband.

"Can you tell me more about what kind of money we're talking here," I asked them.

"These guys own half the property in Hunters Point. They've been buying it up for years. The retail space they're planning . . . Whoever ends up in control of that is going to make more money than God. And then there's the residential units . . ."

"So setting you up was just about protecting an investment," I said.

But I still wasn't sure I believed it was a setup. Like Ma, I'd heard such stories often enough from clients who insisted the evidence against them was fabricated, that it was a conspiracy to frame them for crimes they'd never think of committing. I'd always treated these tales with the disregard they seemed to deserve, viewing them as extraordinary fabrications no different, in my mind, from admissions of guilt. Except that they further decreased the trustworthiness of the person who told them.

The consequence of not believing Cho was to accept that the opposite was true, that he was the one with the organized crime connections, and that he'd leveraged those connections for illicit sexual favors. Which led me once again to the conclusion that I was now in great danger. Once more my eyes went to the gun.

"Why'd you file a whistle-blower case instead of going to the DA?"

His answer was surprisingly honest. "There's no payday in going to the DA. A whistle-blower, on the other hand, stands to reap a substantial reward, a cut of the money recovered on behalf of the government." A consolation prize, perhaps, for someone who'd missed out on the graft. "I knew if I succeeded, the criminal investigation would come."

"And when things turned bad, why didn't you drop the case?"

"I had the chance. It's true," Cho said. "One evening, a few months before trial, I came down to the parking garage from my lawyer's office and found two men waiting for me. They forced me to drive with them up to Twin Peaks. There they explained I had two choices. Either I could be arrested for sex with a minor, or I could drop the case.

"I refused because I thought we could turn it against them, use the threat as a means of convincing the jury that the accounting records they'd produced were manufactured. However, the next week they sent my lawyer the video and an affidavit from the kid I was supposedly with. As I said, it was completely false, but the judge allowed it into evidence.

"The week after the verdict, I was arrested. After I made bail I decided not to stick around. One afternoon I left my car at the bridge, stuck a suicide note in the driver's seat, and stole a van. Eventually I worked my way here. The place belongs to an old friend."

Lydia's arms had tightened around him.

"Tell me about Jordan," I said.

"Since I've been here, I've bought the *Chronicle* whenever I make my weekly supply run to town. I had enough cash to last well into the winter if I needed to. I was biding my time. I didn't know what I was waiting for, but I recognized it when it came. It was the Rodriguez case. There was a story in the *Chronicle*, and it mentioned Jordan's name and yours as Rodriguez's attorneys.

"During the Kairos trial, Jordan was one of Tom Benton's associates, a corporate attorney neck-deep in the fraud for all I knew." He paused. "Now, it seemed, she was working for the public defender's office. The only way to explain the change was that she'd gotten a whiff of what they'd been up to and decided she didn't want any more part of it. The few times I'd met her she'd struck me as cut from a different cloth from the rest of her colleagues. I think it was simply that she seemed honest.

"They'd destroyed me, taken away the possibility of ever working in business again. And they'd threatened me with more than that. I wanted revenge, but I also wanted my life back. I didn't think, acting alone, that I could have both those things."

I said nothing, letting him continue.

"I decided to contact Jordan. The first time I spoke with her was right before the Rodriguez trial. I called her at your office. She didn't want to talk to me at first, but in the end her curiosity got the better of her distrust. I told her much of what I've explained to you. She was skeptical, and wary of the situation. She had no reason to believe what I was telling her, yet at the same time she didn't seem surprised. She wanted to meet in person, make sure I was who I claimed to be. So I agreed to come into the city.

"We set the meeting for a Friday night a week after the Rodriguez trial ended. I was keeping watch, and saw her bring you back to her apartment. I was certain I hadn't been followed, that I'd taken every necessary precaution with our communications. Still, I remained very concerned Jordan might be under surveillance. After all, she'd made such a sudden exit from the firm, Mauldin was likely to have arrived at the same conclusions I had.

"Having observed her building for a long period and seen nothing, I texted her. 'Get rid of him.'"

Just as Benton had said.

"She was aware of the possible danger, and so took a long cab ride, she told me later, having the driver make all sorts of turns and stops. Her destination, of course, was her apartment, right back where she'd started. It seemed safer to both of us than meeting out in public. I waited until she got out, then met her at the building entrance, where she let me in."

This was awful for me to hear. But Cho, focused on his own misfortune, was oblivious.

"We talked for maybe an hour. She kept her cards close, not trusting me completely. Nonetheless, by the end of our meeting, she told me she intended to return to work at Baker. To get proof that the company had submitted false books in the trial, and, if I was right, fix the damage.

"I left at around two AM. I saw no one lurking around, didn't notice any watchers. My idea was to come back up here, wait for the story to break, then reclaim my life. Of course, the story that eventually broke was very different from the one I'd expected. From then on I knew I was a hunted man. I took a Greyhound north, and have been here ever since."

Chapter 20

I suggested we go inside. I wanted him to walk me through it again, so I could make the mental effort required to believe his self-serving story as Jordan evidently had come to believe it that night. She'd given his tale sufficient credence that she'd decided to go back on one of the most important decisions of her life. Because of that, I felt Cho deserved as much time as he needed to convince me as he had her. I didn't want to believe she'd been fooled by him—her opponent in that contentious litigation—any more than I'd wanted to believe she'd been fooled by Rodriguez, her own client.

It all seemed so implausible. Yet I wanted desperately to see what she'd seen.

Cho didn't want to go in. "You can't hear anything inside." Then, by way of explanation, he added, "About an hour ago, there was a car. Just shortly before I came back into the cabin. It stopped maybe a mile down the road. We don't have many people down this way at night."

Someone was looking for Cho. The man at Lydia's house was dead, but there would be other of Mauldin's "security guards," if that's who the man had been. I hadn't wanted to believe Hayes, but after this morning's events, anything seemed possible.

Lydia went to the farthest corner of the house, scanning the dark woods at the edge of the clearing, then returned.

"What do you think?" Cho asked her. "You're still sure you two weren't followed?"

"I don't see how," she said impatiently. "But even if we weren't, how long can we go on hiding here?"

"Depends on what the alternative is."

I spoke up. "We need to prove our case. One way to do it is through the judge who presided over the trial. If we can convince him Kairos won it by fraud, he's the only one with the power to fix it."

"I don't have any more proof now than I had at the trial," Cho said angrily. "If it wasn't enough then, how could it possibly be enough now? You were with Jordan the night she died. Just like you were at the house with Lydia earlier today. You're undoubtedly a suspect, and if I say I'd met with Jordan that night, then so am I. How much credibility will any of us have, really?"

"I'm not sure. But I don't think going to ground here is a serious long-term plan."

I could see that Lydia agreed with this.

"Jordan had credibility," Cho said, not telling me anything I didn't know. "That's why I went to her. When they killed her, it all fell apart. That is, unless we can show they had her killed, staged the rape to stop her from talking."

"Look," I said. "What about Benton? After all, he was running the show. Maybe we should approach him. Try to get him to open up."

Cho scoffed at this. "The first thing Benton'll do is tell Mauldin, who'll sic his dogs on us. Probably the very same ones who lost one of their own this afternoon."

"I'm not so sure. It seems obvious Benton and Jordan had been sleeping together. The chronology of their affair's not clear to me, but I find it hard to believe he was knowingly involved in her murder. If I'm right about him, he's got to be looking for a way out. It's even possible he'd like to see Jordan's death avenged."

Cho shook his head. "People are dead. Jacob has nothing to lose by killing a few more. By now, he'd probably consider even Tom Benton to be expendable."

"You intend to spend the rest of your life, however long it is, running from these men?" I challenged him.

Lydia paused midpace and turned to look at her husband, waiting for his answer to my question. Cho met her gaze in the moonlight. "All right," he finally said, nodding to me, his mouth tightening. "We'll go back to San Francisco."

We loaded the Beemer with Lydia's suitcase and a backpack Cho had ready. His escape bag, he called it, though how he'd planned on getting out if he needed to leave in a hurry I couldn't tell. The only visible transportation at the cabin was the mountain bike. Cho drove, Lydia seated beside him, me in the back.

We'd gone half a mile when the headlights picked out an SUV parked lengthwise across the gravel road ahead, blocking our exit.

Fifty yards from this obstacle, Cho stopped. "You brought them with you."

I flinched and raised my hand as a spotlight shone out from the SUV. Even squinting, I could see nothing ahead. They'd be coming now, approaching on either side of the car. Cho slammed the Beemer into reverse, turning around in his seat and using the illumination of the spotlight to navigate in lurching turns between the trees.

"I don't know where you think you're going," Lydia said. "The road *ends*."

The SUV had pulled forward and was keeping pace, the spotlight leveled at blinding height. "There's an abandoned logging road,"

Cho said. "That's how I get to town when I need to. I ride my bike. I've got an old pickup parked at the end of it, covered with branches. The trip's about four miles. We'll have to leave the car. I've never done it in the dark, but—"

"Where?"

"Here. We'll have to run." Cho stopped. The SUV didn't. "Lydia!" he shouted as the passenger door swung open. I glanced back in time to see her spotlighted, jumping out and running for the woods. Maybe she expected us to follow her, but there wasn't time. Before I could open my door, the SUV slammed into our front bumper, driving the Beemer backward.

My head snapped forward and I fell into the foot well between the front and back seats. We were being pushed down over the rocky river bank. The car stalled and the noise of rushing water filled our ears, the spotlight suddenly raking the sky overhead. I felt us tip and roll; then we were upside down. I fell onto the roof, then found the door handle and tried to open the door. It wouldn't budge, but breaking the seal caused the water, breathtakingly cold, to flow in faster.

For a moment all was dark, then the spotlight began probing outside the windows, as if searching for a way in. "Through the windows," I heard Cho say, but mine wouldn't go down. The glass shattered. Hearing a strangled cry over the liquid sound of the river being sucked into the car, I saw Cho, still inverted in his seat belt, clutch his throat, the glow from the spotlight illuminating him. Then his head was underwater and he made no attempt to lift it out.

I heard bullets thunking against the underside of the car. There remained only pockets of air. My head was pressed against the seat. Frigid water splashed my chin and mouth. Again I fumbled for the door handle, grabbed it, tugged, and also shoved against it with my shoulder. This time, with the pressure equalized, it came open and I was able to float out.

I ducked beneath the surface, hugged my knees and tried to let the current take me. But the piercing cold made me gasp and my throat filled with water. As I was flailing, the spotlight found me. Gunshots rang out and bullets hit the water. I felt the current quicken, snatching me away from the insistent beam, the bottom dropping away as a thundering noise approached. *Waterfall*, my brain had time to register. Then with a sickening rush I was falling through the darkness, my stomach in my throat.

The impact drove the air from my lungs. My injured ribs were on fire. The water solidified around me like cement, pounding me against the fine pebbles at the bottom of the pool, where I was pinned for a helpless second, my need to breathe like a scream. I popped loose and slammed into one rock, then another. The river widened and lost its momentum, leaving me half-floating in a foot and a half of swirling water, spinning from rock to rock until my knees gained purchase and I staggered coughing through the shallows to my feet.

I expected the spotlight to locate me again but I didn't see it. Of course they couldn't drive their truck down here. My breath came fast, every muscle in my body tight with cold and fear and the bruising I'd taken over the last five days, my ribs a searing mass of pain, the injuries from my motorcycle accident reinflamed. Cho was dead. Lydia likely was, too.

Too cold to stay where I was, I decided to follow the current. The only way forward seemed to be ahead. I had a vague idea that staying in the water was my safest bet. I could only take two or three steps at a time before I had to stop and steel myself against the pain, the stillness of the mountains seeming to dissolve my being each time I listened for pursuit. I was deliriously certain there'd be dogs, or copters. If there were helicopters I was screwed, but everyone knew dogs couldn't track in water. My feet were numb, indifferent to whether I was walking in the current or on the spits of sand that appeared on either side, broken by sheer rock walls that forced me again and again back into the water. I could no longer feel my hands, and even my face and lips had lost sensation. The sentient part of me seemed to have shrunken to a core of protothought. I knew I couldn't go on.

Luckily this realization seemed not to have reached my legs, and I kept walking, throwing one foot in front of the other, moving in and out of the water, my shoes heavy, my eyes steady on the gap in the trees ahead. The gorge widened, the trees on either side growing more distant, the mountains again coming into view. I came to a large bar, stretching perhaps a hundred yards between the current and the trees, the silvery glint of river stones showing against the dark sand. I'd gone perhaps a mile and knew I was at the limit of my endurance.

I veered inland, walking on the relatively flat surface, though in my fatigue the going seemed no easier than before. About two-thirds of the distance to the trees I tripped over a stone and heard something light and metallic skitter away in the darkness. I stumbled forward and tripped again, my foot coming down this time with a crunch. I was standing in someone's fire ring, surrounded by empty beer cans. Nearby stood a twisted heap of branches and driftwood.

Whoever had been here had chosen the site because a large tree still bearing its roots was half-embedded in the sand, forming a natural bench. I huddled against it and drew my knees to my shoulders. This brought no warmth. But the shivering had stopped. My head nodded and I forced my eyes open. I didn't know much about the outdoors but it's undoubtedly true that to sleep in such a situation means certain death.

I ran my hands over the smooth log, stripped of its bark, then started feeling around on hands and knees. Lots of beer cans, other garbage. Cigarette butts. At last my hands closed on what felt like a flattened cylinder. A disposable lighter, but when I shook it there was nothing inside. Confirming the fluid was out, I struck the wheel with my thumb and was rewarded with sparks but no flame.

I stumbled stiff-legged to the woods for something small to burn and found an armful of last year's pine needles and a long-dried snag of dry grass and brush. I brought these back to the fire ring and dumped them on the sand near the firewood the partyers had left. I stuck the lighter in my pile of dry grass and moss and thumbed the wheel again and again.

Finally a pair of sparks landed, fizzing in the nest I'd built for them. I grabbed the nest in my fist and balled it up, wrapping my fingers tightly around the grass and moss to make a sealed, crucible-like chamber with the spark at its core, and blew through the hole my thumb and forefinger made, like I was trying to inflate a balloon. After a dozen puffs the heat burned my palm and I had to drop the flaring ball of moss.

In five minutes, I had a small fire. My palm was blistered badly, but the pain told me I was alive. I was aware of the likelihood it might lead my pursuers to me, but it was either freeze to death or take the risk of being shot. With any luck, they'd think I'd been killed in the stream, raked by the bullets that had strafed the current around me. Besides, if they had helicopters and night-vision goggles, the fire wouldn't make much difference. And if they were determined to find me, they would. Why not be comfortable?

I sat close enough to the flames that steam rose off my clothes. When those on my front side were stiff and dry, I turned and roasted my back. I fed the flames but tried to keep the fire small. Warming at last, my body was a solid mass of pain. As the flames faded to embers, I eased onto the sand in a fetal position, pillowed my head on my arm, and dozed.

Chapter 21

I woke frequently through the night to feed the fire, and at first light I was slowly, painfully on the move. A Jeep track from the gravel bar led me to a logging road, which ended a few miles later at the main highway along the Trinity River. I had to stop frequently to rest, leaning against a tree or simply lying down beside the road. By 9:00 AM I was walking the shoulder of the highway toward Weaverville. I wasn't sure what I'd do, but I knew I couldn't hide in the woods for six months like Gary Cho.

The grades were steep and the curves frequent. A few cars passed, but none was going my way. I had to rest again and sat down on the shoulder, then eased onto my side. I was still lying in the fetal position ten minutes later when a sheriff's patrol car approached.

The eyes of the uniformed man at the wheel met mine and he slowly reversed to a stop on the shoulder beside me. I rolled onto my back as his passenger window slid down. I sat up and shakily got to my feet, my eyes filling with tears at the pain this effort brought. Standing, I had to lean on his car for support.

Sipping from a coffee mug, he balanced it carefully on the dashboard as he regarded me. I couldn't keep my eyes off it, and he seemed to notice this with a faint smile. "You're a long way from home," he said with easy humor, as if he had nothing better to do than stop and talk with me.

At first I thought he already knew who I was, and that I was from San Francisco. A stunned moment passed before I realized anyone walking on this road would be a long way from home, wherever home happened to be.

"Got stuck in the woods last night," I told him.

"'Stuck' covers a lot of ground. We've got a phone at the office you can use to sort out what you need." He seemed to take it for granted I didn't have a cell, or he knew that, if I did, there'd be no service here.

When he reached across to open the door, I sat down. "Todd Burke," he said, shaking my hand. He retrieved the coffee mug from the dash as he pulled forward. "I'm the sheriff here."

I wondered if he knew anything about last night's events, if the car had been discovered in the stream with Cho's body in it. I didn't dare ask, of course. When I introduced myself, all he said was: "Must have been a cold night for sleeping on the ground."

I didn't know how to explain what had happened, so for now I said nothing. In twenty minutes we were at his headquarters. He fed me coffee and donuts and showed me to an empty desk with a phone. Then he went into his own office and closed the door. A few uniformed deputies were at their desks, and a female dispatch officer sat behind glass. Not surprisingly, I was the object of their curiosity.

I didn't know where to start. Probably, what I needed most was a lawyer. After yesterday's events, it seemed to me I had as little chance of walking away from the situation as I did of pitching in the World Series. It would be vital later that I not be seen as having hidden information. Besides, Lydia Cho might still be alive—lost or wounded in the forest.

Feeling a sudden determination, I rose and knocked on the sheriff's door. He called, "Come in," and I did. "You make your calls?" he asked. I told him I hadn't, but that I'd realized there were a few things I needed to discuss with him. With a gesture, he invited me to sit.

It was a strange story, I said, and I asked him not to stop me until I'd told it through. Throughout my narrative, his demeanor held neither belief nor disbelief. He sat regarding me with the weary look of a man precisely calculating in his head the vast amount of paperwork my tale was going to generate for him. When I'd finished, he opened his computer, found the number for the San Mateo County sheriff, and connected the call. He asked me for the Chos' address, repeated it into the phone, and requested the house be checked for a possible shooting victim. He replaced the phone, rose, and said, "Let's go."

On our way out, he beckoned a deputy to join us. This time I rode in the back.

At first, I was worried I wouldn't be able to find the place. Last night we'd arrived in the dark, and I'd been half-asleep as Lydia drove, my sense of direction left miles behind us. Now, by the light of a cool early autumn day, I wasn't sure we had the right logging road until the cabin appeared at the end of it. The bicycle and the running shoes were gone from the porch, but, otherwise, nothing seemed to have changed since I'd last been there. Somehow, though, we'd evidently driven right past the wrecked car in the water without noticing it.

Burke turned the cruiser around and proceeded more slowly back the way we'd come. On this second pass, I spotted the site easily enough. Multiple sets of ruts descended from the gravel road down the bank into the river, showing where Lydia's BMW had been pushed over the edge. But it was gone now. The brush was flattened between the ruts, the leaves of the few broad-leaf plants just beginning to wilt, as the deputy pointed out. The current flowed without unnatural interruption toward the bend.

"You can see the tracks," I said.

"I can see what I can see," Burke answered, his friendly attitude now evaporated into a cop's inquisitive suspicion. He made his way down the bank, holding on to the broken bushes for support, then stood scanning the water, hands on his hips. Something caught his eye and he rolled his sleeve, stepped with one foot onto a boulder at the edge, and stooped to thrust his hand beneath the current, coming up with a shard he studied in his palm. "Window glass," he announced in a tone of personal affront.

The deputy, kicking through grass at the edge of the road, bent and parted the stalks. "Shell casings here."

"You'll find spent shells in every square foot within twenty feet of a passable road in this county," the sheriff responded. "Seems like people around here have nothing better to do than get drunk and waste good ammunition on trees. Shell casings don't tell me much."

I was astounded, my alarm growing by the minute. "There were two people with me in the car. A man named Gary Cho and his wife, Lydia. I saw Gary shot in the throat. He was in the driver's seat. Lydia had made it out before the car went in the water."

Burke surveyed the stream. His cell phone rang and he held it to his ear, then said, "Any sign of the homeowners?" He listened again, his face betraying nothing. He pocketed the phone and climbed back up the steep bank. "Looks like we've got a missing person case, after all." To the deputy he said, "Jim, we're going to need everyone we can spare out here in river boots and waders." To me: "Turn around and put your hands behind your back."

"What'd they find in Portola?"

"Nothing," Burke said, snapping on the cuffs. "Same as here. There's one consistent theme to your story, and that's this woman,

Lydia Cho. Her car is gone, and your rental's still parked at the market near her house. That puts you on the scene. You've told me she was with you. We're going to have to keep you around until we get to the bottom of this."

"Everything I've told you is the truth."

"Then you'll be the first. My more immediate problem is I've got to search these woods for a missing woman who had no business here, but according to you this is where she was. I don't think she's anywhere near here, but I still have to look." He studied me for another moment, seemingly giving me the chance to say something more, then signaled to the deputy. "Miranda him, drive him back to the station, and put him in a room."

The deputy's mumbled warnings were hardly needed. Even if I hadn't been a lawyer and, thus, fully aware of my rights, I had nothing to say as we drove back toward Weaverville along the mountain road. I'd dreaded having to explain my involvement in these killings. But that dilemma now seemed preferable to the murky netherworld into which I'd been plunged, one controlled by secretive forces that apparently had the power to erase events as if they'd never occurred—at least two killings and one wrecked car.

My tale of shootings bookmarked by a three-hundred-mile drive for an interview with a man who'd committed suicide months before sounded crazy even to me. I didn't blame Burke for not believing a word of it. I'd felt the same way listening to Cho last night.

The interview room the deputy led me to was more comfortable than most of its kind. The door locked from the outside, but at least it wasn't a cell. There was a couch, or rather a loveseat, a stained and battered specimen that appeared to have been retired from a doctor's reception room. The female dispatcher soon brought me a peanut-butter sandwich and more coffee. Then, when I knocked on the door, a deputy appeared to escort me to the restroom. In the early evening another deputy brought me a sack of McDonald's.

I asked to make a phone call, and he showed me to the same unused desk as before. I said I wanted to call my lawyer, and he hesitated, then let me use the phone in the sheriff's private office. My first call was to my brother, who was stunned by the news and so upset that I quickly reassured him I was fine, even though I wasn't certain this was true. Teddy promised to let our father know, despite the fact that neither of them could do anything to help me. My next call was to Nina Schuyler, my friend, who'd promised to defend me on the gun case.

As I poured my voice into the silence on her end of the phone, I sensed she didn't believe me, either. I was aware of the doubts she'd had about all of us back during my father's trial.

"Don't say a word," she advised me once I'd finished talking. "And don't think you can talk your way out of it. You've said far too much already."

"All of it true."

"You've been in this business long enough, Leo, to know truth doesn't matter. Truth is relative, and a mistake's the same as a lie. They can't use your silence against you, but I guarantee they'll find a way to twist whatever it is you've told them into a hanging rope."

"I know, but I've got more than just myself to think about. My investigation of Jordan's murder's what brought me to this. I need to finish what I started. But in order for me to do that, you've got to get me out."

Her reply was grudging. "I'll make a few calls and see what I can learn."

I thanked her, then went back to my little room.

I was still there five hours later when the door flew open and three men walked in. The first, in muddy boots and a sweat-stained uniform shirt, was Burke. Behind him came a stocky, dark-haired guy in pressed blue jeans, a striped button-down, and a leather jacket with a badge and gun on his belt. Last came Detective Mark Chen, wearing a dark blue suit and no tie.

"Sorry to keep you waiting," Burke said. "It's been a hell of a day. Not that I want to make it any longer, but these men have driven up from the peninsula and need to start back first thing. Leo Maxwell, Lou Suarez. He's up here from Portola Valley. I understand Mr. Maxwell and Detective Chen are already acquainted."

With this, Burke lifted the suspect's chair away from the table and moved it to one side of the room, sat, and tilted it against the wall, his arms folded as if signaling the end of his participation. I was on the couch. The guy from Portola took the interrogator's chair, with Chen standing against the wall behind him. The room seemed to have shrunk to a tenth of its previous size.

"Why don't you start by telling us what brings you to Trinity County," Burke suggested.

"Investigating a murder," I answered, letting my eyes rise to meet Chen's. "I came here to speak to the last person who saw Jordan Walker alive the night she was murdered in San Francisco two months ago. In other words, I was doing Detective Chen's work for him."

"*You* were the last person who saw her alive," Chen said. "And now, according to you, you were also the last person to see Lydia Cho."

I shook my head. "The SFPD knows the man it's arrested for Jordan's murder may be innocent. They're willing to let him take the fall if that means closing the case."

Suarez didn't acknowledge Chen's presence. "Sheriff Burke's question was a good one. Why don't you finish answering it? Care to explain why you thought the man you were looking for was here in Trinity County?"

"His name was Gary Cho. He's the owner of a construction company called Lizhi, and he'd filed a whistle-blower lawsuit against Kairos, one of the main subcontractors on the big Candlestick project. He claimed they were cooking their books and defrauding the taxpayers. Kairos hit back hard—and dirty. They had a phony video of Cho having sex with a fourteen-year-old kid in a Chinatown bath-house. He faked his suicide to keep from being sent to prison. After a few months in hiding up here, he went back down to the city to see Jordan. She listened to him, and his story meshed with her own suspicions. But they killed her before she could pursue it any further. Cho hid himself successfully until he was killed in an ambush last night. I didn't see what happened to Lydia after I escaped from the car."

"How do you know Lydia Cho?" Suarez spoke as if he hadn't heard a word I'd said. His manner was patient, his tone the one an interrogator would use with a man who, though outwardly rational, was clearly insane. Say, a suspect like Randall Rodriguez.

"I don't know her. I was looking for her husband. His suicide didn't sit right with me, especially in the context of Jordan's murder. As part of my investigation, I went to their house and found Lydia being attacked. A man was trying to drown her in the Jacuzzi on her deck. I surprised him, and we struggled. During the struggle, she got hold of his gun and shot him with it. He was floating in the hot tub when we left the house."

Suarez gave me a look that seemed to express regret over my easily disprovable lies. "I was at the house myself this morning and went over every inch of the place. We couldn't find any body, and there was no blood. What we did turn up, later, were some very worried people. Ms. Cho's sister expected her to meet her for din-ner yesterday evening. Everyone's sure she would've at least called, unless someone physically prevented her from doing so."

Chen cut in. "So what you're telling us is you helped cover up a murder?"

I tried to answer them both. "For what it's worth, what hap-pened at the house was self-defense. She forced me to go with her, not the other way around. I didn't feel right about not reporting it. On the other hand, she'd revealed that her husband was alive. It was him I'd hoped to find—alive not dead."

"Now you're just trying to cover your ass," Chen said.

"I was trying to do the best thing in a complex situation. Once Lydia told me her husband was alive, I knew all the guesses I'd made were probably correct. Jordan had been killed because she was planning to expose the fraud in the Kairos trial. Cho had faked his death.

"The night Jordan was killed, she'd received a text. I was there when it came, but didn't see what it said. At that point, she got us a cab and dropped me at home. Later, I located the cab driver, who said he'd taken her back to her apartment. When I spoke with Cho last night, he said the text had been from him. He met with her that night after I'd gone to my room.

"When Cho told Jordan about the fraud, she felt it was her duty to get to the bottom of it. But she was being watched by people who decided she needed to be stopped. They framed Randall Rodriguez for her murder, knowing he'd confess. They tracked me here, ambushed us, and murdered Gary Cho last night."

"Then disposed of the car and the bodies and vanished without a trace," Burke said from his chair against the wall. "It's a great mystery you've sprung on us."

"Is there anyone who can corroborate what you're saying?" Suarez asked.

"Jacob Mauldin is the owner of Kairos. Tom Benton is his attorney. They'll know what I'm telling you is true.

"First, though, you should talk to a man named Walter Hayes. He'll confirm that Kairos employs a private security squad, ostensibly to support the SFPD in clearing out undesirables from public housing projects slated for demolition. In reality, these 'security guards' are mercenaries, ex-military. What they're *really* doing is shooting it out with gangbangers, provoking incidents that can be used to justify rewriting the city's mixed-income housing plan. Kairos's goal is to maximize the value of the new housing units for the well-to-do, presumably by relocating all the public housing into a ghetto-style high-rise.

"I'm confident the man who attacked Lydia Cho is one of these so-called security guards, paid off the books with money skimmed from other aspects of the project. These same individuals had to have been the ones who ambushed us last night. Start asking questions about them, and you'll get to the bottom of what happened here."

"Let's assume Benton and Mauldin both deny there was any such conspiracy," Suarez said with seemingly infinite patience. "What else can you tell me? I'm talking hard evidence here, stuff I can verify. If what you're saying is true, I'd like to help."

"Check their phone records. I assume Detective Chen has pulled Jordan's by now. Did she call Benton that night?" In response Chen simply met my stare without saying a word, a man who wouldn't have given me a sip of water in the desert if I were dying of thirst.

"That's it?" Suarez asked with disappointment. "That's all you got?"

"My next step would have been to speak with Tom Benton."

Suarez looked puzzled. "You figured he'd just break down and confess?"

"I planned to appeal to his conscience. To his grief over Jordan's death. And his guilt. Maybe bluff him a little, suggest Cho had given me something that would sway a judge." I repeated what I'd expressed to Cho last night. "Whatever Benton had done, Jordan's murder couldn't have been part of his plan."

"You know a lot of upscale cars are tracked with GPS units installed by the car manufacturer, right? As an antitheft measure?" Suarez studied me for a reaction. Behind him Chen had a knowing look.

My blood froze. I could only wait while they sprung their trap.

Chen spoke up. "Where do you think we found her? Take a guess."

That couch had seemed comfortable at first, but it wasn't now. The cushions were too soft, the springs shot. Also, there was a smell, one I now identified as sweat and fear. "You probably ought to Miranda me again if you're gonna start asking such tricky questions."

A suitable silence passed, long enough to have encompassed the pointless exercise of reading that obsolete litany off a detective's pocket card if anyone had cared to bother. Apparently no one did.

"Where would you have put her, if you'd done it?" Chen said.

"Did you find her body or didn't you?" I countered, not letting myself be played like this.

Burke cleared his throat. Ignoring Chen's icy stare, he said, "Supposing she were still alive, wouldn't we be wasting precious time?"

Suarez took the handoff. "The way I see it, if we find her alive, that keeps you out of the injection chamber. You'll still do time if she's alive, but if you help us find her it'll be a lot less time than you'd otherwise serve. Plus, unlike a lot of folks we deal with, you'd go in knowing you could survive it. A lawyer like you would be useful inside. You'd be protected."

"Lawrence Maxwell must still have plenty of buddies in the system," Chen said, ignored by the other two. "Course he's bound to have enemies, too. And then there'll be guys that you'll lie awake at night wondering where you stand with them. Bo Wilder, for instance."

I addressed Suarez. "So you haven't found the car." I knew I should keep my mouth shut now but I'd never been much good at it.

"We were hoping you could help us there."

"So you're telling me the GPS was deactivated?"

"How would a person even go about doing that?" Suarez asked.

Chen said, "I suppose you'd just Google it. Be right there in the search history."

"You're welcome to mine," I told Suarez. They had nothing, I realized. They were just fishing, killing time in the hope I'd offer an indication of guilt. Knowing this didn't make me happy. What they didn't know I also didn't know. But I did know I didn't want to be on the run from men who could make a car and two bodies disappear out of a ravine in a remote wood overnight.

"Look, if there's anything I can tell you that might help you find her, ask it, because I want the same thing as you. I want Lydia Cho found, and I want her to be alive. Otherwise, why don't you show me where I'm sleeping tonight?"

Suarez glanced over his shoulder at Chen, whose expression mingled frustration and resignation. Sheriff Burke returned his chair to level and stood with a yawn, stretching his arms. "We have a cozy little jail here. You'll sleep like a baby tonight. I give you my money-back guarantee on that."

Chapter 22

In the morning, after a night spent restlessly tossing and turning despite my exhaustion, Suarez and I were on the road by seven. He was driving, with me loosely handcuffed in back. I'd spoken to Nina and learned I had a court appearance scheduled that afternoon in Redwood City, where the San Mateo County courthouse and jail were located.

Suarez's attitude was different today, less tolerant. More wary. I wondered whether he'd concluded I was the kind of nut no interviewer could crack in one session.

"Tell me about Detective Chen," he said. "What'd you do to piss him off?"

I told him about the Rodriguez trial, me embarrassing Chen's colleague Harold Cole, and how Jordan's subsequent murder seemed to offer the SFPD a perfect opportunity for revenge. Suarez listened with an occasional dry laugh, his eyes on the road. Finally, he said, "He says that if we have to cut you loose on this case he wants you in San Francisco. Evidently they're getting ready to charge you with the murder of that witness in your father's case. Russell Bell."

"I never even wanted my father released from prison," I said. "I certainly wouldn't have committed murder to keep him free."

"If I were you, I'd shut my trap rather than to try to talk my way out of it without ever accounting for how the murder weapon ended up in your girlfriend's apartment."

"Thanks for the advice."

"Don't mention it. But don't worry on that score. I like you for Lydia Cho, at least until a better suspect comes along. You were the last one with her, and your story's way out there. So, for now, you're my man. Chen can wait his turn."

"If I killed her, how'd I get rid of the car?"

"I don't know. But they're going to find her eventually, and when they do, I won't have to wonder where *you* are."

I wasn't as confident as Suarez that the Chos would turn up. The body at the house in Portola Valley had disappeared. Both Gary and Lydia were unaccounted for. Then our adversaries had upped the ante by repeating the vanishing act with Lydia's BMW. Powerless to show I was telling the truth, I felt enormously depressed. I dozed the rest of the trip, waking each time in a cocoon of pain from my still-unhealed injuries.

At the end of the five-hour drive, Suarez delivered me into the custody of the deputies at the San Mateo County courthouse. Stripped of my belt and valuables, I was placed in a holding cell with a bunch of jittery guys evidently in the early stages of detox. One by one, the others were called by a deputy and led out. At last, late in the afternoon, it was my turn.

In the courtroom I found Nina talking to the DA at the prosecutor's table, an unpleasant expression of shock and disbelief on her face. The judge wasn't on the bench, and the gallery was empty. Seeing me, she came over. "They just got around to telling me that Lydia Cho turned up at her house this morning. She won't talk to the police, claims never to have met you. They asked her about her husband, about the supposed dead guy in the hot tub, and she blew them off, then lawyered up. Long story short, San Mateo has to cut you loose. So you're bound for the big city, courtesy of the SFPD."

"Who's her lawyer?" I asked. But I'd already guessed.

"A guy called Tom Benton."

~ ~ ~

Three days, three different jail cells. This time, I was the guest of the city and county of San Francisco. It wasn't my first visit to County Jail Number 5 downtown, but familiarity hadn't improved my view of the place. Once again, I was being charged as an accessory in the murder of Russell Bell.

"They want you to roll over on your father," Nina said when she came to see me the third morning of my jailing. "They're offering a bullshit deal. You testify against Lawrence, detail his role in Bell's murder, and the DA will recommend probation for you."

I started to respond with indignation, but she held up a hand. "I can't go any further," she said. "Remember, I represented your father. I have a conflict of interest."

I should have seen this coming, but after three nearly sleepless nights, the blow hit me hard. For a moment, I couldn't speak. I felt like we'd lost the case, and I realized how much I'd counted on having Nina as my lawyer, fighting for me with the same grit and fire with which she'd handled my father's defense.

"At least pretend you're not relieved," I said.

"I *am* relieved. Because a conflict of interest, a *real* one like this, isn't fun. I don't know who killed Bell. It's never looked good to me, and I've always sensed the three of you—you, your father, and Teddy—haven't told the whole story. That was probably for the best, and so is this. The upside of not being your lawyer means I get to be your friend."

"You could still represent me with my father's and my consent."

"But not without mine," she made clear. "Your arraignment's tomorrow. Maybe the PD's office can help you. You still work for them, right?"

In fact, the boss herself showed up to represent me. Unlike Nina, Gabriela was willing to look past such a small thing as a conflict of interest. "I'm not going to fire you based on anything you confide in me," she promised, though this wasn't stated on the waiver form she had me sign.

She held a press conference that afternoon. "Our justice system can't function if defense lawyers are viewed by the police and prosecutors as indistinguishable from the criminals they represent . . ." This was all I heard, however, before another inmate demanded to change the channel. I was still in jail, you see. For all her skill, Gabriela had been unsuccessful in arguing I should be released on my own recognizance.

During this time, Rodriguez pleaded guilty to Jordan's murder and was sentenced to life in prison without parole. I wondered whether, if I'd been out of jail, I'd have gone to the hearing, sat there mute and powerless while "justice" was done.

The morning after my arraignment, my father and brother came to visit me. "This should blow over in a few days," Lawrence promised, after arguing I should let him post my bond. I'd refused, guessing the money would come from Bo Wilder.

"If 'blow over' means what I think it means, I'd rather stay in here." I knew we couldn't speak freely. Given that the police wanted to use the charges against me as leverage to return my father to prison, our conversation was almost certainly recorded. Any mention of Bo Wilder's name in this context would be damning to all of us.

A few mornings later, Gabriela brought a glow of satisfaction with her into the attorney consultation room at the jail. "A witness has come forward," she said when we'd sat down. "He'll testify that on the night of Jordan's murder, he was detained by two undercover officers in the TL with a vial of crack. There's no report because they never arrested him. Harold Cole showed up on the scene, handed the guy a key, and told him he wanted him to plant a gun in your room in the Seward."

"He's not called Roland McEwan, is he?" I asked. Gabriela shook her head, offering me a different name.

"Then he's lying," I told her. "I got that gun from a former client."

She didn't want to hear it. "This is your ticket out. You could be back trying cases next week." She paused. "Look, maybe our guy switched guns on you. I don't doubt he'd say that, if I put the question to him. I'd rather not, and I don't think I'll have to. There are more interested parties to the situation than you know. You and I are aware that Cole's lazy and doesn't like doing his job. Turns out there's a reason. I've been told in confidence he has a problem with prescription drugs. The Rodriguez case isn't the first investigation he's screwed up, and the DA's office would like to wash their hands of him. This witness gives them the political cover they need to do that."

"It's dirty," I insisted. "The guy's lying and I don't want to accept the benefit of that."

"If our situations were reversed, and you were the lawyer and I the client, what would you do?"

I just shook my head. If the guy were credible, even though his story seemed too good to be true, I knew what my obligation would be. Though told a witness must be lying, an attorney must be able to envision scenarios in which he isn't. Gabriela was toeing the ethical line, as any good defense lawyer must, but her feet were planted on the correct side. One good shove would do it. All I had to do was tell her my father had gone to Bo Wilder and Bo had procured this witness, just as he'd put my former client up to delivering me the weapon in the first place—all with the intent of drawing us into an ever-tighter web of obligation and corruption. But saying that would mean the end of my career, the end of everything good in my life. Gabriela and the PD's office would wash their hands of me, and I still needed the safety net of this job.

"You can't put the guy on the witness stand," I said, with a feeling of sliding past a boundary I hadn't crossed before: the willingness to avoid personal injustice by inflicting injustice on someone else.

"Like I said, I very much doubt I'll have to," Gabriela said. "Leave the details to me."

Three days later, I was out of jail and Detective Cole was out of a job, temporarily suspended while the district attorney's office investigated the accusations of Gabriela's "witness."

I ought to have been relieved but I was filled with dread, wondering what my father had promised Bo Wilder as the price for my get-out-of-jail-free card.

~ ~ ~

The Saturday after my release from jail, Teddy and Tamara invited me to their house for dinner. I rode the commuter train over. Normally I'd have walked the rest of the way, a half-mile stroll that usually succeeded in clearing my head. Today, however, still suffering from numerous injuries that made walking painful, I took a cab.

For me, that little bungalow had come to represent an ideal of domestic life that comforted me all the more because I didn't want it for myself and knew I probably could never achieve it if I did. Today, however, my headache began the moment I strode down the piss-scented stairs of the Civic Center station. The pain was like a chisel between my eyes by the time the cab turned onto my brother's street from Martin Luther King Jr. Way and I saw the twin Harleys parked out front.

Dot and Tamara were in the front room, supervising Carly at the easel, newspapers spread on the floor at their feet. The door was open, the family's fat yellow Lab lying across the wide threshold. It was eight months since I'd last seen Dot. Today was hot, and she was wearing a sleeveless top and jeans, her leather jacket and chaps lying discarded over the arm of the couch. When I stepped over the dog and said hello, each woman looked away, as if I'd brought shame on the family. In many households the source of their coldness would have been my recent stay in jail. In ours, it was how I'd gotten out.

Dot gathered herself, and rose for a brief embrace. "I'm sure you're glad to be back," I said as she stepped away. She'd lost weight, and her hair was cut shorter and had, I imagined, more gray in it. But on her face was still the same no-nonsense expression I remembered from the first time we'd met, a look that promised woe to any man who crossed her.

She stepped back, sizing me up and apparently not liking what she saw. "Yes and no. If I'd guessed the kind of trouble you were in, I'd have kept Lawrence as far away as possible." I nodded. She'd provided an alibi for Lawrence in the trial, but I'd sensed it was a lie. Bell had been a sadistic, unrepentant rapist, a true psychopath, and had sought to cover his own crimes by offering himself as a snitch against my father. No man deserves to die, but his death hadn't added to the world's sorrows.

"Whatever Lawrence has done, I didn't want or ask for it," I said. But that was no excuse. He was my father and I was his son. He'd make any sacrifice for me and she knew it.

Her face seemed to harden in response and she turned back to Carly and Tamara. Carly wiped her hands and ran to me. I hugged her, touched her mother's arm with silent acknowledgment, then went out through the kitchen to the backyard, where I found Teddy and Lawrence in plastic Adirondack chairs by the lemon tree, drinking from sweating bottles of Red Tail.

"Grab yourself one," Lawrence said. I declined.

Teddy watched me like a kid waiting to be called out for some misdeed, but Lawrence was riding high. I'd helped assure his freedom, and now he'd returned the favor. He was magnanimous in his new role of benefactor. "Congratulations," he said. "Twenty days or twenty years, it's just a matter of degree. You're out."

"Quit bullshitting. I didn't need anyone to spring me."

"I didn't have anything to do with it." He gave me a wink.

I straddled one of the chairs and returned his gaze with dismay. During his twenty-one years behind bars, he'd mastered San Quentin's Darwinian rules and emerged as shrewd as a fox among wolves, and I now saw he was utterly without moral qualms where his or his family's survival was concerned. An innocent man indeed.

"What now?" I wanted to know.

"You go back to the public defender's office."

"And you?"

"I need to make a living. And for a man who's spent more than two decades in prison, there aren't many ways to do that."

"We won't be breaking any laws," Teddy put in. "Bo Wilder, this big, bad white supremacist prison gang leader, he invests all his spare cash in real estate. He's some kind of absentee slum lord. He's got plenty of people he trusts to do his dirty work. But he needs ones he can trust to handle the clean side of his business."

"You believe there's such a thing as a clean side?"

My father shook his head like I just wasn't getting it. "He's got six hundred rental units and a dozen resident managers all currently doing whatever they want. What he wants us to do is clean it up, get everything in compliance with the law, file articles of incorporation, hire experienced staff, get the operation running like a proper business."

"And this's why Teddy was in fear for his life, and why you had to run halfway around the world, and why our office was firebombed. All because Wilder needs a couple of guys with no experience in property management to handle his rental business."

I didn't for a second believe that they'd merely be keeping his rental books.

"There ought to be plenty of money coming in with an operation like this. Right now, though, there's not. He wants us to find out why and fix it." Lawrence shrugged. "It's accounting, not rocket science. I called a few people who are in a position to know, and what I hear is Bo's stepped back. He's taken his money out of the game. Which makes sense, given he's in prison. He saw what happened to Santorez."

"Because he was the man holding the knife. He sent us the man's *ears*."

"Right. Meaning, Bo knows better than anyone the game is finished for him. He has a family, just like Teddy does, and he wants them looked after. That's his priority now. He doesn't trust his old associates for a job like that."

"He trusts *you*?"

"Like it or not, I owe him. If he hadn't put out the hit on Bell, I'd be in prison now. I didn't ask him for that, but it doesn't mean I'm not grateful. He gave me back my family. I can't turn away from such a serious obligation, nor would I want to." It was as if he'd forgotten entirely about his sojourn in Croatia. "And then there's leverage. I think he's demonstrated that there's a downside to not doing as he asks."

"He threatened your family, Teddy," I said in a quiet voice.

Teddy's face looked pale beneath the lemon tree. "To be accurate, what he told me was I could walk away, but in that case he couldn't guarantee my family's safety."

"And what if working for him puts you where he is?"

Teddy didn't have an answer to that. "It won't," my father said, as if his assurance ought to be good enough for the two of us.

"So it's done." I had to swallow back an enormous bitterness. I hadn't been conscious of a progress in our lives, or what we might be progressing toward. Normality, I thought now, the kind of easy domestic existence the rest of the world seemed to take for granted. I could feel all the achievements of the last six years slipping away, as if a great wave had lifted us nearly to safety but now was sweeping us back out to sea.

"So this is how the two of you plan to make your living from now on. Have you told Tam and Dot?" I couldn't keep the belligerence from seeping into my voice.

"Dot knows," Lawrence said. "I'm not sure what Teddy's told Tam."

"I haven't told her anything. She wouldn't understand. The fire . . ."

"What wouldn't I understand?"

We turned. Tamara was at the open kitchen window. She must have come to the sink to wash her hands, then paused there when she heard her name. Teddy rose and took a step toward the house, but something in her face made him stop.

"I didn't mean that," he told her.

She didn't respond. The screen partially masked her expression and made her seem far away, the way I sometimes saw my mother in dreams.

"We'll be safe from now on," Teddy told her. "I won't be doing anything illegal. Just managing the man's real estate and ensuring his family gets paid."

When Tamara spoke again, her voice seemed far away. "What if he's lying to you about what he wants? Last time he burned your office. If you try to say no to something he asks, what's next? He burns us out of our house, murders us in our beds?"

Blame swung in me like a compass needle, honing magnetically toward my father as it'd done at all such moments in the past. Lawrence had been the bogeyman and scapegoat of my childhood. As an adult, I knew the truth was more complicated. Then again, maybe it wasn't. Tamara deserved peace, and each of us would have given it to her if we could.

Oblivious to the chasm over which we seemed poised, Carly called for her mother from inside the house. Tamara threw a glance over her shoulder, then stepped back from the window and out of sight.

Chapter 23

Rachel Stone had left me several messages since my release, but I hadn't returned them. When her name appeared on my phone's screen after my visit to Teddy's, however, I pressed Talk, despite knowing nothing good could come of it.

"Has Rodriguez's guilty plea changed your feelings about him being innocent?" She spoke as if she expected me to have come around on this.

"I'm just as sure as ever that he's innocent. He didn't kill Jordan, no matter what he says."

"Who did?"

"How about Jacob Mauldin."

"You want me to print that?"

"Only if your lawyers will let you."

"Give me a break. I've got to have proof before I start making accusations of murder. Stop wasting my time."

I knew I shouldn't have, but I gave her the short version of my recent activities, going easy on the blood and leaving Lydia Cho mostly out of it. Instead, I focused on what Walter Hayes had told me about Mauldin's private security guards provoking bloodshed in Double Rock.

She listened. When I was finished, she sighed and said in a defeated voice, "Leo, I'm going to do you a favor and not print a word of what you've just said."

"So you don't believe me?"

"In a word? Maybe. But without proof, what's the point? Hayes is a man with an agenda. Just like you. Speaking of things I can't print, my sources tell me he's only against the Candlestick project because he's been secretly taking a piece of the action in Double Rock, and he doesn't want to lose out."

I decided to change the subject. "What about the Panther?"

"I'm talking to the man who conjured him. You tell me."

"Benton knows what they did to her. Make him tell you the story. All of it."

"Tommy's out of it. He's taken a leave from his law firm. A sailing trip, evidently, the big one he's been planning for years. Jordan's death hit him hard. He loved her, you know. He tells me you were jealous. Shall I print *that*?"

"Print whatever you like," I told her.

I called Benton's office but instead of his secretary answering, I got his voice mail, the message confirming his temporary absence. Taking a cab to the Sausalito boat docks was my next idea. There was no guarantee he wasn't already out to sea, but if I didn't find him I'd only be out the fare.

I called from a box at the gate. After a few minutes he appeared on the dock, a figure dressed in khaki shorts and a Stanford sweatshirt. He stood looking toward where I leaned against the bars at the entrance gate. He took his time getting to me.

"You won," I told him as he approached. "You and your client got away with it."

He shook his head, opened the gate, and let me through. I felt as if he'd been expecting me. "I went to see her father," he told me as we walked toward the end of the pier. "The man was filled with ideas. He said Rodriguez was innocent of Jordan's murder, that he'd been framed. I asked him who was guilty, if that were the case. And do you know whom he accused? Me."

Benton gave a sudden laugh that died in his throat almost as soon as it'd begun. Then he shook his head again. "Someone filled his head with conspiracy theories. You?"

"He wants Jordan to have been right about Rodriguez," I said. "Before she was killed he told her she was foolish to believe her client was innocent. Called her naïve. Now he wants more than anything to be wrong. That's not a conspiracy theory. It's a father's heart."

"The poor bastard," Benton said. "Torturing himself that way."

"I suppose you set his mind straight and told him the truth."

"I told him Rodriguez had confessed, pleaded guilty, and he'd be spending the rest of his life in prison. I said that was the most justice any of us was likely to see in this world."

"You couldn't lie to his face, in other words. And you also couldn't tell the truth."

"I loved her," Benton said. "By now you must realize that."

We stood at the end of the sailboat pier, shoulder to shoulder in uncomfortable proximity. "Then do something about it. Her father deserves to know the truth about her death."

Benton gave an irritated shrug. "It was a pointless visit. One that only gave him more pain."

"But it helped you see things more clearly. It made you realize you had to leave. Just like she did."

"Look," Benton said sharply, the façade finally dropping. "I don't know if you believe your own accusations. Just remember, nothing is ever so simple or so complicated as it seems."

"Your secrets sail with you, I suppose." I wanted to remind him there was no safety in renunciation.

"Here's what you need to know. When a case is done, I put it behind me. I don't ask myself whether I was on the right side, or what was true. The moment you start second-guessing, you're finished in this business. That's where Jordan went wrong. She couldn't move on."

"She called you after Cho first approached her, back from the grave. You told Mauldin that Cho had communicated with her, and that she was listening to what he had to say."

"Even if you were correct, which you aren't, I would have a clear duty to speak with my client regarding anything that touched on his case."

"You did your duty and look what happened. Even now, the only thing that allows you to face yourself is you keep telling yourself you didn't know they were going to kill her. The more you repeat it, the more it might be true. Is that the deal you've made?"

When he answered this time, his voice was thick. "My mind's made up. I'm sailing tonight. I understand your frustrations, but they're no longer my problem. I wish to God Jordan was still alive . . . But she's gone, and nothing I say can bring her back."

"Does Rodriguez deserve to be framed for a murder he didn't commit?" I asked.

He looked at me, hesitating. "I don't know what anyone deserves." Then he walked away.

~ ~ ~

It didn't surprise me when I heard, a few weeks later, that his boat had been found adrift and empty. Then, complicating the picture, it was revealed that several million dollars were missing from the client trust fund at Benton's firm, with suspicion focused solely on him. It wasn't hard to picture the situation in which he'd found himself. Everyone else with direct knowledge of what'd happened was either dead or neutralized by threats. Benton, haunted by Jordan's murder and his role in it, was a liability and a loose end.

I wondered what his plan had been. And whether it had been thwarted by his enemies—which is to say, by his former client—or just bad luck. Maybe, like Cho, Benton had found himself in a situation with no winning outcome and had decided to fake his death. These thoughts and more filled my mind as I went about my daily routine at the public defender's office, where I'd at last returned after my own leave of absence.

~ ~ ~

Walking back to the office from court one fall morning, I felt a tap between my shoulder blades. I turned and was handed an envelope. "You've been served."

Inside was a subpoena commanding me to appear in Superior Court. *Cho v. Kairos*, the subpoena heading read. The clerk's office couldn't tell me what it was about, and the court's electronic filing system had no information. In the morning, with no clue what I was walking into, I headed over to the federal courthouse.

The courtroom was locked. I pressed the buzzer at the door of the judge's chambers and was admitted. "They're waiting," a serious young woman said, and led me down a hallway.

Beyond another door lay Judge Parker's chambers. He was responsible for the complex litigation docket and handled exclusively civil cases, and I'd never appeared in front of him. A court reporter sat ready. Two lawyers occupied high-backed chairs at a conference table a short distance from the judge's desk. A third attorney sat at the head of the conference table. None of the three appeared on friendly terms with the others.

Dressed in a dark suit, Lydia Cho sat behind one of them, staring intensely at me.

The judge indicated a chair and waited until I sat before he began. "Thank you for appearing so promptly, Mr. Maxwell. I have a few questions for you, and when I'm finished, these lawyers may wish to ask a few questions of their own. The only questions you're required to answer are mine."

He then took a moment to briefly introduce the lawyers in the room. One from Benton's firm represented Kairos. Another represented Lydia Cho. The third was introduced as being from the US Attorney's Office. "I see you've arrived without counsel. Do you wish to consult an attorney before we begin?"

My head was spinning. "Why don't you give me a little more context. If it looks like I need a lawyer, I'll pipe up. Right now, I can't imagine why I would."

"Very well. You're here because your name was mentioned prominently in a letter to me written by a lawyer named Tom Benton. His letter claims you have knowledge of a conspiracy between his client and others to commit a fraud on this court and defame a man named Gary Cho, and to commit other crimes in furtherance of that conspiracy, including possible murders. I brought you here to tell us what knowledge you may have."

The court reporter finished typing. Silence seemed to swell from every surface. The judge's desk had a marble inlay holding a fine tracery of cracks that appeared to me like a spider's web. "Are you sure this letter is authentic?" I asked, to buy time while my mind scrambled to guess what this was about.

"That's not your concern. For the moment, we'll assume for our purposes that it is."

"You'll have to ask me more specific questions. My involvement has to do with investigating the murder of Jordan Walker. She worked with me at the public defender's office after leaving Benton's firm. She was Tom Benton's associate in the Kairos trial, as you already know. Their client was Jacob Mauldin, who I believe was involved in Jordan's death. But I can't prove it."

"You're aware that a man named Randall Rodriguez has pleaded guilty to her murder?"

"Of course. He was our client. But that doesn't mean he killed her. He'd confess to killing JFK if anyone thought to ask him about it. Whoever framed him knows that."

"Which only raises the question of who did frame him—and, if you know, why?"

The question was a softball. It seemed as if the judge was on my side rather than seeking to silence or intimidate me as I'd expected. I forced myself to breathe. The room had suddenly become airless. "I believe that Jacob Mauldin had Jordan Walker murdered and framed Randall Rodriguez for it because she was planning on exposing the conspiracy evidently described in Benton's letter. What does it say about her?"

"I can't tell you that," the judge said. "This matter has become the subject of an inquiry by the US Attorney's Office. Such criminal matters are beyond the scope of my jurisdiction. What I need to determine is whether to reverse the judgment for Kairos, order a new trial, or do nothing at all. The problem is tricky because in the government's view, revealing the contents of Benton's letter would compromise an ongoing investigation. But that doesn't stop me from compelling testimony from private citizens with pertinent knowledge. Do you have any knowledge that would suggest the judgment was obtained as a result of fraud?"

"I do," I told him, because I sensed he wanted the answer to be yes. However, I knew that nothing I might tell him could possibly be other than hearsay and speculation. Following the judge's prompting, acutely aware that every word I spoke was being taken down by the court reporter, I proceeded to tell what I knew and suspected. Relying on what Cho had told me the night of his death, I described how Mauldin and Kairos had manufactured the case against him, forging an incriminating video and contriving false evidence to suggest that Cho's allegations of fraud were baseless. I told of Cho faking his death, then of the chain of events that had ended with Jordan's murder. Finally I told of the long day that had begun with me finding a man apparently drowning Lydia Cho in her Jacuzzi, his shooting, our trip to her husband's hiding place up in Trinity County, and Cho's murder there. I also described my fruitless meetings with Tom Benton.

When I'd finished, the judge asked if there were any questions from the lawyers. Lydia leaned forward and whispered to her attorney, who shook his head, refusing to ask me what she'd suggested. No one else spoke up.

The judge then thanked me for my testimony and told me I was free to leave.

"I'd like to ask a question," I said before I went. "I heard Benton is missing at sea, presumed dead. How'd he come to send this letter?"

"I'll read you his opening paragraph. 'Hon. Judge Parker,' it begins. 'It's with sadness I write this. I am a lawyer and duty-bound to keep my clients' secrets. But I also have an obligation to the court when I know a fraud has been committed. Because my desire for self-preservation is stronger than my ethical conscience, according to the instructions I've left my attorney, this letter will only be delivered if and when I'm dead."

The judge broke off and raised his eyes to the lawyer representing Kairos. He stared straight ahead. The judge regarded him for a moment before addressing me. "Curiosity satisfied? Because that's all I can read, according to our friend from the government."

"Not even close," I said. "But I guess it'll have to do."

Chapter 24

Rodriguez remained behind bars. The *Chronicle* sued to have Benton's letter made public, but the judge dismissed the suit in a one-line order stating that the document in question had been turned over to the US Attorney's Office, and the paper would have to seek it there. The *Chronicle*'s request to that office was denied.

Rachel Stone's story summarizing these strange events contained another tidbit gleaned from an interview with Rodriguez's lawyer. It appeared that prison had worked a change in her client, because he now was ready to protest his innocence. The trouble was that, after the judgment, it was too late to withdraw his plea. The only way to wind back the clock and regain his right to a jury trial was through a petition for habeas corpus, and the standard for a successful habeas petition required him to present proof of innocence.

A judge had unwound the Kairos case with the stroke of a pen, but all Rodriguez and his lawyer had was speculation and conspiracy theories with no apparent basis in fact.

A few weeks after these articles appeared, Stone got in touch with me. "You calling to apologize?" I asked her.

"For being right?"

"Now you're giving yourself too much credit."

"Nothing I've printed is provably incorrect. A great deal is still unknown, of course. And we both know there was no way I could take seriously your freakish story about hot tubs and hit men. We're not the *National Enquirer*."

"Don't you think you need to admit Jacob Mauldin's the guy you should be talking to now? A judge just ruled he committed fraud in court. Instead of harassing me why don't you get him to talk?"

"He has, after a fashion. That's actually the reason I'm calling. He, Lydia Cho, and the government have announced a settlement of her husband's lawsuit against Kairos."

I had a sense of foreboding. "Well, I hope she took him for all he's worth, just like he did to her husband. Right down to the scorched earth."

"Many of the terms are confidential, but I'm told she'll be assuming a fifty-one percent stake in Kairos. Mauldin will retain a forty-nine percent stake and will have no involvement in its day-to-day operations. The company will be required to open its books to auditors but will retain its contracts. Care to comment?"

My mind reeled. "You mean they'll be working together?"

"She won't comment one way or another on the fraud allegations. Still, it's the kind of 'no comment' that suggests the allegations are true. Evidently, though, she believes her husband really was a scumbag. Otherwise, how could you explain her going to work with Mauldin?"

"Maybe she believes in forgiveness. Or maybe the settlement included enough cash to convince her to keep her mouth shut, to let bygones be bygones." I didn't think that I could go for forgiveness, were I in Lydia's place. Even if it really were her husband on that video. I also remembered Benton's comment: *I don't know what anyone deserves.*

"There's more," Stone informed me. "She insists the events of October twenty-seventh never happened as you claim. There was no man in her hot tub. She never took you to her husband. He was never killed by hit men. Rather, he committed suicide by jumping from the Golden Gate Bridge months ago. She turns out to be not much of a fan of your imagination, either."

"Yeah, I was just out on a hike one morning and I dreamed it all up. Have you considered the idea maybe she was in on the fraud from the beginning?"

After a pause, she said, "You want me to print that?"

"Print whatever you want," I told her. "As long as it's not too critical of Jacob Mauldin."

After this conversation, I seethed for half a day; then I calmed down as I realized I wasn't completely at an impasse. I'd actually seen the face of the man who'd been brutally questioning Lydia in her hot tub, a man I now believed had been working for Jacob Mauldin, one of the "security" men he'd brought in to shoot up drug dealers in Double Rock.

I wondered if Lydia had intentionally led the killers to her husband's hiding place that night. Perhaps neither of us had been meant to walk out of those woods alive.

I called Cho's former lawyer, Ma, on the pretext of congratulating him on a settlement that ought to eliminate his malpractice liability. But while I had him on the phone, I asked if he might still have in his files an employee directory or similar document from the Kairos litigation. Preferably one with pictures.

He replied that me he might be able to put his hands on material like that. But, naturally, he was curious. "What are you looking for, if you don't mind me asking?"

"I'm just trying to determine whether any of Kairos's employees recently turned up dead."

"I'm not on the case anymore. Which means I'm not supposed to have any case documents. But you know how electronic storage is. Nothing really ever disappears."

"I'd like to match a face. Or, more likely, rule out the possibility that the guy I'm interested in was one of theirs. No one will find out about it."

He told me to come to his office Saturday morning at eight thirty. "Wear jogging clothes," he suggested.

To make our meeting on the weekend look legit, he insisted we jog a few desultory miles in the rain and wind after I'd met him in the lobby of his Embarcadero Center building. When we returned, we rode the elevator up to his small suite, which was deserted. Unlocking his office door, he turned on his computer, logged in, and opened a folder.

"Now I'm going to use the john," he said. "Try not to get my chair sweaty."

The window he'd opened was a folder tree of Kairos documents. A subfolder contained files labeled with the name of an employee and a numeric identifier. These turned out to be resumes, each with an attached color headshot. These the company presumably would submit to the government when bidding on contracts. Each dossier was stamped: HIGHLY CONFIDENTIAL.

I'd had no idea that Kairos had so many employees. My fascination made me almost forget my purpose. I clicked through dozens of resumes and headshots. Then after opening the file of a man named Carl Hastings with the job title of "seismic engineer," I saw a face I'd never forget. I'd been afraid I wouldn't recognize him even if he was there, but the minute the headshot appeared on the screen a pulse of fear moved down my spine.

It was the man I'd last seen floating dead in a hot tub at Lydia Cho's. I hit Print and the copier in the other room spat out what I wanted.

Ma returned a few minutes later. "Find what you need?"

I told him I had, thanked him, and got out of there, promising again to keep my mouth shut about the favor.

I thought of calling Rachel Stone but knew I still had nothing definite to tell her. In spite of my discovery, I seemed to be at a dead end, so I decided to take a chance. I put a copy of the printout of Carl Hastings's dossier in an envelope with one of my business cards and sent it to Lydia Cho.

Two days later, I was drinking a beer after work, studying the chess problem in the *Chronicle* and thinking of Rodriguez while delaying the inevitable return to my room. Suddenly, a man moved through my peripheral vision and sat on the bar stool beside me. I swiveled and locked eyes with Jacob Mauldin.

He was about five five and round bellied, with a shock of white hair above a face like the moon. Not the bland familiar features but the dark side peppered with craters. He would have been ugly even without the acne scars. He had on pressed slacks and buffed shoes. When the bartender turned to him Mauldin ordered a Plymouth Gin and tonic.

"I know who you are," I said, trying to hide my impulse to put as much distance between the two of us as possible. From all my online digging, I obviously recognized him. His easy comfort on my turf struck me as a sign of danger.

"That saves me having to think up a suitable pickup line. How are you, Leo?"

"Not so good," I said after a suitable pause. "I miss my friend."

"We all miss someone." He accepted his drink from the bartender. "An insightful woman once told me men are disposed to looking backward, fixating on the one who got away. The perfect girl who, if we could just get her back, would make everything all right. Women, on the other hand, look forward. They believe the best is yet to come."

"Is that what Lydia Cho believes?"

"Lydia knows how to make a silk purse out of a sow's ear."

"And you're the sow. I guess you had to pay her seriously big bucks. It's too bad killing her didn't work."

"I'd appreciate if you'd refrain from making reckless accusations. You'll find yourself saddled with a defamation suit, if you're not careful."

"I'd welcome it."

"Would you?"

I'd had a few pints by then and didn't give a shit. I had the accusations ready and they rolled out of me with easy momentum. "What'd it take to bring her over to the side of the formerly bitter adversary who had her husband killed? After framing him? Five million? Ten? Come on, it's just you and me talking, Mauldin. Don't forget, I was there that night. I saw Gary Cho take a bullet in the throat."

"So you say. Lydia, on the other hand, denies it ever happened."

"Yes. But it isn't too hard to figure out why."

"You think so?" He inclined his head. "Maybe you're the one looking for a payoff, to keep you from talking about what you claim happened that night. But you've *already* gone on and on about it. And no one believed you. If I offered you money, it would only give credence to a story the world has already dismissed."

I held up my glass, signaling for another. "I'm not looking for money. Gary Cho's murder isn't the one that keeps me awake at night. I want to know who killed Jordan, and why. I figure if anyone knows, you must."

He sighed patiently.

"Your former client has already been convicted of that crime, based on his own confession. I came here tonight because Lydia said you'd contacted her, and when she provided me with what you sent her, it was evident you'd somehow come into possession of confidential personnel information relating to one of my employees. That concerns me. My sole purpose in coming here is to get to the bottom of the leak, if there is one. Let's be clear: I'm not here to lend credibility to your theories."

"Then I may as well send that printout to Rachel Stone at the *Chronicle* and tell her Carl Hastings happens to be the guy who'd been drowning Lydia in her own hot tub, the one she shot. He was trying to get her to tell him where her husband was, and when she went up there, Cho was killed. A real company man; he was right there on your payroll, I have no doubt. Listed as an 'engineer' but his real job was something far more sinister."

"I'm sure you don't have any doubts."

"While Rachel may not trust every word out of my mouth, I'm sure she's interested in knowing why Kairos was settling a case it'd already won. She must be wondering what leverage Lydia could possibly have that placed her in a position to obtain such a significant stake in your company."

"A lot of our dirty laundry has been aired. Not to mention Benton's letter, which contained only lies. Naturally, I'd have preferred a great deal of what's come out never to have seen the light of day, but it's behind us now. Happily." He paused. "I don't dispute that we had a problem on our hands. We needed a fresh presence at the helm, a public face able to convince the world we're ready to do business as usual. Who better than the widow of the person who brought the fraud to light?"

"You knew nothing about it, of course."

"Sometimes the man at the top is the last to know. You don't want to believe it, but when you learn the undeniable truth, you do what you have to do to make amends."

"You're the one who sent Hastings to her house. Obviously, one of the terms of this arrangement would be her continued silence."

"Kairos doesn't yield to extortion. If anyone had made such an attempt, we'd have immediately reported that person to the authorities." He sipped his drink.

"The beauty of a settlement agreement is that it transforms extortion into a mutual agreement to compromise a disputed claim."

Mauldin shook his head again. "The individual on the print-out you sent Lydia, a file stolen from my company, is no longer employed. If your account were true, he would be dead. They'd have found him in that Jacuzzi. But I can assure you he's alive and well."

"If he's alive, I'd like to talk to him. Can you tell me where to find him?"

"I'm not at liberty to give out such information. I wouldn't concern myself with his well-being, if I were you."

"If anybody should be concerned, it's the police."

He ignored this. "Do you care to tell me how you obtained the document you sent to Lydia?" he inquired politely.

I didn't.

"Well, one way or another I'll find out. Now about your proposed conversation with Ms. Stone. Naturally, you're free to do whatever you wish. Still, I'd advise against it."

"Because . . .?"

"I merely wish to suggest you consider the risk to yourself in proceeding down the road of further publicity. You have your phone on you?"

"Why?"

His smile this time held a bit more menace. "I'd just like you to refresh your memory for a moment about what sorts of incriminating evidence might be stored on these phones. Go ahead, take a look. Try the videos."

I stared at him. A rushing sound filled my ears. I was distantly aware of a need not to panic, but the sparkle in his eye told me what I was about to find was something very bad indeed.

Still, I wasn't prepared. Nothing could have prepared me for the horror of what I saw.

In the videos on my phone were six files I was sure had never been there before. Not that I'd opened the videos folder very often in the previous months. They could have been there for weeks and I wouldn't have known, except I was pretty sure that if these videos had been on the phone either of the two times I'd been arrested since Jordan's death, the police would have found them. They were titled "Jordan1" through "Jordan6."

"I suppose the Panther, if he exists, must enjoy the suffering of the women he rapes." Mauldin was relaxed now. "In fact, their suffering may be more important to him than the physical release of the act itself." He took another sip of his drink, set it down, and rubbed drops of condensation from the glass between his thumb and forefinger, then tossed me a package of cheap drugstore earbuds from his pocket. "Let's move to a booth."

I slid down from the stool, still feeling like I'd been punched in the groin. My life was open to these people, I realized. They'd stop at nothing.

In the booth I inserted the earbuds and played the first video, which was agonizing to watch, a pornography of death. It was a clip showing Jordan, still alive, tied to the bed in which I remembered having made love to her for the last time that night, no doubt only hours before this video was taken. Her face was wan, her eyes vacant and terrified, wasted by the ordeal she must already have endured.

"Please," she said, looking up into the face of the person holding the camera or, more likely, the phone that had been used to capture these moments. Her tongue licked her lips dryly. "Please, Leo, why are you doing this?"

I tore the buds from my ears with a cry that momentarily silenced the restaurant. Across from me in the booth, Mauldin, ignoring the disturbance I'd caused, reached across and took my chin, pressing his thumb painfully into the hollow beneath my jaw, forcing my head up until he was able to look me in the eyes.

"You understand now?" he asked in the gentle tone inquisitors learn, a voice as caressing as the purr of a cat toying with maimed prey. "The stakes are quite high for all of us," he went on. "You, me, and Lydia. We each have everything to gain or lose. I'd hate to think we weren't pulling for the same side."

The other video clips were worse. I watched each of them, sitting in the booth across from Mauldin, because I had to know what was at stake for me. Each showed Jordan pleading for her life, begging, which was evidently where her faceless, voiceless attacker's pleasure came from. His face wasn't shown, but in each video, Jordan's voice had been made to speak my name. The fakery was undetectable to me. From video to video, her spirit declined. By the third one she was weeping uncontrollably as her attacker violently raped her, her body shaking with seizure-like spasms, his face carefully kept out of the frame.

The final video showed her after she'd been bound on the toilet in the position in which Rebecca and I'd found her. "Please, Leo, let me go," she said, her voice slurred after hours of brutal abuse. "I won't tell anyone it was you. I promise." *Prom-ith* is how the word came out. Then the camera was covered for an instant, and when the lens was uncovered a strip of duct tape had been placed across Jordan's mouth. The last frames of the video showed the door slowly closing, never to be opened again while Jordan remained alive.

For a long time I couldn't breathe. I stared down at the phone on the tabletop, beyond rage. Mauldin's face was almost sorrowful, as if he pitied what I was going through. I knew better. I knew I had to keep my cool for Jordan's sake. Obviously the videos, though undetectably altered, were legitimate. Mauldin possessed them either because he was the killer or because they'd come into his possession from the person who'd made them—a person whom Jordan no doubt would have been able to identify if she'd lived. In his mind, the pleasure he'd taken in her terror must have outweighed the risk of leaving her alive.

Suddenly I remembered Lydia taking the cell phone from her attacker's truck. Her power over Mauldin was now crystal clear. His employee had raped and murdered Jordan, perhaps at Mauldin's direction or perhaps not. In any case, Mauldin had protected him and Lydia had found this out.

"There must have been a video that showed his face," I said. "And Lydia must still have it. As long as she stays happy and healthy, it never goes public. Is that your deal?"

Mauldin shook his head like nothing I said possibly could matter to him. "The clips you just watched would be enough to put you in prison for the rest of your life. Given that risk, I'm surprised you're willing to go on blaming others for your crimes. Rodriguez has confessed. He's in prison. All along, you've had the key to his freedom right there on your phone. Who knows where else you have it, even? It's really none of my business. In fact, I'm not even sure what you were watching there. But if I were you, I'd take a hard look in the mirror before you accuse anyone else."

His words reverberated in my ears. Presumably no Internet-connected device I owned or used was safe from Kairos's tampering, the insinuating electronic fingers of Mauldin's sophisticated friends. When Bo Wilder had used his proxy to place the murder gun in my hands, it had been a lesson in his power over me. Mauldin and Kairos had raised such instruction to a higher level.

"What do you want from me?" I asked.

"You tell me what *you* want," Mauldin insisted.

"Nothing from you."

"That's a shame. I want people to want things. The act of exchange creates trust. Trust allows people to let down their guard."

"I pity Lydia if she ever lets down her guard with you."

"Granted. It's always possible she'll soon learn she's not cut out for this business. You ever fish? When a fish wants to fight you, sometimes the best thing to do is let her run with the line. Maybe Lydia will spit out the hook and maybe she'll swallow it. If she swallows, I'll reel her in, slice her open from cunt to kisser, and slop out her guts."

The sudden crassness was shocking, as he intended it to be.

"Is that what your people did with Tom Benton?"

"I don't know where Tommy is. My guess is he's living the good life now, thanks to all that money he embezzled. We should all be so lucky."

Mauldin's face left no doubt Benton was dead and who was responsible. Then his look softened and he placed his hands on the table, preparing to rise. "Look, I know you must be thinking all sorts of terrible things about me right now, but I'm not a bad guy, and not an unreasonable one. I had no reason to want Jordan dead. I was as shocked and saddened by her murder as everyone else. What's more, I'm a businessman. Believe me. These kinds of rumors put Kairos at a terrible competitive disadvantage. We simply can't have them."

I wanted to tell him to go fuck himself but my throat was so dry I couldn't talk. In my mind again I saw Jordan's anguished face and heard her cry: *Leo, no, please, Leo.*

"Think about it," he said. "Think about everything we just discussed."

He left me sitting in the booth and walked out.

~ ~ ~

Ten minutes later I was puking in the alley. When I was finished I leaned against the brick wall, waiting for the feverish sweat that had sprung out all over my body to turn cold. When it did, I took out the phone and thumbed to the videos again. Though a desperate part of me hoped it would all turn out to have been a dream, the videos gone, these digital files were the only evidence connecting Kairos and Mauldin with Jordan's murder. If I could get an expert to examine the phone, it was possible he could trace the path the videos had taken in being placed there and perhaps identify the server they'd come from, enabling me to connect them to Kairos. At the very least, I should be able to prove the videos had been altered, that Jordan in fact hadn't spoken my name.

But the videos were gone. There was no sign the files named "Jordan1" through "Jordan6" had ever existed on the phone, or anywhere else. The folder was empty, just as it'd no doubt been before Mauldin had instructed me to look at them.

I stared in disbelief at the screen. Then I threw the phone to the pavement. I slammed my heel on it, stomping again and again until it shattered. Then I ground the parts against the concrete, making sure nothing was left but a pile of twisted metal and grit.

I stood breathing hard in the alley, momentarily sated.

Then, with renewed energy, I hurried at a fast walk back to the Seward, where ten minutes later I repeated the assault on my laptop, beating it against the tile floor in my bathroom until the neighbor downstairs banged on the pipes.

Chapter 25

Mauldin's technology-based extortion confirmed to me that he, not Cho, was the one in bed with the Chinatown mafia. No mere construction CEO had access to the expertise displayed in his threatening gambit. It was, of course, both a repeat and an amplification of the methods Kairos had used to discredit Cho.

After a week of sleepless nights, I decided to pay a visit to Jordan's father. The truth could bring him no peace, but he deserved to know what I knew. Also, I had a plan for turning Mauldin's threats on their head.

Walker had lost weight, his already gaunt frame reduced to a skeletal appearance, so that his shirt gaped slightly at the throat. Most shocking, though, was his hair, which had gone completely white since I'd last seen him.

We met in his tiny office at the city attorney's suite. Walker was a true civil servant, and it showed in everything from his drab sport coat to the neatly labeled file boxes stacked waist-high under the window behind his desk. He listened motionless as I brought him up to date, his head leaning against the back of his chair as if he lacked the strength to hold it up. If knowing the truth about his daughter's last hours gave him comfort he didn't show it. "There's something else you need to know," I said when I'd described what I'd seen. "The videos have been altered. When Jordan's begging for her life, it's my name she speaks."

I watched him and wasn't surprised to see a flicker of suspicion. He was likely wondering whether the answer had been in front of him from the start. Purposefully, I went on. "What all this means is at the very least, Mauldin covered for Hastings, his errand boy. Even if he didn't okay Jordan's murder, he protected the man."

"They're hoping the doctored video will silence you," he said. I couldn't look at his face for more than an instant because of the pain I saw there.

"Mauldin's right. I have no proof Kairos was behind it, other than the file I located identifying the man I saw as a Kairos employee."

Walker ran his hands through his hair. "This is all so awful. I don't think I told you, but Benton came to see me before he left. To let me know of his supposed feelings for my daughter. In the heat of the moment I may have wrongly accused the man. From what you're saying now, Mauldin had him murdered because he wouldn't go along with the cover-up of Jordan's death."

"Benton was a link in a chain," I said. "Afterward, when he realized the part he'd played, I think he found it hard to live with himself."

"He wanted forgiveness, he said. 'Forgiveness for what?' I wanted to know. 'I can't forgive you if you won't tell me what you've done.' He wouldn't, but he promised me he'd never practice law again. Thinking I'd approve. I *chose* this line of work. I don't spend my days moaning over how miserable I am. The law's my livelihood, and now it's all I have, and I've always practiced it honorably. It doesn't disgust me, and I don't disgust myself. That's what I tried to share with Jordan after she took up the profession. That's what

Tom Benton ripped away from her. He made her despise herself and regret her choices. She felt I'd deceived her, perhaps. Maybe that makes *me* responsible for her death, since she learned her regard for the law from me."

I let my sympathy go unspoken. Probably it helped to have a listener, but, at the same time, he wasn't speaking for my benefit, or because he expected a response. "I'm glad you didn't have to see the videos," I told him. "I hope you never do."

"But I need to see them," he said, looking up. "No matter how horrific they are, I need to know what happened."

"Because of the demonstration Mauldin put on for me at the bar, they're counting on me backing down. I don't intend to back down."

"I believe you, Leo, but how can we control what the police—" He broke off.

"We know whom we're dealing with now, and what the tactics are. Remember, they handled Cho the same way, discredited him by framing him. In his case, they cooked up a video showing him having sex with a fourteen-year-old kid in some place in Chinatown."

"And it worked," Walker said. "Or it would have worked, if Benton hadn't sent that letter to the judge. You think the police are just going to take your word for it that the videos of Jordan's death have been doctored to make her say your name?"

"No. That's why we're going to need the best network forensic tech we can afford to hire. One who can work in real time. Their little demonstration tells us how it'll happen. We'll need to find someone capable of detecting the intrusion when it occurs, monitoring it, and tracing it back to its source. We document it, then we go to the police."

"And how do you plan to provoke this intrusion, as you call it?"

"Simple," I said. "You'll file a wrongful-death lawsuit against Kairos and Mauldin. We'll name Carl Hastings as Jordan's killer and do exactly what Mauldin warned me not to do. That is, we'll allege he was an employee of Kairos, acting at his boss's direction."

Walker was staring at me strangely.

"What?" I asked.

He looked bemused. "I'm just surprised. That's all. It's a very civilized tactic for a man with your reputation. I was envisioning a midnight meeting in a ruined factory, night-vision goggles, that sort of thing. This sounds too straightforward. Though sensible, of course."

"You want justice. If the police won't or can't hold her killers accountable, we have to do it ourselves. The question is: should we use the legal system, or is there another way you want to go?" On the tip of my tongue was the other option I'd considered during recent sleepless nights as the horrible images from the videos cycled through my mind.

That is, I could tell my father about my encounter with Mauldin and be reasonably sure he'd contact Bo Wilder to arrange for his swift end. But doing this would mean obligating myself to the man, Wilder, for life. Not to mention, it'd be wrong. I'd once believed justice and revenge were the same, but I'd learned there were crucial differences, chief among them being what happened afterward. Justice stopped the cycle of violence, but retribution had a life of its own, each act sparking the next in an endless chain.

"I'm a lawyer," I said. "No matter how much I'd like to take a can of gasoline to this man Mauldin's house and light the place on fire, I believe in the rule of law."

"So do I," he said. "Okay, then. We'll sue the bastards."

Over the next weeks, we consulted experts and settled on Marty Ferris, whom Jeanie had recommended. I acquired a new cell phone and laptop. To each, prior to its activation, our expert attached a device that allowed him to remotely mirror every piece of data it sent or received. If anyone tried to plant a video on the computer or phone, he'd see it happening in real time, and, more importantly, he'd be able to meticulously document the event. In addition, he'd make every attempt to trace the illicit connection to its source, though this, he warned me, would be extremely difficult. He'd also preserve the video, analyzing it for signs of alteration.

With our expert retained, we met on a Saturday morning at the Walkers' house to draft the complaint, which would trigger, we hoped, the reaction Mauldin had threatened.

Framed photos of Jordan at all stages of her life seemed to occupy every surface in the house. I wondered how her father could stand it, and I noticed his eyes seeming to flit from place to place like a climber seeking holds over a precipice. His wife was out, he explained. She spent most of her spare time with Jordan's sister and the grandkids these days. He offered me a seat at the kitchen table and poured us coffee. Paranoid about using a computer that could be infiltrated by Kairos's hackers, he insisted on working longhand. He had a stack of yellow pads for each of us and a box of new pens. Also, he had several treatises he'd brought home from the office, every source we could possibly want to consult about the intricacies of the law that would govern the case.

Between the two of us, we set out to tell the story of Jordan's death in numbered paragraphs that Mauldin and Kairos would be required to admit or deny. Walker was a meticulous drafter, far more prone to fiddling with sentences and word choice than I was. He insisted on including much that at first seemed to me irrelevant: Jordan's upbringing, her community involvement. "A complaint like this, you have to draft it for the press," he told me, as if he'd been filing civil actions all his life. "It's the details that bring her alive. Mauldin, he probably won't even read it. But Rachel Stone will."

His details were the kind that at the memorial had turned me off, being what I thought of as a public façade over the real, live woman I'd known. I realized that I'd known her only briefly, but in that limited sense, I'd known her well. My interest was narrower than her father's, yet no less intense for that. The paragraphs where my name appeared were the springs of the trap we were setting for Jacob Mauldin.

In several concise, declarative sentences, the finalized document narrated my arrival at Lydia Cho's, the carnage that followed, and my identification of Carl Hastings as an employee of Kairos. For now, however, I omitted any explanation of how I'd made this connection. Finally, there was my encounter with Mauldin: "Mauldin showed Maxwell videos depicting the rape and murder of Jordan Walker, obtained from the phone of Kairos's former employee," and "Mauldin threatened that if Maxwell revealed what he knew, he would be framed for Jordan Walker's murder."

Walker filed the complaint the following Monday in Superior Court. The next day, he called me on a burner phone I'd picked up, a throwaway with no camera or data capabilities. Mauldin was successfully served. Everything was ready. My phone and laptop were safe in the offices of our network technician, hooked to his monitoring equipment.

For three days, nothing happened. Then, for the second time in the past several months, I was awakened by a knock on my door. It was the police, with a warrant to seize and examine the contents of every electronic device I possessed.

I agreed to accompany the officers to Southern Station to answer Detective Chen's questions while the men searched my room. Once seated at the interview table, I signed the form acknowledging I was speaking to the police voluntarily. Then I explained to Chen exactly what Walker and I had done.

Chen listened without interruption, then said, "And your explanation for destroying your phone and computer is?"

"Altered videos had appeared and disappeared on my phone. Mauldin had as good as told me that they could plant incriminating evidence on any device I owned whenever they chose."

"But, according to you, the evidence was already gone, so—"

It wasn't lost on me that destroying evidence was the reaction of a man who'd just been confronted with proof of his crimes. "If I'd been thinking clearly I'd have taken the phone to an expert immediately. Or gone to the police. But I was just too freaked out."

"I don't mind telling you that Jacob Mauldin is the one who called in the report. According to him, you requested the meeting at the bar. When he arrived, you showed him a cell phone. You claimed it had been taken from the man who you say attacked Lydia Cho."

"It's true that I strongly suspect that's where the videos came from. I think Lydia turned them over to Kairos as part of the settlement of her husband's case."

"Mauldin claims his meeting with you at the bar was the first he'd heard about this cell phone, or any videos. According to him, you identified the man you claimed to have taken the phone from as a former Kairos employee. He says you showed him a confidential company personnel document that you used to lend surface credibility to your story."

They would find a copy of that file in my hotel room, I knew.

Chen went on: "Now you've admitted to destroying a cell phone that evening, perhaps the very one Mauldin claims contained the graphic videos showing Jordan Walker's rape and murder. He believes you're the one in those videos, that you were trying to blackmail him over a crime you committed yourself. According to him, you offered to delete the videos if he paid you three million dollars. Do you have any response to these allegations?"

"They're utterly false." I now realized Mauldin had taken the allegations in Jordan's father's lawsuit and flipped them on their head. It was his word against mine.

Chen's gaze was skeptical, the look of a cop who'd heard far wilder stories, none of which had turned out to be true. He still wanted me for Bell's death and was skeptical of the way I'd slipped that noose. "It doesn't help you that Lydia Cho continues to deny the events you've described, including the dead body in her hot tub and the subsequent killing of her husband. Her whereabouts *are* unaccounted for during the time period in question. After she reappeared, she reported her car stolen. However, it was never found. Sheriff Burke documented tire tracks, broken glass, and shell casings in the place where you say her husband was killed. Then comes Thomas Benton's letter, the allegations of fraud in the civil trial, and Lydia's sudden settlement with the company. None of it makes any sense."

"I agree."

Chen pondered a minute, studying my face like he could read the truth there. "You need to give me more," he finally said. "Mauldin's story puts you on the hook for extortion, if he's willing to testify. My guess is he'd settle for convincing Walker to drop his suit. Yet, according to you, Mauldin's the real extortionist here. And if what you claim is true, he in turn was extorted by Lydia Cho. Isn't it funny how her name keeps coming up?"

"What are you thinking?" I asked.

"Let's assume for now everything is as you say, but Mauldin doesn't fall for your trap, and the videos never mysteriously appear on your phone. What would you think about trying your plan on Lydia?"

~ ~ ~

A few days later I called Lydia Cho from one of the interview rooms at Southern Station. "Please don't hang up," I told Lydia when I reached her. "It's Leo Maxwell. Something awful's happened. I'm in trouble and I don't know where to turn."

Detective Chen sat across from me, gazing down at the wire I'd be wearing if this worked.

On her end there was only silence, making me afraid I'd over-played my part, sounded too desperate. Finally, Lydia said, "What kind of trouble?"

"Videos just appeared on my phone. Out of nowhere. Videos of Jordan's death. But they've been altered. In at least two of them she says my name."

"The same phone you're using now?"

"No. This is a prepaid."

"Thank God. Look, there's nothing I can do for you, Leo. All I can say is whatever they want from you, you should give it to them. They'll get it in the end. Make a deal while you can."

"It may be too late for that. We need to talk in person."

"I can't. I won't. I told you before. You shouldn't be calling me."

"I know the deal you made with them," I said, talking quickly to keep her on the line. "I have proof, and I'll use it if I have to. I'd just prefer not to drag you in. I need a copy of the original video. You still have it, or they wouldn't have settled with you. You'd be dead."

"I'd be dead if anyone knew we were having this conversation."

"It's not too late to do the right thing," I said, making my final pitch. "I want to give you that chance."

She took a deep breath, audible over the phone. "I'll come to you. Three PM."

I gave her the address of the Seward.

Chapter 26

I sat on my bed, phone in my hand, trying to resist the urge to sit straighter or scratch the place at the small of my back where the transmitter was taped on. I'd checked from all angles in the scratched mirror of my tiny bathroom to be sure it didn't show. Chen had a crew stationed in the room directly above mine. I'd done a sound check a few minutes ago and received a text on my prepaid that we were good to go.

Now there was nothing to do but wait. My goal, according to Chen, was to get Lydia to say on tape that I'd been telling the truth about the hot tub scene, the phone she'd taken from the dead man, and the shooting of her husband at the cabin. If she confirmed the existence of the videos, even better.

Ever since Chen had suggested his plan, my mind had been running at full throttle. Now, even as my thoughts raced in circles, I felt an odd sensation. A presence, for lack of a better word. For the first time in a long while, I didn't feel alone, and it wasn't because of the cops in the room upstairs. Somehow, it was easy to imagine

Jordan sitting right beside me on the bed where we'd made love a handful of times, listening with a pensive frown as I tried to script a scene that couldn't be scripted. The Rodriguez trial and our nights together seemed another life, and I remembered Tom Benton, who'd kept the pajamas she'd worn.

"Try listening to other people rather than yourself for once," she'd probably have said. It was an instruction she'd given more than once as we were preparing for trial. It was good advice.

My phone buzzed and I held it to my ear.

"It's Lydia. I'm downstairs. I think this guy's convinced I'm a hooker. He won't let me come up."

"I'll be down," I told her.

It was good to exit my too-small room, if only for a moment. It would've been better to meet in the open air, but Lydia hadn't wanted a public place. Finding her in the lobby, I shot a look at the front desk guy leering behind his Plexiglas shield. Her face was a mask of distaste verging on panic. In my room, I closed the door and double-locked it behind us.

"This is a real shithole," Lydia said, moving to the space between my desk and the bathroom door where the window was, one of the few places to stand without blocking the movement of anyone else who happened to be there. She wore designer jeans and a denim jacket over a ribbed sweater. Her hair was different from when I'd last seen it. Now she had a ponytail with bangs that made her look younger.

After a moment, she turned. "I never thanked you properly for saving my life."

"You're welcome," I told her.

"It occurs to me I should have offered you some sort of compensation. A reward, so to speak. I guess it's old-fashioned but that's the word to use. I wasn't in a position to be able to offer you one before. I am now. Is that what I'm really here to talk about or am I jumping the gun?"

"I called because of the videos that showed up on my phone. I don't know what to do. I—"

"Quit bullshitting!" she interrupted. After a pause, she went on: "I know about the lawsuit. You called their bluff. Mauldin knows you don't have any evidence. All he has to do is deny everything. He's not taking any risks."

I dropped the act. "But *you* have evidence."

She shrugged. "I stay safe. Isn't that all any of us wants?"

"Mauldin showed me the videos. Altered versions, like I said. The killer's face isn't shown, but there's a glimpse of his hands. It's clearly not Rodriguez. What I'm trying to say is an innocent man's behind bars and you have evidence that would free him."

"I'm not saying you couldn't cause me a lot of problems. I just can't give you what you want. Money can't make up for losing your friend, but even her father's bound to settle his lawsuit. Everybody settles. It's just a question of how much."

I shook my head, a terrible taste in my mouth. "You're smarter than your husband."

"Carl Hastings is already dead. All you know is you came to my house and saw him attacking me, which I'll continue to deny. The man who attacked me is dead, and they'll never find him, so they won't be able to connect him to Kairos. Even if they did, you can't get justice from a corpse."

"Isn't what you've done called 'making a deal with the devil'?"

"You've got your mind made up about what a bitch I am, so there's no sense in me trying to change it. Even if I could, what do I care? Why don't you just tell me what I'm doing here?"

"Gary's death isn't the one that keeps me awake at night," I said. "I want to know why I shouldn't go after your friend Mauldin for Jordan's."

She stared out the window a moment, then said, "I can only tell you what I've learned. The night Gary showed up at Jordan's place, Hastings was on surveillance detail, watching Jordan, because she'd left the firm and no one knew what she intended to do. He must have seen you leave, and he must have seen Gary arrive. He was supposed to alert his superiors and await instructions, but he took matters into his own hands. He forced his way in, stripped her naked, tied her up, and made her repeat everything Gary had told her. After he'd raped and tortured her, and taken a few videos for his own private pleasure, I guess, he left her to die. Jacob only learned what happened after I showed him the videos from the phone and we settled my husband's case."

I made a noise of disbelief. "That's what he told *you.*"

"It's true. He never intended anyone to come after me. They were out of control, bent on revenge, acting at Hastings's direction, not Mauldin's. These guys enjoy settling scores."

"You're telling me Mauldin's men were acting on their own when they murdered Gary? They showed every sign of wanting to kill me. Yet they were happy to let you escape? The only truth here is that these killers need to be brought to justice and you're telling me Mauldin won't allow that. The hell with him."

"Hastings is just a ghost. You can't send a ghost to jail. You can't kill him. Anyway, it's not Mauldin who won't allow it. It's his connected friends." She suddenly switched tacks. "For a week, I believed Gary had committed suicide. When he first contacted me to let me know he'd faked his death I felt like I'd been tricked. I'd already been making plans. I didn't want him to come back. Does that make me a monster?"

"Maybe," I told her. "But at least you know what you are."

"Oh, I know who and what I am. There's no doubting that." She turned to the window.

This seemed to confirm what I'd previously guessed. "Someone led those killers to Gary's hiding place that night. It wasn't me, so the only person it could have been was you. You knew we'd be followed. You've gotten everything you wanted. Mauldin bought your silence, and now you want to buy mine about what really happened to your husband."

She didn't answer. And I realized I was right. I wondered if I hadn't known it all along. She'd seen the same video the jury had seen. And like the jury, she'd believed it.

"I want to see the video that shows Hastings's face. The one you're holding back."

"I couldn't retrieve it for you even if I wanted to. It's in something called an electronic lockbox. A company runs this service. You give them your files, and instructions on how to dispose of them if a certain event happens. For me, the lockbox will only be opened if I die. When I'm dead the contents will be distributed to a select e-mail list. You're on it. So is that reporter, Rachel Stone. I've told Jacob this, and he understands it's better to have me with him rather than against him. I hope you see that, too."

"So as long as you're alive and in control of the company, the real facts about what happened that night and the connection to Kairos stay buried. But if something happens to you, the video gets sent to the right people. Just like Tom Benton's letter." I was struck with awe at the coup she'd engineered, the victory she'd managed over both her husband and Mauldin.

My bathroom door swung open. The first thing I saw was the barrel of the gun. Lydia's eyes went wide and she stepped back, stumbled, and fell as Hastings came out. He looked down at her.

"Bitch, in about five minutes you're going to wish you'd killed me." He grabbed Lydia under the arm and half pushed, half tossed her toward the bed, where she dropped onto the mattress beside me. Then he had to rest, leaning his free hand on the windowsill, using it to take some of his weight.

I'd last seen him floating in that hot tub, the water swirling pink with his blood. Lydia had emptied his pockets, then I'd left him floating there as I painfully followed her into the house. If I'd glanced back, would I have seen him lift his head and gasp?

And what would I have done then? I wondered. Tell Lydia?

By the look of him, he hadn't recovered from being shot point-blank in the chest. He was pale, thinner than I remembered, the bones visible in the forearm above his clenched fist holding the gun. He hadn't been in the bathroom while I was waiting for Lydia to arrive. Somehow, he'd slipped through the cordon of police.

"Strip her," he said to me. "Rip her clothes off."

"If you kill her, your face will be all over the evening news. You heard her. Everyone's going to know what happened to Jordan."

Lydia sat rigidly, staring at Hastings like he was the ghost she'd labeled him a moment before.

He stepped forward, seized her sweater, and yanked the neck downward. She pitched forward, the fabric holding. He grabbed a better handful and pulled again, the sweater ripping at the neck. A scream escaped her and his hand was instantly at her throat, squeezing tight enough to cut off sound.

His eyes flashed. "You know where that bullet went you put in me? I can't even get a hard-on no more."

The look in her eyes must have expressed mockery, because he twisted her around, pressing her face into the bed, and began tugging at the waistband of her pants. He was breathing hard. "That's all right, honey," he said close to her ear. "Doesn't mean I can't fuck you the way I fucked the others. And I'm still gonna kill you when it's done."

"You heard what she said about the electronic lockbox," I said, my voice rising in panic as what he had in mind became clear. Lydia Cho dead in my room. Me probably dead, too. "You kill her and the video gets sent to the newspaper, gets sent to the police."

"You really think there's a video showing my face?" he asked contemptuously. "You really believe that?"

He paused, allowing the truth to sink in. Lydia's posture was unreadable. She made no move to rise. If he was wrong, surely she'd speak up now to assure him there was a video and she'd seen it. But she said nothing. If I hadn't believed I was about to die, I'd be applauding her. She'd actually scammed Mauldin. The trouble was, she hadn't counted on the only person who could contradict her story coming back to life.

Our visitor suddenly straightened and half turned, listening. In the next instant, the door crashed in. I saw a flash of movement as whoever had kicked in the door ducked back out, Hastings firing an instant too late, the room filling with gun smoke. I heard someone shout: "Police! Throw down your weapon!"

I drove my shoulder into the center of his torso, my hands going to his wrist above the gun. He grunted in pain and wrenched himself free.

"Get down!" came a shout.

The barrel of Hastings's gun followed me as I threw myself to the floor, but gunshots sounded before he could fire, and three red holes bloomed in his shirt.

Six months later my father and I are drinking in a Tenderloin watering hole. Earlier, after a brief hearing, Rodriguez's petition for habeas corpus was denied based on the lack of any clear-cut evidence of his innocence. I'm not sure how I feel about this. I keep thinking of that wink he gave me during the Janelle Fitzpatrick trial, his excitement as Jordan held his hand. Walker's lawsuit against Mauldin and Kairos, by contrast, is proceeding.

Kairos, in the meantime, has lost the Candlestick contract. Rachel Stone's exposé of Mauldin's private security guards' misconduct in support of his scheme to undermine the city's mixed-housing plan ran on the front page in a three-part series that was picked up widely in the national news. She even managed to dig up his connections to the Chinatown mafia. A federal investigation is proceeding now, and according to her, indictments are expected. So much for Lydia Cho's deal with the devil. She still has her interest in Lizhi, however, which remains positioned to take Kairos's place in the sweet spot of the deal.

Hiram Walker talks about forcing the case over his daughter's death to trial no matter how much money is offered, but he'll see the light. In the end, as Lydia said, everybody settles. Walker will realize the time has come to bury Jordan. The settlement, of course, will be confidential. Jacob Mauldin may be held civilly responsible for Jordan's murder to the tune of tens of millions of dollars. Meanwhile, Rodriguez remains in prison indefinitely, his criminal conviction seemingly beyond attack. Such is the beauty of our justice system.

The place is filling up, the noise covering the fact that my father and I've run out of things to say to one another. We've talked it over from front to back and back to front again. He's repeatedly reminded me there's nothing I can do to help a man who won't help himself, and the sooner I accept this the better. His scowl is his scornful verdict on any man who'd voluntarily put himself behind prison bars.

"You're sure about Mauldin?" he finally asks.

I nod. "I'm sure."

"And you're positive the cops aren't going to charge him as an accessory to murder?"

"We have no proof Hastings was the one who killed her. He didn't confess."

Lawrence sips his bourbon, then wipes his mustache. "I'm glad you can tell me stuff that's bothering you. It's good to know we have that kind of relationship." He hesitates. "Something bad could happen to this guy Mauldin, you know. Maybe a lot worse than having to write a big check. You think having to open his wallet to Jordan's daddy is enough?"

"Not even close," I tell him. "But, satisfying as it might be, it's not my job to punish the man."

"That's what I thought. I just wanted to make sure. Stay true to your principles."

Lawrence leaves crisp twenties on the bar. Dot's expecting him. Whatever their problems might have been while they were abroad, they've seemingly patched things up. Having money must help.

These days, he seems to have plenty.

~ ~ ~

Not a night goes by without dozens of arrests, people plucked from their homes, from their cars, but most of all off the streets. Most probably need to be arrested, but many just are in the wrong place, of the wrong skin color, at the wrong time. Some are hardened but many are scared, homeless, addicted to drugs and alcohol, caught in the hustle like rats on a wheel. The system dehumanizes equally all whom it catches.

I often think of Jordan. I can no longer remember what her body felt like against mine in the dark, except when she returns to me in dreams.

What remains after the gut punch fades is my certainty that Jordan would've gone on doing this work. She'd never have turned cynical, and she'd never have taken out her frustrations on her clients. She'd have fought for them day after day, brushing aside the inevitable defeats, choosing the side of the least powerful among us against the blind power of the state that seeks to destroy the lives of all who get caught in its machinery, which repays harm with harm in an endless cycle that doesn't deserve the name of justice.

Each case is a new case, but each case is also the same case.

Because of her, I'm proud to call myself a public defender.

Only, it can't last. The ultimatum comes when I least expect it. I'm in jail to meet a client when the guards bring in another man. I'm about to inform them of their mistake when he gives me a look that shuts my mouth.

The deputies gone, the inmate tells me, using short, rehearsed-sounding sentences, about the details of my niece's life. Carly's preschool, the names of her teachers. The books on the shelf beside her bed. Descriptions of her stuffed animals. What she eats for breakfast.

"What're you wasting your time in the public defender's office for?" the man asks next. "You could be making real money, buy that sweet girl some pretty things."

Bo Wilder's name isn't mentioned.

It doesn't need to be.

No threat is made.

But that afternoon I put in my two-week notice, giving as my explanation that I intend to return to private practice. I don't tell my brother and father the real reason, but they must guess. My brother looks at me sorrowfully, probably thinking I've at last consented to the inevitability of corruption.

He's wrong, but I can't tell anyone that for now. I'm biding my time, hoping for the opportunity to make everything right.

In the meantime, I do a brisk business representing Wilder's foot soldiers, pleading out men who don't need me to remind them not to talk. For now, I'm not asked to perform any unethical acts, or to do anything illegal. But I know it's only a matter of time. One of these days, I'll get the midnight call, the bag of cash I'll be expected to hold until the right person comes to retrieve it. When that day arrives, I'll be ready with a plan to save my family.

If such a plan exists.

If my family wants to be saved.

For Carly's sake, I tell myself, they must.

Acknowledgments

I'm grateful to Otto Penzler for believing in this series—and for continuing to support it. Without him, Leo Maxwell would still be a figment of my imagination. Michele Slung, my top-notch editor, has saved me from embarrassments and improved these books in more ways than anyone can know. I'm indebted to the team at Grove Atlantic, especially Allison Malecha, Peter Blackstock, Deb Seager, Charles Rue Woods, Julia Berner-Tobin, and Paula Cooper Hughes, along with others who've worked behind the scenes. I'm still awed that Gail Hochman, my amazing agent, stuck with me for years before I ever published a word. Many thanks to Matt DeClaire for website help.

My good fortune from the people named above pales in comparison with the love and support of my dear wife, our parents, our extended families, and our children. Thank you and my love to all.